Jasper

Michael Easterling

Other books by Michael Easterling

The Water at the End of the World

Christmas Eve on the Underground Railroad and Other Christmas Stories

Sweet Hope: an Appalachian Ghost Story

ISBN: 978-0-578-58430-0

VALLEY OAK PUBLICATIONS

To the reader:

At night, when the troubles of this world weigh heavy upon me and worry has me tangled in my sheets, I tempt sleep by concocting stories, stories of a man who sought, and found, peace. I have compiled these stories into the collection that follows.

Likely they will put you to sleep too.

Table of Contents

A Veteran of the Great War Comes Looking for
Gold in California   1

Mud and Mosquitos   7

Bakelite   13

Lessons in Prospecting and a Meeting with the Devil   20

The Sanitary Fund   31

Madame Coyote   41

Dreaming   50

Sarah Petruzelli, Attorney and Baby Sitter   58

Assaying the Ore   64

Desert Rose   70

The Miners' Ball   77

Love Letters   96

Job   118

Ode to Cholla   127

Utterly Brilliant   132

A Few Consequential Errors   144

An Unlikely Parade   157

Sonya   171

Right-O, Daddy-O   186

Laying Ghosts to Rest   198

The Colberts   212

Sleep   230

A Veteran of the Great War Comes Looking for Gold in California

"Stars in your eyes." It was an expression Jacob Harmon had heard, but it was not until that warm May morning in the desert town of Inyo that he witnessed the actual phenomenon. Hunched over the counter of his general store, he had just begun to write out his weekly orders for goods when the light of a sudden went dim, as if someone had pulled the curtain down upon the day. He looked up to see the outline of a man who not only came near to filling the doorway, but appeared an apparition due to the aura of sunlight surrounding him. As the man strode forward across the worn wooden floor, Mr. Harmon could see the man's height was augmented by a trench hat used by soldiers in the recent war. The man also wore trousers of dark khaki serge tucked into calf-length boots. In contrast to these articles of military attire was a red-checkered flannel shirt which clashed with the near orange of the man's hair and beard.

But it was the man's eyes, like sunlight drawing up life from a newly sprouted seed, that caused Mr. Harmon to unfold his slumped figure and produced a smile upon his careworn face.

"Good morning," Mr. Harmon said.

"Bore da," replied the man, and in response to the confused looked on Mr. Harmon's face, added, "That is how we say 'good morning' in Welsh." Then he slapped down five, crisp twenty-dollar bills upon the counter. "I have come to prospect for gold!"

Plunk! went the front legs of a chair in the back of the store where Shoshone Sam, leaning back against the wall, reading the plays of Euripides, suddenly sat forward.

"Ah," Mr. Harmon said, staring at the treasure lying upon his counter. "Yes, well…"

Quickly, silently, Shoshone Sam stole forward. "Did I hear you say, 'prospect for gold'?" he said.

"You did indeed, sir," the stranger replied, rubbing his hands together and looking altogether like a boy about to open his Christmas presents.

"So what kind of mining are you intending to do?" Shoshone Sam said. "Are you planning to file a placer claim or a lode claim? Or perhaps you're wanting to do some reclamation work?"

As Mr. Harmon waited for the stranger to reply, he reflected upon the difference in skin color between the sun-polished bronze of Shoshone Sam, whose ancestors had inhabited the California desert for thousands of years, and the "peaches and cream" complexion of the stranger. As he sought the appropriate phrase that might summarize this difference, he noticed the stars in the stranger's luminous eyes grow dimmer, this in response to Shoshone Sam's interrogation. It came to Mr. Harmon that before him stood not someone with knowledge of mining, but a seeker of romance, a Francisco Coronado in quest of the golden cities of Cibola, a Jason in search of the golden fleece. In short, one of those self-deluded ignoramuses who thinks he's going to gather up gold nuggets as if they were Easter eggs lying around on the ground. That stated, Mr. Harmon was the last person to puncture a man's dream.

"Let's not bother our friend with technicalities right now, Sam. He wishes to prospect for gold, and that's enough for the time being."

Shaking his head, Shoshone Sam returned to his Euripides.

"Now, then," Mr. Harmon said, "first off you'll need some grub." Turning, he hollered, "Jake!" As he waited for Jacob Jr. to come from the back storeroom, Mr. Harmon wrote down a list of the foodstuffs the stranger would need. This he handed to his son. "Gather up these goods for Mr. …" He turned toward the stranger. "I'm sorry, I didn't get your name."

The stranger's smile broadened. "It's Aurfryn Owen."

The stranger spoke fast; Mr. Harmon was not sure if that was all one name or two. "For Mr...."

"Owen," Aurfryn supplied.

"Thank you. And I'm Jacob Harmon, and this is my son, Jacob Jr. While Jake's getting these supplies, let's go over yonder and take a look at some tools."

Though it may have been implied that Mr. Harmon thought little of the gold seeker, in point of fact, he did stock a certain amount of supplies for prospectors, though over the years the demand for these goods had grown less and less. Nowadays most mining was done by large companies, using heavy mining equipment. Almost gone was the lone prospector who eked out a living, scratching in the dirt.

"You'll need a shovel, of course," Mr. Harmon said, lifting one off the rack. "And a pick." Mr. Harmon ran his eyes over a dusty shelf. He still had a few packets of chemicals used to identify minerals. He had streak plates, and sets of minerals for testing hardness. He even carried a small balance beam made of brass. But he suspected these tools of the miner's trade would only confuse Aurfryn Owen at this nascent stage in his prospecting career.

"Well, these should do you for now," he said, carrying the pick and shovel back to the counter. He then took a closer look at Aurfryn's apparel. "You're going to find wool rather uncomfortable in our desert climate." Ascertaining Aurfryn's measurements, he then selected a pair of denim jeans, an additional flannel shirt, a large bandanna and a lined denim jacket. "You'd be surprised how cold our desert nights can get."

Aurfryn lifted the clothes off the counter. "Have you a place where I might change?"

Mr. Harmon directed Aurfryn toward the stockroom then he selected blankets for a bedroll for Aurfryn. To these he added cooking utensils along with a box of matches. When all these goods were placed upon the counter alongside the foodstuffs Jacob Jr. had gathered, they made a considerable pile, making Mr. Harmon wonder how Aurfryn was going to carry it all.

Aurfryn returned, looking more the prospector and less the soldier.

"You'll need a different hat," Mr. Harmon said.

Aurfryn removed his trench hat and ran his fingers along the brim. "What is the matter with this one?"

"It won't do for the desert. With your pale skin, you'll be burnt to a crisp in no time." Mr. Harmon selected a wide brim felt hat of a light color. "See if this fits."

Aurfryn settled the hat upon his head. "How do I look?"

"There's a mirror over there."

Aurfryn returned from an examination of his reflection obviously pleased. He placed his old trench hat upon the head of Jacob Jr. "Here you go, lad, a gift from a Welshman to an American."

The boy beamed.

"What do you say to Mr. Owen?" Mr. Harmon said.

"Thank you, sir."

"You're welcome, lad. May it bring you luck, as it has me."

"Now then," Mr. Harmon said, "you'll need some means of carrying all this. I know a man here in town who'll sell you a good burro at a very reasonable price."

"No burro," Aurfryn said. He pointed to the far wall. "I would prefer one of those."

On the wall, next to a pair of broken snowshoes, hung an old trapper's pack made of wood and canvas. Both were decorations hung by the store's previous owner, though what either had to do with the desert, Mr. Harmon had never fathomed. That said, the pack appeared large enough to accommodate a great amount of gear.

Having assigned Jacob Jr. the task of getting the pack down off the wall, Mr. Harmon studied the mound of goods with regards to perhaps lessening Aurfryn's load. He then remembered a new line of lightweight goods he had recently began to stock. He went to a nearby shelf and returned with a canteen. "Feel the heft of that," he said, placing the canteen in Aurfryn's hands.

Aurfryn tossed the canteen lightly into the air. " 'Tis light as a feather. What is it made of?"

"It's a brand-new material called Bakelite. It may be light, but it's tough as nails." Jacob Jr. returned, bearing the pack, and Mr. Harmon instructed him to fill the canteen while he himself made a tally of Aurfryn's purchases.

In the meantime, Aurfryn began to load his pack, which did indeed prove commodious; everything other than the bedroll and the tools fit within. The bedroll Aurfryn tied upon the top of the pack with rope Mr. Harmon provided. The tools were hung from loops already sewn into the sides of the pack.

Running an eye over the pack, Mr. Harmon doubted he could lift it. Yet its weight seemed of little consequence to Aurfryn, who swung it up off the floor and, leaning forward, balanced it upon his back while he threaded his arms through the shoulder straps. When he straightened up and stood looking down upon Mr. Harmon, his eyes were more like comets than mere stars.

"One more thing," Aurfryn said. "I'll need a pan."

"A pan?" Mr. Harmon had already supplied Aurfryn with cooking pots.

"A mining pan, like the one used for panning gold in a river."

Mr. Harmon ignored the guffaw coming from the back of the store where Shoshone Sam had obviously been listening. In point of fact, Mr. Harmon did possess such a pan, something also left by the store's former owner. It resided beneath the counter and functioned as a repository for buttons, hair pins, paper clips and lost articles waiting for customers to claim. Mr. Harmon pulled the pan from the shelf, emptied its contents into a bushel basket and set it upon the counter. "I'll throw this in for free. Now your bill comes to nineteen dollars and seventeen cents." He slid all but one of the twenty dollar bills across the counter toward Aurfryn.

Aurfryn pushed them back. "I'll ask you to keep the rest on account. Now if you would be so kind as to point me to the river."

Mr. Harmon scowled at Shoshone Sam's half-hearted attempt to mask his laughter with a cough. Moving from behind the counter, Mr. Harmon went to the front door and held it open as Aurfryn, his pack still on, squeezed through the opening. Then Mr. Harmon stepped to the edge of the porch and pointed east. "Do you see that long line of willows way off there in the distance?"

Aurfryn nodded.

"That's the Owens River."

Aurfryn quickly turned to look at Mr. Harmon. "'Owen,' you say? As in 'Aurfryn Owen'?"

"Uh… yes, I suppose so."

Aurfryn beamed. "'Tis a lucky omen, a sign that this was meant to be." He breathed a satisfied sigh. "Ah, the mighty Owens River."

Mr. Harmon pushed a clod of dirt off the edge of the porch floor with his shoe. "Well, I'm not sure 'mighty' is the word you'd use to describe the Owens River."

Aurfryn held out a large hand. "I thank you, Mr. Harmon, for all your help. You cannot imagine how I have dreamed of this day."

Mr. Harmon clasped Aurfryn's hand. "Now, you be careful. It's only May, but it's already devilishly hot out there. Make sure you always carry plenty of water."

As Mr. Harmon watched Aurfryn cross the dirt road and set out across the scrub-dotted desert, he was joined by Shoshone Sam.

"How in heaven's name did the likes of him end up here, Sam?"

Shoshone Sam watched as the Welshman wove his way around the creosote bushes and rabbit brush, the handles of his pick and shovel swinging back and forth like pendulums. "I'll give him three, maybe four days. After that he'll be dead."

Mr. Harmon wiped his hands on his apron. "You may be right, Sam. I'm afraid you may be right."

Mud and Mosquitoes

The answer to Harmon's question, as to how a Welshman came to be in the California desert, involved a boat, a train, and a bus. But as to *why* Aurfryn Owen wished to seek his fortune in this harsh clime, that was a more difficult question to answer. Initially, his desire had been triggered by reading *Roughing It* by Mark Twain, a book which, as a soldier fighting in France, Aurfryn had somehow come into possession of. Twain's flair for depicting the untamed West and romanticizing the Comstock's glory days had captured Aurfryn's imagination and afflicted his battle-weary brain with gold fever. Now as Aurfryn loped across the desert, he could just imagine that a distant streak of windblown sand marked the trail of a bounding stagecoach, atop which were perched a young Mark Twain and his brother Orion who, like Aurfryn, were off to find whatever adventures awaited them in this odd angle of the world.

Aurfryn adjusted the tilt of his new hat to better shield his face from the sun's rays. Despite his exertions, he was surprised at how little he sweated and reasoned it had to be the air, unusually dry in his experience. What was it Mr. Harmon had said about water? To always carry it with him? Aurfryn could hear the slosh of his Bakelite canteen each time he veered around a bush, and the sound served to intensify his already considerable thirst. But months spent fighting in the trenches had steeled him against physical discomforts; he would drink when he reached the Owens River, that is if he were not too busy gathering up gold nuggets.

Topping a rise, Aurfryn saw a dry lake, a feature he had read about. He had also read that a man crossing a dry lake might imagine he sees water in the distance, only to find that the water continues to stay in the distance. Such a phenomenon is a mirage, made by the wavering heat rising off the desert floor. Had Aurfryn realized that the dry lake was Owens Lake, he might have modified his thinking concerning the "mighty" Owens River.

He stopped to shift the weight of his pack and to adjust the straps, which were starting to chafe his shoulders. Though he loathed to admit it, he was beginning to think Mr. Harmon's suggestion of a donkey not a bad idea. His refusal of that suggestion had been based on his memory of how ill-used were the horses and mules that hauled the army's artillery, and his determination to never let an animal suffer as they had. Keeping that in mind, he went forward, using the strength of his arms to lift the pack up off his shoulders until the muscles of his arms cried out in pain. He would then walk for a quarter mile or so, bearing the full weight of the pack upon his shoulders until they made similar complaints, and he would be forced to enlist the strength of his arms once more. By this alternate use of arms and shoulders, he found he could bear his burden well enough. Yet it surprised him how the line of trees that marked the Owens River did not appear to be getting any closer. When he had stood upon the porch of Mr. Harmon's general store, the line of trees had seemed but a hop, skip and a jump away. He was now learning that distances are deceiving in a land where everything is wide open. Yet this was a part of the desert's allure, to be able to see countless miles in every direction.

Another attraction of the desert was the ground itself. Aurfryn had never been in a place where so much raw earth lay exposed. In Wales, the land of his birth, all was swathed in green. Aurfryn never imagined that hills and plains of bare ground could be so picturesque, yet here the hand of nature had brushed the earth with every color from dove gray to dark vermilion.

He came to a small arroyo which forced him to sidestep down the steep slope until he reached the sandy bottom whose white sand radiated back the sun's heat. Despite the heat, wildflowers grew in abundance. Later Aurfryn would learn their names–purple mat, globe mallow, indigo bush, chia sage, sand verbena—but for the present it was enough just to partake of their beauty and to marvel at their profusion.

Though anxious to get to the Owens River, Aurfryn could not resist spending a little time in this oasis of color. Besides, he could no longer ignore his thirst. He slipped out of his pack and let it fall to the ground where it lodged itself upright in the sand. He rubbed his shoulders, made raw by the straps. Yet this was a small price to pay for his being here, in this storied land, living out his dream.

As he drank deeply from his canteen, a large lizard went scurrying past, leaving tiny tracks in the sand. Aurfryn noticed other tracks as well, mostly bird tracks, but one large set that looked as if it had been made by a dog. Here was something else to marvel at, the evidence of abundant wildlife amidst such seeming desolation. The winding path of flowers enticed him to explore, and he followed the streambed downhill for perhaps a half of a mile, all the while keeping a sharp lookout for nuggets of gold. In places, the arroyo was little more than a wide crack in the earth. In other places, it was a wide wash filled with ankle-deep sand, difficult to walk across. Finally, he came to an abrupt drop-off and could go no further. Looking south he again saw Owens Lake, framed by ochre-colored cliffs and, in the distance, the snowcapped peaks of the Sierra Nevada mountains. As he gazed upon this far-flung wilderness, he saw no evidence of the hand of man, save for a dirt road that skirted the northern edge of the dry lake bed. Spellbound, he would have been glad to have stood there for hours, just admiring the scenery, had not his stomach, which had been grumbling for the last hour or so, not been quite so complaining as to its wants. With a sigh, he turned from the vista, curious to see what kind of a meal he could make from the stores Mr. Harmon had provided.

As he went back along the wash, he happened to glance left and saw atop a bank a large desert tortoise resting in the shade of a honey mesquite bush. In response to a prodding finger, the tortoise retracted its head into its carapace, but made no move to leave the relative coolness of its shady spot.

Aurfryn received a second surprise when he returned to see two pocket mice go scurrying out of his backpack. Pulling back the top flap, he saw a bag of flour had been nibbled on, and, like an upturned hour glass, was slowly spilling its contents. He removed the bag of flour and set it down upon the sand. A quick inspection revealed he had returned in time to prevent further ransacking. He also discovered that, aside from several tins of sardines there was nothing to eat that did not involve cooking. No matter. He was used to meager fare, and as he began to unwind the lid on a sardine can, he marveled that a man could lunch on seafood here in the midst of the desert. Such a reflection was itself a reflection on the man himself, for Aurfryn had never lost his childlike sense of wonder, and was often willing to suffer any number of aches and pains in order to gratify that sense, which was why he ignored the pain when, having finished his lunch, he once more shouldered his backpack. It seemed odd that, minus the weight of water and a can of sardines, the pack seemed heavier than before, particularly as he labored to climb up out of the arroyo and onto level ground.

Finally, he reached the line of willow trees, and too excited to even stop to remove his pack, plunged headlong though the thicket and found himself at once knee deep in mud. He also managed to stir up a cloud of mosquitoes, who lost no time tucking into the providential repast his flesh provided. Firmly anchored in the mud, madly waving his arms to fend off his attackers, Aurfryn looked like a whirligig gone berserk. He knew he must somehow extricate himself from the mud, yet to do so would require breaking off attempts to defend himself.

Whatever action he might have taken, it certainly would not have been to lose his balance and fall backwards into the mud. Now he was stuck from head to toe, staring up into a fog of mosquitoes. By rocking side to side, he managed to wiggle out of his shoulder straps then turn face down into the ooze. He reached out, grabbed the trunk of a willow and dragged himself out of the muck, all the while suffering an invasion of mosquitoes into his mouth, nostrils, and ears. Despite not being able to see for the mud and mosquitoes in his eyes, he stood up and ran, tripped over a rock, picked himself up, and ran blindly on. The second time he fell, reason reasserted itself, and he fished a bandana out of his pocket and used it to wipe the mud and mosquitoes out of his eyes before continuing his flight across the desert, not stopping until the last of the mosquitoes had given up pursuit.

As he stood, hands upon knees, trying to catch his breath, globs of mud fell from his beard and spattered the ground. His state brought to mind a time he hoped to forget, a month-long period of torrential rains spent in the muddy trenches at Ypres.

Aurfryn began to scratch his innumerable bites. The more he scratched, the more he itched, the more he itched, the more he scratched. He continued in this escalating cycle until his fingers were coated with blood as well as mud. Upon reflection, he was not certain whether the mosquitoes were not a worse adversary than the Germans had been. What made matters worse was that he must trespass again upon the mosquitoes' domain if he wished to rescue his backpack. This time, however, he knew what to expect, and he conducted the rescue of his pack as if it were a military operation. He approached the willows along a dry creek bed, keeping low so as not to be seen by the mosquitoes. When he encountered the first of the buzzing sentries, he broke cover and made a charge toward the river. His rescue might have succeeded with few new wounds suffered had not the mud gripped his backpack like a miser his loot. It was not a real wet mud, more like a paste, or modeler's clay that had molded itself around the pack. It did not help that the pack weighed as much as a good-sized boulder, or that Aurfryn could find no solid ground to stand upon except at the near end of the pack where the flap that covered the opening lay spread out in the mud. He tried yanking on this, but it soon began to tear. He sank his hands into the mud, found the pack frame, pulled with all his might, but the pack was glued to the earth. He leaned forward, gripped the far end of the frame and pulled. At first nothing happened, then with a sort of *slurp* and a *pop*, the pack broke free and both it and Aurfryn fell backwards, half in and half out of the mud. He wasted no time, but cradling the backpack like an enormous child, ran from the mighty Owens River as fast as his legs could carry him.

It would have been understandable, at this point, had Aurfryn been dispossessed of any romantic notions concerning prospecting for gold. But, surprisingly, he was overcome by an inexplicable feeling of joy. How long had it been since he had felt joy in any measure? And how that joy contrasted with his recent experience of war, where the predominant emotion was that of fear. Yet even fear becomes a casualty of war, for to be constantly afraid requires an energy that cannot be sustained, and eventually fear, along with every other emotion, is worn away, leaving nothing but all-encompassing numbness.

Part of his joy came from the release of something in his own basic nature suppressed by war: the capacity to see the humorous side of life. Though he had planned the rescue of his backpack as a kind of military operation, there was nothing of the tragedy of war about it; the stuff with the mud and the mosquitoes was pure comedy.

The rest of the joy he felt came from the realization that he need not treat nature as if she were an enemy, for though she may at times seem maddeningly perverse, nature, unlike humans, was never actually malevolent. He realized that if he could live here, in the California desert, then he might lay down the psychic weight of war as he had his bolt-action rifle; that he could live in peace with nature and never again fear the destruction to his spirit made by hatred and bloodshed.

Aurfryn continued to run, but this time for the joy of it. What a sight his fleet figure must have presented to the eyes of those creatures hiding in the brush! A mud god, clutching, not just a backpack, but a divine truth, racing across the California desert, laughing fit to shame a pack of hyenas.

Bakelite

As Aurfryn sat with his back against a fallen cottonwood tree at the edge of a dry lake, his thoughts were far from happy. "Bakelite," he muttered. "Bakelite."

Though his head projected above the fallen tree trunk, thanks to the broad-billed hat sold to him by Jacob Harmon, Aurfryn was able to shield his sunburned face from the sun's blistering rays.

Two and one-half days ago, he had been living his dream, sort of. He had been panning for gold in the Owens River. In truth, the Owens River is not much of river, there being many places where a man of Aurfryn's height could jump across it without getting his boots wet. But the Owens River's diminutive size did not deter Aurfryn from attempting to pan for gold. He selected a spot away from the willow thickets where most, though not all, of the mosquitoes lurked, and near to where the Owens River emptied into Owens Lake, or rather would have emptied had there been any actual water in the lake for the river to empty into. In the absence of water, the river just petered out, disappearing into the sand about one hundred feet past a line of salts that marked where the shoreline once had been.

Aurfryn knew the theory behind gold panning, for he had read about it in a book. The prospector submerges his pan into the river, scooping up some of the sediment from the bottom. He then sluices the water around in the pan, slowly casting off the lighter sediments until only the heavier particles, gold in particular, remain. The problem with the sediment in the Owens River was that it was uniform in nature, a fine silt, and when Aurfryn succeeded in casting off what he thought were the lighter particles, nothing else remained. Still it was exciting to be actually prospecting, and Aurfryn happily went about panning until darkness overtook him, leaving him with sore knees, a sunburned neck, and a somewhat diminished expectation of striking it rich any time soon.

Yet hope rises with the sun, and the next morning Aurfryn decided he would forsake panning and try his hand at hard rock mining, something he had read about also. He shouldered his heavy backpack, and with pick in hand, strode east across a broad alluvial plain, aiming toward a range of chocolate-colored mountains. He made frequent stops to pick away at anything that glittered or to crack open unusually colorful rocks. Such efforts gave him satisfaction and earned him a fine set of blisters.

When he reached the mountains, he struggled up a narrow canyon, sending down a clatter of rocks as he continued to pick away at every tempting crevice wherein gold might be hiding. Upon reaching the top of the mountain, he shed his backpack and sat on the hard ground, too tired to fish his canteen out of his pack. Though he had yet to find any gold, he was not disheartened, for it had been worth all his exertions just to be where he was, for never in his life had he been upon a mountain so high, the mountains of Wales being mere bumps by comparison. He thought himself nearly level with the crest of the Sierras, the great wall of granite and ice clearly visible to the west. In the opposite direction, there was a broad basin, which also featured a dry lake bed, and beyond that, range after range of mountains, each separated by broad valleys and looking like islands rising up out of the sea, and none showing any evidence of ever having been visited by man. Aurfryn felt himself the sole proprietor of a vast untouched realm.

But that was over two days ago. Now Aurfryn, leaning against the downed cottonwood, reflected upon the vicissitudes of life, for at that moment, he gladly would have traded his wilderness kingdom for a cup of water. He knew now that it had been a mistake to head off into that vast wilderness with so little water and encumbered by the weight of his pack. But he been possessed with a yearning to go and see and do; to find that El Dorado which so far had eluded all gold seekers. And the fates seemed to reward his enthusiasm, for he had not gotten halfway down the far side of that chocolate-colored mountain range when he came upon a band of vitreous rock through which colors swirled like red and orange liqueur. He knew the band of rock was not gold, but felt certain it had value nonetheless. He could just imagine a piece of it polished and set into a ring for some lady of fashion.

Yet when he went to break the rock out of its matrix, he found he could not bring himself to use his pick, for that seemed a sacrilege, something on the order of taking a hammer to a David. Instead he used his pocket knife to lever out a piece no bigger than would fit into his shirt pocket, deciding he would return to harvest the rest should the rock prove of value.

Two days later, Aurfryn still carried that rock specimen. He took it from his shirt pocket and held it in the light. The streaks of color appeared to undulate as he moved it back and forth. He was certain it would have appeared even more lustrous had he water to wash away the film of dirt. Parched as he was, he could not even summon up a little spit.

"Bakelite," he muttered. "Bakelite!"

His second day of prospecting had ended with expectations of finding El Dorado sadly diminished. Tired and hungry, he used a little of his precious water to make a thick pancake batter, which he mixed right in his skillet before setting it to cook over a fire of resinous brittle bush. As his skillet grew hot, Aurfryn tried to picture where exactly he was. He knew he was in a canyon several mountain ranges east of Owens Lake. But as to how far east, or whether he was north or south of that dry lake, he did not know. This was not to say he was lost; in his quest for gold, he had not abandoned all common sense. He had made note of the fact that the mountain ranges he had crossed ran north-south, and all the canyons he had explored roughly east-west. To find his way back to Owens Lake, he only needed to head west.

Hungry as he was, he found the dry pancake stuck in his throat, yet he dared not wash it down with water he must save for his return journey. He managed a couple of bites before tossing the rest into a nearby bush, knowing a creature would find it, just as a creature had his found his bag of sugar the night before. Determined not to contribute to the diet of anymore wildlife, Aurfryn made a cache, using rocks stacked tightly together, and sealed up his foodstuffs within. It never occurred to him to take similar precautions with his Bakelite canteen.

Bakelite! How Aurfryn wished he had never heard the word! He repositioned himself against the downed cottonwood tree in an attempt to achieve a more comfortable position. He thought it odd that his backrest was the sole tree, dead or alive, anywhere in sight. It was as if it had fallen from the heavens. It spoke of a wetter era when there must have been at least some water in the dry lake bed.

Water. All his thoughts kept returning to this subject. Aurfryn recalled his dismay when upon waking this very morning, he discovered his canteen empty. Some creature, he knew not what, but obviously one possessing teeth tougher than nails, had gnawed a hole in the bottom of his Bakelite canteen, and what water the creature had not imbibed had gone to moisten the desert sand, leaving Aurfryn with nary a drop to wet his whistle. Aurfryn immediately realized he was in a bad situation, for he had counted upon that water to see him through the long trek back to the Owens River. Not bothering with his backpack, he immediately set out to the west, just as the sun rose behind him. His plan was to walk as far and as fast as he could while the day was still cool, then hole up somewhere in the afternoon when the heat was at its worst.

And that was how he came to be sitting at the edge of a dry lake bed, taking advantage of the scant shade the downed cottonwood provided. Since sunrise, he had crossed two mountain ranges, two dusty basins, with another mountain range to surmount before he would be in sight of Owens Lake, or so he hoped. Only one thing he knew for certain: he needed to be up and going.

Yet when he tried to stand, he became so dizzy he had to sit back down again. After a while the dizziness passed, but not so the pounding in his skull that had accompanied his dizzy spell. Aurfryn told himself to ignore the pain in his head, the ache in his joints, his chapped and bleeding lips, his swollen tongue; to get up and get moving. Instead he closed his eyes and rested some more. He must have fallen asleep, for he dreamed someone was talking to him.

"Had enough of prospecting, pilgrim?"

Aurfryn looked up into the face of Shoshone Sam.

"You look like you could use a drink," Shoshone Sam said, and tossed Aurfryn his canteen. Aurfryn nearly dropped it in his rush to unscrew the lid. The water was warm with a metallic taste, and was the most delicious water he had ever tasted.

"Where…" Aurfryn said, when could speak. "How…"

"How did we find you? Me and Jake Jr. have been following you for the last day and a half. Jake Sr. thought it a good idea to keep an eye on you." Shoshone Sam took in Aurfryn's sorry state. "Looks like it was a good thing we did, too."

If Aurfryn's dry ducts could have produced grateful tears, they would have. "I am greatly in your debt. Thank you."

"No thanks necessary. Jacob just wanted to make sure he didn't lose a paying customer. Now, should we head on back, or do you need more time to bake in the sun? By the looks of it, I'd say you're already properly cooked."

Aurfryn started to get up, and found he couldn't. Shoshone Sam offered him a hand, and found he had to use two. "What do white folks feed their children to make them so big?"

Standing, Aurfryn still felt a little dizzy, but the pain in his head had lessened. He watched as Shoshone Sam picked up the canteen then started walking east.

Aurfryn was confused. "Wait a minute."

Shoshone Sam turned.

Aurfryn pointed in the direction he thought west. "Are we not supposed to go that way?"

Shoshone Sam shrugged. "You can if you want. Me, I'd rather ride back in the store's delivery van, which is just a little way over that hill yonder. Of course, if you prefer to walk, I'll lend you my canteen."

Aurfryn did his best to catch up. "No, it is a nice day for a ride in a van."

As they walked along, side by side, Shoshone Sam repeated his earlier question. "Had enough of prospecting?"

Aurfryn thought before replying. "Despite the current situation you find me in, I do not believe I have."

Shoshone shook his head. " 'Experience keeps a dear school, but a fool will learn in no other.' "

"Am I a fool?"

"All dreamers are fools, and I took you for a dreamer first time I laid eyes on you."

Aurfryn asked for some more water. As he again drank deeply he thought about what Shoshone Sam said and had to admit that "dreamer," was an apt description of himself. But sometime within the last three days his dream of finding gold had given over to something richer. Despite sore knees, aching back, sunburned skin, chapped lips and nearly perishing from thirst, he had fallen in love with the desert, though it was quite obvious the desert did not return his love. Then again, the desert was not possessed of human feelings. It was just a place. A magical place. And what are dreamers but seekers after magic?

Aurfryn returned Shoshone Sam his canteen, and they walked on.

"So, do you have anything to show for all your efforts?" Shoshone Sam said.

Aurfryn handed Shoshone Sam his treasure, the orange and red rock.

Shoshone Sam grunted. "That's it?"

Aurfryn nodded.

"Do you know what this is?"

"No, but I believe it to be of great value."

Shoshone Sam again shook his head. "You come to a place you know nothing about and expect to find riches when you can't even tell the difference between gold and garbage. This little rock, which you believe to be of great value, is jasper, a type of chert. If you had a ton of it, you couldn't swap it for the price of a cup of coffee. Admittedly, it's a nice sample. In fact, one of my ancestors could've made a nice arrowhead out of it, but as to great value, it's practically worthless. I suggest you pitch it."

"No," Aurfryn said, taking the rock back, "let it be a reminder of my own ignorance." He pocketed the rock. "Jasper is a curious name for a rock, do you not think? Do you know who Jasper was?"

"You're talking to someone who spent seven years at a Jesuit school. Jasper was one of the three wise men, following a star, looking for the baby Jesus."

"It was not just the baby Jesus the wise men were seeking. They were the scholars of their day, wandering in the desert, seeking knowledge."

"Well, maybe you should call yourself Jasper; you've certainly done enough 'wandering in the desert.'"

Aurfryn ran his fingers through his rough beard, thinking about Shoshone Sam's suggestion. The more he thought, the more he liked the idea. "I believe I shall do just that. Here I am in a new country, trying my hand at a new occupation. It seems fitting that I should have a new name as well." He tapped the rock in his shirt pocket. "And as Jasper, I shall be like the wise men, a seeker after knowledge, for this little rock tells me there is much I need to know if I am ever to make a go of it as a prospector."

"Well, one thing's for sure," Shoshone Sam said, "'Jasper' is a sight easier to pronounce than that mouthful your parents stuck you with."

They reached the top of a rise from where the van could be seen. "Jake, Jr. has your gear in the back," Shoshone Sam said. "We figured that while we were following you around, we might as well pick up after you."

"I do hope you did not bother to save the Bakelite canteen."

The corners of Shoshone Sam's mouth drew up into what, for him, passed for a grin. "I had my doubts about that newfangled stuff when I saw Jacob Harmon putting it out on his shelves." He held up his canteen. "Give me a canteen made of metal any day."

Lessons in Prospecting and a Meeting with the Devil

Three people stood upon a rise at the edge of a broad desert plain. One of the three, Eros Slaughter, a prospector of vast experience and the author of two books on the subject, was lecturing his new student upon the subject of finding gold.

"Now then, Jasper, I want you to imagine you're a nugget made of gold. Contrary to the belief held by medieval alchemists, there is no power on earth that could've created you. Volcanism could not have done it. Mountain-building forces can melt you, can extrude you through the fissures of rock, but no force here on earth could actually have created you.

"No, you were created when the very stars themselves were formed, for only the stupendous forces of star creation could slam together enough atoms to create heavy metals. Yet even those forces could not produce gold in great quantities. If you put together all the gold that's ever been discovered here on earth, it would make a mound hardly bigger than the one we are standing on.

"Now, forget that you are gold, but a prospector looking for gold. How do you go about it? Well, the good news is that gold is everywhere: in the oceans, the rivers, in practically every shovelful of earth. The bad news is that it is in such exceedingly minute amounts as to be of no practical value to the prospector. The trick is to find those places where gold is concentrated."

Eros swept his arm in a wide arc. "Look out there and tell me what you see."

Jasper followed the motion of Eros's arm. "I see a broad valley, mostly flat except where it swoops up to meet the hills."

" 'Swoops,' that's an accurate description. We call those 'swoops' alluvial fans. Now, concentrate upon those hills. Do you see anything unusual?"

"You mean the way some of them are colored in distinct bands, appearing lighter in color toward the top."

"That's not all that unusual, though I'll say right now that the ability to distinguish between rock types will help determine whether gold may be present. No, I want you to look for something that's common to all the hills that surround us. It's subtle."

Subtle thought Jasper as he slowly turned in a circle. "I don't see…" Then he detected a line, perhaps a ledge that circled the hills at the same elevation, and this brought to mind something he had read recently in one of the geology books at the Nevada State Library. "My goodness!" he exclaimed. "This valley was once a lake."

Eros slapped Jasper on the back. "We'll make a prospector out of you yet, son."

"I don't understand how you deduced that." This statement came from the third member of the group, Margaret Rutherford, a librarian at the Nevada State Library who had befriended Jasper when he had asked for help on finding books about prospecting. She was the one who introduced Jasper to Eros Slaughter, and had also organized this outing.

Jasper pointed out the nearly continuous line. "It's like the ring left in the tub after a bath."

"And it's not just this valley that was once a lake," Eros said. "Nearly every valley from here on down to Barstow was once a lake, each one emptying into the other. A prospector must understand the geologic history of a region. In this case, knowing that this was once a lake can tell you where to look for gold, for water works to expose gold. Back before there were lakes here—even before there were hills— this all was a vast inland sea. Then subsequent geologic forces pushed up the hills that surround the valleys, cutting off the sea, which eventually dried up. Now, the central portion of any uplift will not have much mineral formation, for it is at the edges, where the underlying rock hits against the overlying rock that mineralization occurs, and that's where a prospector wants to look for gold, in the fault zone created where the underlying rock pushes against the overlying."

"I read about faults," Jasper said. "But how do you go about finding one?"

"Think back to when there were lakes here. Obviously, it was a much wetter period. Storms were frequent, and water, in the form of rain, washed down and eroded the hills. Where most of the erosion occurred would have been along faults, for that was where the earth was most disturbed, where it was weaker."

Jasper pointed. "So those canyons we see are fault lines, where the rain came down and formed the canyons and gullies."

"That's right, and that's where you want to be looking for gold. Just don't expect to find it."

"Is that because someone has already looked for it?" Mrs. Rutherford said.

Eros smiled. "Well, there's that, Maggie. Hardly a speck of earth exists that some miner hasn't gone over. But I was thinking in terms of the forces of erosion."

"Meaning, the water will carry the gold away," Jasper said.

"Correct. Even with gold being as heavy as it is, it can be carried away by the action of flowing water. Think of a stream acting upon a rock. Maybe it is not flowing swiftly enough to dislodge the rock. But were that stream to double in speed, it would increase its carrying capacity by sixty-four times."

"So, where do you find gold?" Mrs. Rutherford said.

"Well, Maggie, let's find out. Why don't you drive us in that jalopy of yours up to that ledge that marks the edge of the ancient lake."

Mrs. Rutherford's 'jalopy' was a recently purchased Model-T Ford. She drove them several miles east, stopping just off the gravel of the road.

"I dare not get too far off the road," she said. "Otherwise, I'm sure to get stuck in the sand."

"We're fine right here, Maggie," Eros replied.

The three got out of the car. Despite the elevation, over five thousand feet where they stood, it was hot.

"Now then," Eros said, pointing with his walking stick, "there is the shoreline of the ancient lake, and any gold carried by streams into that lake would have settled out right there. Of course, to have made it that far downstream, the gold would likely be in the form of what we call 'flour,' having been ground down by the forces of erosion as it was pushed downstream." He pointed left. "That canyon you see was initially carved by the stream that entered the lake. Near the top of the canyon, gold, if present, would most likely be lying within a matrix of country rock. As the gold was washed downstream, it would've been broken into smaller pieces, which you would expect to find nestled within cracks and fissures."

"I explored canyons similar to this," Jasper said, "and nary a flake of gold did I see."

Eros smiled. "If gold were easy to find, then it wouldn't be valuable. Now then, why don't we mosey on up the canyon and see if we have better luck finding gold than you did?"

Jasper and Mrs. Rutherford's younger legs soon outpaced Eros', and they stopped to wait for him. Eros motioned them on. "Just wait for me up there where it gets really steep."

The crunch of their boots upon the coarse sand was the only sound to be heard. A bit of cloud passed before the sun, momentarily casting them in shade. "I forget how hot it is out here until a speck of cloud comes along," Jasper said.

"Despite the heat, are you enjoying your day, Jasper?"

"Indeed, I am, Mrs. Rutherford."

"Oh, please don't call me that; it makes me feel so old. Call me Margaret, or Maggie like Eros does."

"And where is Mr. Rutherford today?"

"Sadly, the same place he's been for the last twenty years. In a cemetery, outside of Carson City."

Jasper turned toward Maggie. "I'm sorry. I did not wish to bring up a sad memory."

Maggie waved away his concern. "Time is a great healer. The sadness disappears, leaving only good memories, which is why our outing today means so much to me. Harold, my late husband, was quite the amateur botanist, and we used to spend many days hiking the old desert trails, especially in the springtime when the wildflowers were in bloom. You cannot imagine the profusion of wildflowers after we've had a rainy winter."

"I had a taste of that, walking along a little wash down by Owens Lake. Yet even without the flowers, I've come to love the desert." He stopped and pointed. "Just look at those hills, Maggie. You cannot match them for color. They are like a rainbow captured in stone."

Looking back, they saw that Eros using his walking stick to pry something out of the ground.

"Should we wait for him?" Jasper said.

"We'd better not," she said, continuing to walk up the canyon. "It would just make him feel as if we were treating him like an old man, which, of course, he is."

"How old do you think?"

"I'm not sure, but he was here during Virginia City's heyday."

"Is that a fact? I wonder if he ever met Mark Twain?"

"I wouldn't be surprised. Eros has wonderful tales to tell."

Something shiny caught Jasper's eye, and he stopped to pry it out of the gravel bed. The rock was the shape and size of a small sugar cube, and reflected the sunlight off its metallic surface.

"Do you think it's gold?" Maggie said.

Jasper had been reading a lot about minerals and their crystal structure. "I don't think so," he said. "Gold does not have a cubic crystalline structure." Nevertheless, he saved the rock to ask Eros about it.

When they had gone about a quarter of a mile farther, the canyon abruptly divided into three smaller canyons, each very steep.

"I think this is where Eros wanted us to wait," Maggie said. She leaned against a large boulder and ran her hand across her forehead. "I wish I had thought to bring water."

Jasper removed a canteen from the small backpack he carried. "New as I am to this country, I have already learned my lesson about not carrying water." He unscrewed the lid and offered Maggie the canteen.

Maggie took several sips before handing it back. "Thank you."

Jasper drank in turn. As he was screwing the lid back on, Eros emerged from a bend in the canyon. "Would you care for some water?" Jasper said, holding high the canteen.

Eros shook his head. "I'm an old desert rat. Over the years I've conditioned myself to drink very little. You might say I'm like a camel in that respect."

"Jasper," Maggie said, "show Eros the rock you found."

Jasper held out the metallic cube. From his pocket, Eros took a similar rock, only twice the size of Jasper's.

"What are they?" Jasper said.

"They're pyrite crystals, and they're your first lesson in how to make a living as a prospector. Gold isn't the only thing of economic value. Now these little crystals aren't worth much–a boy might pay a nickel for one like this at a rock shop–but a large pyrite crystal is worth a lot more. I once found one that measured over three inches on each side, and at the Smithsonian Institute in Washington, D.C., they have one over seven inches square. Crystals that size are worth a lot to a collector."

"How much would you say?" Maggie said.

"I wouldn't take fifty dollars for the one I've got."

"If I found such a large crystal," Jasper said, "who would I sell it to? One of those rock shops you mentioned?"

Eros shook his head. "A rock shop would only give you pennies on the dollar for anything you brought them. What you need to do is to deal directly with collectors, those people who are willing to pay good money for an unusual specimen. My advice is for you to wait until you've got a sizeable collection of specimens then run an ad in one of the big city newspapers. Once you've built up a base of customers, you'll have a ready market for whatever you find."

Eros directed their attention to the canyons before them. "This spot is not exactly what I was looking for, but it will serve." He pointed straight ahead, using his stick. "Likely this wider canyon was the primary stream that once entered into the ancient lake. It might prove worthwhile to sift through the gravel here, especially near the outside edges where the gold would've settled." He changed the direction of his stick. "This side canyon was obviously a smaller stream, entering the main stream at a steeper angle. Where one stream joins another is also a good place to look for gold, as the contents of the side stream will settle out into the larger one. I suggest we poke around here and see if we can find any signs of what we old prospectors call 'color.' "

Jasper and Maggie, using only their hands, began to sift through the gravel.

"Our task is made difficult by the absence of water," Eros said. "If we had water, we could set up a rocker and sift through a lot more debris."

Jasper searched upward along the dry streambed while Maggie explored downstream. Eros was content to sit upon a flat rock and bask in the sun. After an hour of searching, Jasper and Maggie were about a quarter mile apart, which is why she had to shout to be heard. Jasper and Eros hurried to join her at the entrance to a wide wash.

"Find something, Maggie?" Eros called out as he drew close.

"I think so."

"Likely it's just some more pyrite," Eros said.

Jasper and Eros came to stand, looking over Maggie's shoulder.

"Is it gold?" she said. "It looks like gold."

"Where exactly did you find that, Maggie?" Eros said.

Maggie pointed. "Right there where you can see I've gouged out a place in the sand. Is it gold, Eros?"

Eros smiled. "Gold it is, Maggie."

Maggie gave a squeal of delight. "Is it worth much?"

"Not a piece that size, but it does indicate the presence of gold. I've got a hunch we may find more somewhere up this little wash."

This time Eros joined in the search. It was because he had spent so many years doing this exact same thing that he spotted gold the others had walked past, not seeing. "Here!" he called out.

Jasper and Maggie hurried back to join him. "That's gold right there," Eros said, pointing.

Jasper squatted down and gently brushed away bits of gravel to expose two small flakes, which he placed in Eros' palm.

"Small flakes, such as these, indicate that we're likely a good distance from the main gold vein." Eros said. "Let me know if you spot any more flakes like these."

The three spent nearly an hour in that area, shifting through gravel and turning over rocks, but found nothing resembling gold.

"That's all right," Eros said. "We may have better luck farther up the wash."

Two hours passed before the next discovery was made, and it was Jasper who made it. He had been going along turning over stones. He turned over a rock that looked like a toppled tombstone and found pressed into the soil not flakes of gold, but seven small nuggets strung out like shiny stars in a constellation.

"Eureka!" he shouted and danced a little jig.

Maggie was the first to join him. Seeing the nuggets, she gasped.

"What's all the excitement?" Eros said, hurrying forward. He looked down where Jasper was pointing. "Well, if that ain't a case of beginner's luck, I don't know what is! Don't just stand there, pick them up!"

In prying up the nuggets, Jasper unearthed two more, both larger than the rest.

"It's not supposed to be like this," Eros said, shaking his head. "It gives the wrong impression. A prospector might look for a month of Sundays and not find anything. Now here you are on your very first day, picking up nuggets like they were as common as peas in a pea patch."

"Believe me, I'll not let this discovery go to my head," Jasper said, then instructed his new friends to hold out their hands. He divided the nine nuggets between them, giving the largest to Maggie.

"But Jasper," she said, "they're your discovery. You should keep them for yourself."

"That's right, son," Eros said. "These nuggets could easily keep you in grub for a month."

Jasper shook his head. "Without the kindness you've both shown to a stranger, I'd never have found them." He tossed his nuggets lightly in his hand. "Besides, I have me a feeling there's a lot more where these came from."

"What we want to do now is find the source of these nuggets," Eros said. "If we can find more nuggets, they may point us to the mother lode."

But another hour passed, and not so much as a gold flake did they find. Tired and hungry, the three came together as the sun was well in the west.

"That's the way it goes, sometimes," Eros said. "Most times, in fact. You think you're on the trail of a major strike, and it peters out into nothing. Like I said earlier, if it were easy to find gold, it wouldn't be worth much. Now we need to find a place to camp before the sun sets, and I happen to know a good place not too far from here."

"There needs to be water if I'm to make us dinner," Maggie said.

"The place I'm thinking of has a spring, Maggie."

As they were returning to the automobile, Jasper made an excuse and went off behind a large bush to relieve himself. As he was about to button his fly, he heard a sound like the ticking of Maggie's Ford when the engine was cooling, only louder. He turned to see the biggest snake he had ever seen. It was coiled upon a large rock not two paces from where he stood. The body of the snake was like a massive spring, coiling itself ever tighter. The head swayed side to side like a hypnotist's pocket watch, its little pitch fork of a tongue stabbing the air.

During his time as a soldier, Jasper had been subject to the most harrowing experiences imaginable, yet never before had he felt as frightened as at that moment, so frightened, in fact, he could not move. It was as if his feet were anchored in concrete.

His initial warning having no affect upon his intruder, the snake began to hiss. The sibilance started softly, like a small leak in an inner tube, but quickly rose in volume to that of a swarm of outraged bees. The head of the snake, shaped like an arrowhead, seemed to inflate, while the mouth opened like a trapdoor on a stage to reveal needle sharp fangs. A creature from the underworld could not have exhibited a more fearsome display, yet Jasper stood as if turned to stone.

Having issued a warning, having amplified that warning, there was nothing left for the snake to do but to strike, and it was then that Jasper's survival instincts took command and sent him leaping back, seemingly just in the nick of time. "The Devil!" he screamed, before falling backwards over a rock, landing hard on his tailbone. Unconscious of the pain, he furiously crawled backwards across the sand. The snake struck a second time, and it seemed to Jasper that, once again, it missed him by just a whisper. The truth was, the snake never came even close to hitting him, for it never left the rock on which it had been sunning itself. Yet to hear Jasper tell of it later, the snake came so near to biting him, he could smell its foul reptilian breath.

In the meantime, Maggie and Eros, having heard the cry of, "The Devil!" turned to see Jasper, crawling backwards through the sand like some strange mechanical toy. When Jasper managed to get to his feet, he streaked past his friends.

"Jasper!" Maggie shouted. "What is it?"

Eventually Jasper stopped running. "The Devil!" he reiterated, pointing back the way he had come.

"What devil?" Eros said.

"Snake!" Jasper yelled.

"Snake?" Eros said. "Is that all?" He strode toward the bush where Jasper had been.

"Where are you going?" Jasper yelled, as he ran back toward them. "Did you not hear what I said? There is a devil of a snake!"

Eros disappeared behind the bush and emerged moments later with the rattlesnake draped over his walking stick. "You mean this little ol' rattler?"

By any standard, the rattlesnake was not little, hanging down as it did two feet to each side of the stick. But it did not stay long on the stick, but wiggled off onto the ground where it began to slither away.

Jasper picked up the biggest rock he could manage.

"Jasper, what are you going to do?" Eros said.

"Why, kill it, of course!"

"Now hold on there! Leave be!"

" 'Thou shalt not suffer a snake to live!' " Jasper quoted, as he advanced upon the snake, which was trying to make a getaway.

"Well, son," Eros said, "you're going to suffer this one." And he jabbed Jasper hard in the stomach with his walking stick.

The rock fell from Jasper's hands as he doubled over.

"I'm sorry, Jasper," Eros said, "I didn't want to hurt you. But I can't let you harm that poor snake."

Jasper slowly unbent. "For the love of God, why not?"

"I'll tell you exactly why not," Eros said. "What did that snake ever do to you? All he was doing was trying to get a little warmth before the cold night comes on, and here comes a big galoot like yourself and scares the wits out him!"

"Scares the wits out of *him*? What of *me*?"

Eros stepped closer, laid on hand upon Jasper's shoulder. "Being scared is not an excuse to kill something. If you're going to be spending your days out here, you're going to have to learn to get along with nature's creatures, the same way I've done for more than sixty years."

Jasper could see some logic in Eros' argument, yet something instinctively made him want to kill the snake. The snake, however, had made its getaway, disappearing under a bush, and Jasper was not about to go in after it.

"Besides," Eros said, "There's a special reason why I'll not hurt a rattlesnake."

"And what might that be?" Jasper said.

Eros patted Jasper on the shoulder. "I'll tell once we've gotten some grub in our bellies. In the meantime, you best button your fly."

The Sanitary Fund

Sitting beside the makeshift kitchen Maggie had created, Jasper sopped up the bean juice on his plate with a chunk of bread. "I've heard it said that hunger is the best sauce, yet were I as full up as Jack Biggers, I still would have found these beans irresistible."

"I would've preferred to have served you my spicy pan-fried chicken," Maggie said, "but Eros insisted I make pork and beans."

"That's because beans are the staple of the prospector," Eros said. "If Jasper is going to be scratching a living out of the dirt, miles from any place where he can get a home-cooked meal, then he's going to have to get used to eating beans."

"Along with this delectable bread, I hope," Jasper said. "May I ask what gives it its special flavor?"

"That's sourdough bread," Eros said. "It's made with the same starter I've been using the past fifty years. The older the starter, the better the bread. I'll be glad to share some with you."

"You don't know how generous Eros' offer is, Jasper," Maggie said. "Most sourdough bread bakers I know guard their starter as if it were the Crown Jewels."

"I've never been one to hoard anything, Maggie. Besides I feel I owe it to Jasper after poking him in the stomach."

Jasper placed a hand on his still sore stomach. "I do not know what came over me, seeing that rattlesnake. Never have I felt weaker in the knees, not even during the war."

"Most people have some fear they can't account for," Eros said. "I guess yours is fear of snakes."

"You mentioned you have a particular reason for not killing a rattlesnake," Jasper said.

"Did I?" Eros said, setting his plate aside. "Funny, I don't remember saying any such thing."

"Oh, fiddlesticks!" Maggie said. "Of course, you do. You just want us to coax the story out of you."

Eros grinned. "You're on to me, Maggie. But if I'm going to be telling this story, we first best find some more wood and build up this campfire."

"I'll let you two do that while I wash up the dishes," Maggie said.

While Eros stirred up the fire, Jasper gathered up what deadwood he could find. Then as Maggie and Jasper made themselves comfortable around the campfire, Eros used a twig to light his pipe. Satisfied that it was drawing well, he rested his back against an upright boulder. "Maggie, did I ever tell you about the time I gave Mark Twain five thousand dollars?"

"Does this have anything to do with snakes?"

"It does."

"Then to answer your question, no, I haven't heard you tell about giving Mark Twain that kind of money, and I'm sure I would have remembered if I had."

Eros blew a stream of tobacco smoke heavenward. "Well, this must've been about 1864 or there about. I'd been living in Virginia City for over a year, working down in the bowels of the earth for the Gould and Curry Mining Company. I figured we must have dug about halfway to hell, and the temperature down there only seemed to confirm this. Try doing calisthenics in a Turkish bath and you'll get some idea of what it was like. A man could only work for about fifteen minutes before having to rest. For ten to twelve hours a day we'd slave away, fifteen minutes on, fifteen minutes off, and every minute wondering if the whole mountain was going to come down on our heads."

"That sounds horrible," Maggie said, "and knowing how you love the wide-open spaces, I wonder why you put up with it."

"Well, the money was good. Working for the Gould and Curry, a man could make about four times the national average. Of course, most miners spent their wages in the saloons, of which there were plenty, but I never cared much for the taste of liquor. Besides, I had something better to do with my wages. I was saving up to get married. Now, don't look so surprised, Maggie. I wasn't always the confirmed bachelor you see today."

Eros leaned forward and emptied the ashes of his pipe into the fire. "Her name was Esmeralda, and she was the prettiest gal this side of the Mississippi, or any side for that matter. Her father owned a hardware store; not the biggest in Virginia City, but by far the busiest because Esmeralda waited on the customers. Men would come into the store: 'I need a bolt, Esmeralda.' Come back five minutes later: 'I forgot to buy a nut to fit the bolt, Esmeralda.' Of course, they didn't need a dag-blasted thing. They just wanted the chance to be near Esmeralda and gaze into her beautiful green eyes.

"But I was certain Esmeralda had a special place in her heart just for me. Many a night we'd sit together on the swing outside her father's house, or go for a walk out where we could look down upon the lights in the Carson Valley, and we'd get to talking, and I'd start boasting how I was going to strike it rich and build a big mansion on Nob Hill in San Francisco, and she and I would get married and live the life of king and queen." Eros laughed as he reached into his pouch for more tobacco. "If a fool's talk was worth something, mine would've come in at a thousand dollars an ounce. A man didn't get rich working for Gould and Curry; it was the Goulds and the Currys who had it rich. But then something happened to change my fortune.

"Down in the mine, we always worked in pairs. The man I'd been partnering with for nearly a year decided to take a job riding shotgun on the Wells Fargo stage. The way he figured it, it was a lot safer guarding a gold shipment, where the worst that could happen would be for somebody to shoot him, than it was working down in the mines. I was assigned a new partner, a German fellow name of Herman Eberhardt, and a more cantankerous and disagreeable man God never created, though like most Germans I've known, he was as smart as a whip. When he wasn't working in the mines, he had his nose in survey maps or was looking over the ground around the mines. After we'd been working together for a couple of months, he confided in me that he knew a way to get rich. All he need was enough money to purchase mining equipment. Of course, getting rich was foremost in my mind, and since I had all that money saved up, I suggested we go in as partners and split the profits fifty-fifty. He agreed, and so the Eberhardt and Slaughter Mining Company was formed.

"Now, there was a mine, the Wide West, known to one and all, for it yielded rich ore. The owners were offered four thousand dollars a foot for that mine and scoffed, declaring it but a paltry offering. Herman, who had been studying the ground around the Wide West, and had even sneaked into the mine when the guard was drunk or asleep, was convinced the main ore-rich vein was a 'blind lead.' A blind lead is a vein of that does not reach the surface, and is only come upon while digging. Herman believed that, unbeknownst to owners of the Wide West, the richest vein of ore was running independent of the ground filed upon. Herman and I immediately filed a new claim and set to work.

"Though we had slaved for the Gould and Curry, it was as nothing compared to the way we worked now that we were mine owners ourselves. We hardly stopped to sleep. In fact, sleep seemed just an unnecessary distraction, for we were fueled by the knowledge that soon we would be joining the ranks of the Goulds and Currys. Seems the only time we stopped digging was to set off some dynamite when the rock proved unyielding to our picks. Herman figured that by digging down at an angle of forty degrees we'd reach the rich vein after we'd dug about one hundred feet. One hundred feet may not sound like much, but the tailings from one hundred feet makes a sizeable mountain. And the effort of hauling all that rock up a slope of forty degrees! We started by packing the rock out on our backs, but soon went to using donkeys, then ran some rails and winched the debris to the surface on an ore cart. Then there was the shoring required to keep the ground above us from coming down on our heads. Dynamite, donkeys, ore carts, timber for shoring–none of that came cheap. But what was a few thousand dollars when untold riches awaited us?"

Eros inhaled upon his pipe and blew a cloud of smoke over our heads. "I started to have my doubts when we'd dug about forty or fifty feet beyond the one hundred feet originally projected. Herman did some more studying of the ground and declared that we just needed to change the angle of our digging a bit to hit the rich vein. This gave me renewed hope until having gone another fifty feet in this new direction we had nothing to show but a mountainous pile of worthless rock.

"Then the hoped-for event happened. I had just finished winching up another ore cart of rock when Herman came running out of the mine, his face flushed with excitement. He handed me a rock. Most of the rock we'd burrowed through you could barely break with a sledge hammer, but this rock crumbled in my hand like a stale piece of bread, and there among the fragments of that rock, sparkling in the sun, were particles of gold and silver.

"Well, I guess we went a bit crazy, but who was to blame us? We whooped and hollered and waved our hats in the air and generally carried on like lunatics until we had a sizeable crowd around us. Word soon spread that a vein of nearly pure gold and silver had been discovered at the Eberhardt and Slaughter Mine. Folks wanted to see for themselves, but we weren't about to let anyone into our mine to steal our precious ore. While I stood guard, Herman went back down into the mine and came back with a shovelful of ore which he spread out upon the ground for all to see. Any fool could see that the dirt was rich. Some speculated that such dirt would assay out at over five thousand dollars a ton!

"Well, that was certainly cause for celebration. We hired a couple of men we could trust to guard our mine while Herman and I adjourned to the nearest saloon. I said before that I never cared much for the taste of spirits, but that night I drank champagne like it was water. Oh, what a glorious feeling, to be intoxicated not only with drink, but with the knowledge that we were rich men! In my mind, I already had that mansion on Nob Hill.

"Not surprisingly, I woke very late the next morning with a

monumental headache, but also with a happy heart, knowing that, from now on, I could sleep as late as I liked and never have to do a lick of work if I didn't feel like it. I do believe I fairly floated over the ground as I made my way to the mine.

"So imagine my dismay when I found it guarded by men other than those we'd hired!"

Eros emptied the ashes of his pipe into the fire then took his time scraping out the bowl with a stick.

"Don't leave us hanging, Eros!" Maggie exclaimed. "Tell us what happened!"

"Well, the long and the short of it, Maggie," Eros said, returning his pipe to the pocket of his vest, "is that Herman Eberhardt, that no-good partner of mine, forged my signature and sold the mine for ten thousand dollars in cash."

"Ten thousand dollars!" Jasper exclaimed. "But that mine must have been worth a king's ransom."

"So you would've thought," Eros said. "But it didn't take the new owners long to figure out that the mine had been salted."

"Salted?" Maggie said.

Jasper remembered coming across "salted" in *Roughing It.* "That is when someone places rich ore inside a mine to give the impression that the mine is valuable when it is not."

Eros nodded. "The way I figured it, Herman knew he had miscalculated, and that the mine was never going to amount to a hill of beans, so he pawned the mine off on some unsuspecting dupes for what cash he could get for it. Then he lit out, leaving me holding the bag, only since I had invested everything I owned in the mine, I didn't have so much as a bag to hold."

"So what did you do?" Maggie said.

"After I finally convinced the new owners that I was as much cheated as they, I enlisted the aid of a sheriff's deputy to help me hunt down Herman, though not knowing where he had gone, there seemed little chance of us catching him. Then my old partner from the Gould and Curry told me he'd seen Herman riding north across the barren desert. The way we figured, Herman was making for the recent gold discovery in the Jarbridge Mountains, up in the northeast corner of Nevada.

"With that in mind, it wasn't long before we found tracks made by his horse. Then we had a bit of luck, for Herman's horse threw a shoe, and that slowed him down. We spotted him on the second day, not far from this spring we're at right now. Unfortunately, he spotted us as well, and he holed up in that jumble of rocks you can see right over there. Those rocks provided Herman with plenty of cover, while we had nothing to hide behind but sage brush.

"Well, it was a standoff. Herman couldn't leave the safety of his hidey-hole, and we couldn't get near him without getting shot. Then while the deputy and I were deliberating on what to do, we heard this horrible scream. At first, I thought it another one of Herman's tricks, something to get us to play our hand, but after about an hour with us not hearing so much as a peep, I decided I'd try to sneak up on Herman while the deputy covered me. I tell you I was shaking in my boots, but I need not have worried, for I discovered Herman lying on the ground as dead as a brick. It didn't take long to figure out what happened. Herman had been attempting to stash the money he stole in a crack in a rock, likely so he wouldn't have the money on him in case he got caught, trying to escape. But he hadn't figured on there being a rattlesnake holed up in that crevice."

Eros tapped the side of his neck. "The snake struck Herman right here in the jugular vein. Had he gotten bitten anywhere else, he most likely would have lived, but the venom went straight to his brain and killed him. I confess I was grateful to that snake, for even while we were chasing Herman, I didn't know what we were going to do once we caught up with him. Much as I disliked the man, I wasn't looking forward to hauling him back to Virginia City to see him put in jail or maybe hanged. That old rattlesnake saved me a heap of trouble."

"And is that why you will not kill a rattlesnake?" Jasper said.

"It is."

"So what happened when you and the deputy returned to Virginia

City?" Maggie said.

"Having retrieved the ten thousand dollars, I offered to buy back the Eberhardt and Slaughter mine, but the new miner owners wouldn't hear of it. It seemed that in my absence they had dug a little deeper and came upon that rich vein of ore that had eluded Herman and me. Eventually the Eberhardt and Slaughter mine yielded over one million dollars in gold and silver."

"But Herman forged your signature," Maggie said. "Wouldn't that have made the sale of the mine invalid? At the very least, you should've gotten one-half of the profits."

Eros shrugged. "Perhaps, but only after a lengthy courtroom battle in which lawyers would've ended up with most of the money. The truth is, I was sick at heart of the whole thing, and wanted nothing more to do with the Eberhardt and Slaughter mine."

"So, what does all this have to do with you giving Mark Twain five thousand dollars?" Jasper said.

Eros smiled. "I was just getting to that. Now, at that time, some of Virginia City's leading citizens, Mark Twain among them, were going from mining town to mining town soliciting contributions to the Sanitary Fund for wounded Union Soldiers. I took the ten thousand dollars, subtracted what I had invested, and donated the rest. I remember the look Twain gave me when I handed him all that money. He stared at that money then at me in my threadbare clothes then back again to the money. I had the feeling the disparity between all that money I'd handed him and my ragged appearance gave him an idea for one of his stories."

"Did he say anything?" Jasper said.

"Not that I remember." Eros stretched out his arms above his head. "And now if you two don't mind, I think I'll turn in."

"One moment," Jasper said. "May I ask what became of Esmeralda and your plans to marry?"

Eros blinked several times. "Eh? What was that?"

"Esmeralda, she…?"

"Oh yes, Esmeralda. Well, she up and married someone else. A very rich man."

"I'm sorry, Eros," Maggie said. "Obviously, she didn't deserve you."

"No, Maggie, it was the other way around; I didn't deserve her. Esmeralda was a sweet, innocent girl who little cared for riches until I went and planted the seed in her head with all my boasting. I only hope her wealth made her happy."

"So you never knew what became of her?" Jasper said.

"I heard she and her rich husband moved to San Francisco. Perhaps she got to live in that mansion I hoped to build for the two of us."

Maggie sighed. "It's a sad story, Eros."

Eros shook his head. "The whole experience was the making of me."

"How so?"

"Well, despite the fact that Herman turned out to be a crook, he taught me practically everything I know about mining. It was that knowledge that gave me my livelihood and allowed me to live life on my own terms."

"But what of your dream of becoming rich?" Jasper said.

"Rich? Why I'm the richest man alive! Just look above you."

Jasper and Maggie peered up into the night sky. Sagittarius, that constellation shaped like a teapot, had risen above the southern horizon, and from its spout poured a stream of glittering stars that flowed clear across the sky.

"Now, that's what I call riches," Eros said, following the arc of the Milky Way with a sweep of his arm. "And the wonder of it is those jewels don't have to be grubbed out of the ground, and you don't have to worry for fear they'll get stolen. For over sixty years, I've called the desert my home, and its beauty far exceeds any mansion built by man. Each sunrise reveals a land with more colors than could fit on an artist's palette, and every night the sky is filled with jewels more lustrous than any worn by a queen. I dare you to show me greater riches than these." And having made that challenge, Eros rose and went off to sleep.

Maggie and Jasper continued to sit, staring at the glowing coals, all that remained of the campfire. In his mind, Jasper reviewed the story Eros had told. "I confess to being somewhat troubled by Eros' story," he said in a low voice.

"In what way?" Maggie said.

Jasper listened a moment. The rattle of Eros' snoring assured him he would not be overheard. "Have you read the book *Roughing It* by Mark Twain?"

"Yes, but it's been years."

"There's a story in it that describes an incident not all that different from what we just heard."

"So you think Eros was borrowing from the pages of Mark Twain?"

"Not necessarily. It might be that Twain, who had a reputation for prevarication, might have based his story on the events of the Eberhardt and Slaughter mine."

"So what is it that bothers you?"

"A specific detail in Eros' story." Jasper looked to the east where the light of the rising moon outlined the rock jumble where Herman Eberhardt had met his end. "It seems more than a coincidence that Eros led us to the very place where Herman was bitten by a snake." Jasper shuddered as a chill ran up his spine. "You don't suppose there are still rattlesnakes here, do you?"

Eros' voice came out of the night. "You better believe there are. Rattlesnakes as big around as my arm." Laughing, Eros turned upon his side. "Sweet dreams."

Madame Coyote

Jasper was working his way up a wash looking for signs of "color." It had been a year since he had entered Jacob Harmon's store and began his career as a prospector. The eighty-plus dollars Mr. Harmon held on account had dwindled as he drew more supplies and had little of value to exchange for them. The amount of gold he had found so far would not have filled the watch pocket of his jeans. His biggest discovery had been a quantity of jewelry-quality turquoise, which he had sold to Shoshone Sam who in turn sold it to (to use his own words) "the crazy Navajos." That discovery had Jasper walking on air for a few days, but since then he had little to show for his efforts.

Behind Jasper trailed Esmeralda, a donkey he had purchased on the advice of Jacob Harmon and whom Jasper named after the girl that his mentor, Eros Slaughter, had once hoped to marry. Eros had described Esmeralda as the prettiest girl this side of the Mississippi, and were it possible for a humble donkey to be considered pretty, then Esmeralda was, being all of a tawny color, save for the charcoal-gray streaks that adorned her long cheeks. Esmeralda had a pleasant disposition, an attribute conditional upon Jasper providing her with a piece of hard candy each morning. If someone had told Jasper he would end up indulging the sweet tooth of a burro, he would have laughed. The manner in which Esmeralda taught Jasper the error in his thinking occurred on the first morning he attempted to put Esmeralda to work. He spread a saddle blanket across her back then bent down to pick up the packs containing his gear. Upon straightening, he found the blanket had slipped to the ground. He set the packs down, repositioned the blanket, bent down, picked up the packs again only to find the blanket lying upon the ground once more. How exactly the blanket came to be there, Jasper was not sure, for it appeared Esmeralda had not moved a muscle. Suspecting some sort of chicanery, Jasper held the blanket in place with one hand while he struggled to lift the heavy packs with one arm. But the moment he succeeded in placing the packs upon Esmeralda's back, she executed a little sidestep, and packs and blanket tumbled to the ground.

At this point Jasper thought it best to sit and think about the situation and his options. First would be to repeat the same process of trying to load the packs, but he was fairly certain the result would be the same. A second option would be to "wallop the hell out of her," which Esmeralda's previous owner had recommended, "should she give you any trouble." During the war, Jasper had seen mule drivers "wallop the hell" out of exhausted horses struggling to pull loads far too heavy for them. The sight had sickened him, and he was not about to resort to such cruel measures with Esmeralda. A third option would be to use ropes to immobilize Esmeralda while he loaded his packs onto her. Jasper felt this would do little to foster an *esprit de corps* and might result in her exacting revenge at some opportune moment in the future. Besides, he needed the ropes to tie down the packs.

Having run out of options, he decided to think about it some more while he indulged himself with a piece of hard candy. He had bought a large bag of these candies and allowed himself one per day as a special treat from his otherwise unvarying diet of beans and sourdough bread. Given the current crisis, however, a candy seemed warranted. He had no sooner gotten the candy unwrapped then he found Esmeralda leaning heavily upon his shoulder, staring avidly at the candy.

"Tell me, friend," Jasper said, "why I should share my candy with such an uncooperative beast such as yourself?"

Then he had an idea. He presented Esmeralda with the candy, and as she stood, crunching it with her big molars, Jasper threw the blanket and packs onto her back. Content with her candy, Esmeralda offered no resistance.

"I must apologize for failing to see the true nature of our relationship," Jasper told Esmeralda, as he cinched the ropes that secured the packs. "Your antics have taught me that you are not to be thought of merely as a beast of burden, but as an equal in our adventures."

Esmeralda responded with a loud hee-haw, shattering the stillness of the desert morning and sending several mourning doves off looking for a quieter neighborhood. Thereafter Esmeralda always got her daily candy and Jasper was never given any trouble concerning the packs.

Jasper bent down and picked up a shiny rock. It was a small piece of chalcopyrite, displaying "peacock" coloration. It was a pretty thing, but too small to be of value to a collector. Yet having studied minerals under the tutelage of Eros Slaughter, Jasper knew chalcopyrite contained copper, and though copper was not gold, Jasper would not turn down a potential copper mine if he should happen upon one.

Jasper proceeded to look for more chalcopyrite. Eros had showed him how to trace a mineral specimen back to its point of origin. A continued search suggested the main source was somewhere along a dry gulch entering the wash from the east. Where the gulch ended, halfway up the side of a hill, Jasper pried up a piece of chalcopyrite as big as his fist. Not only did it exhibit a colorful iridescence, not unlike that of a peacock's feather, but it contained a multitude of slender crystals, some as long as his thumbnail. Jasper was pleased, for here was a specimen which a rock collector would pay several dollars for.

He continued up the hillside following what looked like a game trail. To each side of the trail, the ground was littered with tiny pieces of copper bearing ore. It seemed odd there were so many fragments lying on the surface, and he began to suspect that it was not a game trail he was following, but a man-made footpath. His suspicion was confirmed when the trail ended at the base of what was clearly a mine tailing. He scrambled up over the loose scree and found the opening to a mine partially blocked by fallen rubble. Jasper poked his head inside. It wasn't much of a mine, ending as it did about ten or twelve feet from the entrance.

Jasper turned and examined the ground around him. There were a few short wooden planks and pieces of rusty metal, but little else. Jasper made a bench using one of the planks and sat looking down on the plain below him. He could discern the faint line of a wagon track heading northwest. Together, the mine, the tailings and the wagon track all told a familiar tale. Sometime past, a prospector, likely a man much like Jasper, had noted the presence of copper-bearing ore and had followed it to its source. Yet whatever copper ore he had unearthed must not have been much, judging by the small size of the mine and its tailing.

Though disappointed, Jasper took his failure stoically. It was not the first time he had thought himself hot on the trail of discovery only to find that someone already had been there before him. Eros Slaughter had warned him of this, saying there wasn't a speck of earth that some miner had not gone over. Yet it seemed strange to Jasper that a country so vast, where one could go weeks, months even, without seeing another living soul, could have been so thoroughly picked over by treasure seekers.

Of course, there was always a chance that the miner had given up before finding the main body of copper ore, but Jasper thought that unlikely, for he credited his fellow miner with the same tenacity he himself possessed. No, if the miner had called it quits, it was because there was nothing to gained by going on. Jasper would just have to be content with his nice specimen of chalcopyrite.

Jasper made his way back to where Esmeralda stood patiently waiting. "Well, Esmeralda," he said, picking up the end of her reins, "today has seen little profit, and I would not mind taking comfort in a bowl of beans and some sourdough bread."

It was late afternoon by the time they returned to the spring where Jasper previously had set up camp. He quickly gathered what pieces of wood he could find and made a fire to reheat his pot of beans. As he stirred the pot, he thought about the statement he had made earlier to Esmeralda. Had the day truly been without profit? True, he only had the specimen of chalcopyrite to show for his efforts, but throughout the day he had wandered through fields of spring wildflowers. His spirit, grown weary from months of fruitless prospecting, had been lifted by their beauty. Surely there was profit in that, if not for the pocket, then for the soul.

Jasper caught sight of something out of the corner of his eye and turned to see a coyote standing not forty feet away.

"A pleasant good evening to you, sir." Jasper said. Here was an addition to the day's profit column, for Jasper had acquired an affection for these wild and wily creatures that were as much a part of the desert as cacti. He found the coyote an odd animal, alternately furtive and sociable. Sometimes Jasper only glimpsed a coyote before it disappeared, as if by magic. At other times a coyote might join him of an evening, sitting, or perhaps lying, at the edge of his campfire light, sometimes for hours.

Another aspect of the coyote which amused Jasper was his vocal talent. The natives called the coyote "song dog," and to lie awake at night, listening to a pack of coyotes celebrating the rising of the moon with their chilling canine discord was a thrill Jasper would not have traded for gold, even now when he certainly could use some.

The coyote turned sideways, revealing the absence of a hind leg. That the coyote had managed to survive with such a handicap seemed a miracle, more so because she (her swollen teats testified to her being a she) appeared to be in better health than other coyotes Jasper had encountered, even ones not pregnant, as this one obviously was.

"You must forgive for calling you 'sir' when clearly you are a Madame," Jasper said. He broke off a piece of his bread. "I wonder if you would be inclined to join me for dinner?" He dribbled bean broth over the bread and set it on a tin plate several paces off to one side. Returning to his campfire, Jasper finished his dinner, ignoring the clatter of the tin plate being pushed along by a tongue. Later when he got up to put more wood on the fire, he saw that the bread was gone, as was his new friend, Madame Coyote.

Over the course of the next week, Madame Coyote was a regular dinner guest. Jasper, never presumed upon their friendship, but always allowed his visitor to savor her tidbits at a respectable distance. Then the three-legged coyote stopped coming. Jasper missed her company, but trusted she had discovered better fare elsewhere.

As a result of a very wet winter, the wildflowers continued to bloom into late spring. Across the wide plains, desert poppies colored the ground as if some mighty hand had brushed it with orange paint. The ravines and washes, which had received more moisture, were festooned with the blossoms of the indigo bush, the long clusters of apricot-colored mallow petals, the aromatic trumpet-shaped flowers of sacred datura and the soft lavender stocks of the desert snapdragon. These, as well as other flowers, vied to out compete each other in splendor. Their sheer vibrancy beckoned with a promise of endless glories waiting to be discovered. Like Jasper, Esmeralda caught spring fever and was hard pressed to stand still while Jasper loaded the packs upon her, even given her candy.

Late May marked the first anniversary of Jasper's making his home in the desert. This called for a celebration, a feast, but all Jasper had was beans, flour, a little sugar, half a tin of lard and a small bottle of whiskey kept for medicinal purposes. Yet a dearth of comestibles was not to put a damper on the festivities. Jasper made a dough of flour and lard, sprinkled it with sugar and baked it on the lid of his Dutch oven. He shared this pastry with Esmeralda, careful to stipulate that this treat was not to be considered as a regular thing. Then Jasper toasted the desert, taking a sip of whiskey each time he turned to face the four cardinal directions. He was not sure why he did this, other than it seemed that the occasion demanded that some sort of ceremony be enacted. In conclusion, he held the bottle high and saluted the sun. "Here is to the best year of my life, and may the coming year bring me the pot of gold at the end of the rainbow." Jasper reflected that this was not likely since rainbows in this land of little rain were about as common as sea creatures. "Well, perhaps not a pot of gold, but sufficient gold to supply me with enough beans and flour for—"

Jasper's speech was cut off by a sudden thunderous growl, as if some colossal machine were ripping into the bowels of the earth. The ground began to buck beneath him, pitching him one way then another as if he were on the deck of a ship in a storm. Bushes were set to rocking. A nearby Joshua tree toppled over. Jasper's brain could not come to grips with this sudden deviation from the world as he had known it. On and on the convulsing went. Seconds seemed like minutes. A minute an eternity. Finally, one word emerged from his muddled brain. "Earthquake!" he yelled.

The word acted like a magician's incantation uttered to break a spell, for the earth ceased its shaking. Not so Jasper's knees. Wisely, he decided to sit down and wait for the pounding of his heart to subside. A frightened Esmeralda, who had added to the cacophony with earsplitting hee-haws, came to stand with her head resting upon Jasper's shoulder.

Jasper reached up and patted her cheek. "Well, that was a bit of excitement that I dare say we lacked back in Wales. I cannot say it is an experience I would care to repeat."

As if to assert that Jasper had little say in this matter, the ground began to shake again. It was, however, but a small aftershock, over before Jasper had time to react. Throughout all the shaking, Jasper had managed to hold on to the whiskey bottle. Now he took a sip to settle his nerves. When several minutes passed with no more aftershocks, Jasper set about putting his camp back in order. As he possessed little, there was little damage. The worst was his pot of beans, which had toppled over, dumping its contents. It was when Jasper was at the spring, washing the pot, that he looked up to see the three-legged coyote.

"Well, Madame," he said. "It seems Mother Nature caught a bit of Saint Vitus' Dance, but she is better now, or so we hope."

But matters appeared not well with the three-legged coyote. Restlessly she paced back and forth on three legs. Jasper approached her, looking for injuries, but saw none.

"If it is supper you are after," he said, turning away, "I am afraid that, given the circumstance, I have nothing to offer."

The coyote made a disconcerting sound, a troubled whimper. As

Jasper again approached, she ran about ten feet, stopped, looked back over her shoulder, and once again made that pleading sound.

"Esmeralda," Jasper announced, "I do believe our friend wishes for us to go with her."

Having successfully communicated her wish, the coyote hurried on ahead. Though she ran on just three legs, Jasper still had a hard time keeping up. After nearly a half mile that left him breathless, they came to a hillside covered in recently fallen rock debris. The coyote scrambled a short way up and attempted to dig with one paw. Jasper immediately deduced the problem: the rock slide had blocked the entrance to the coyote's den.

Jasper set to work, tossing rocks left and right as Madame Coyote transmitted her anxiety with soft whimpers "I take it you have little ones in your den. We can but hope they are still alive."

Esmeralda, standing on solid ground at the base of the scree, questioned the whole situation with strident hee-haws.

"Silence, you noisome beast!" Jasper ordered. "Your racket will set the earth to shaking again!"

Jasper worked steadily despite the fact that he held out little hope for the pups. The scree was so loose that no sooner had he shoved rocks aside than others slid down to take their place. He used several large rocks to make a dam above where he was digging and succeeded in exposing an opening in the earth. He shoved a hefty rock aside, exposing more of the hole. Before he could reach inside the den, Madame Coyote passed between his legs to emerge seconds later with a pup held by the scruff of his neck. She carried the pup down off the hill and deposited him at Esmeralda's feet. By the time she returned, Jasper had already extracted the remaining four pups. Madame Coyote took one, and Jasper cradled the remaining three in his arms as he slid down off the hill.

Esmeralda did not know what to make of the small creatures. She nudged one of the pups with her nose, then snorted, blowing dust off the pup and setting it to whimpering. Madame Coyote moved in and began to wash her pups with her tongue.

"Well, now," Jasper said, sitting down to empty his boots of rocks, "I do believe this rescue calls for another celebration. A pity that I left my bottle of whiskey back at camp." He fussed with a knot in his boot lace. "Then again the whiskey might not be such a good idea, considering that the last time I indulged, the earth began to shake."

Yet there was more to celebrate than just the rescue of the coyote pups. As Jasper dumped out the contents of his boots, out dropped nuggets of pure gold!

Dreaming

It was Monday morning in the small town of Inyo, and as was his custom each Monday, Jacob Harmon was making out his weekly orders. It was a task he hated. Not only did it require the use of several different forms, depending which distributor he was ordering from, but it served to remind him once again of his paucity of sales. He wondered why he ever came to this hole-in-the-wall in the first place.

At one time the purchase of the Inyo General Store seemed like a smart decision for two reasons: one, the whole of the eastern Sierras appeared poised to become a great metropolitan area not unlike Los Angeles. The prerequisites were there. There was water, there was land suitable for agriculture, there were mountains rich in minerals. In addition, the dry desert air promised to be the cure for his wife's troublesome cough.

But developments had not followed suit. True, the land was good. Farmers moved in and planted apple orchards. The result was apples delightful to the eye and delicious to the palate, but only on those years when a farmer actually produced a crop. The problem was not with the soil, but the climate. Late frosts, drying winds, years of drought followed by torrential rains meant a farmer would be lucky to get in a good crop one year in four. Then the Los Angeles Department of Water and Power moved in and bought up most of the water rights. Water that might have gone for farms and industry was now being piped to thirsty city dwellers two hundred miles away. Each year less and less water flowed into the Owens River with the result that the once large Owens Lake had all but disappeared.

Worse was the fact that the dry desert air had not proved the cure for his wife, and like Owens Lake, she visibly shrank each year until she finally succumbed.

Jacob pushed one order form aside and took up another. What a nuisance to have to use so many forms when one should do. Across the nations, new chains of markets were springing up. "Supermarkets" they were called, selling everything under the sun, and each one served by one central distribution center. Everything a store manager needed was housed under one roof with no need to order from separate distributors. To be a part of this growing trend of supermarkets was Jacob's dream.

Jacob rubbed his eyes, tired from filling out forms in the dim light. That was another thing about the new supermarkets; each store was bright and cheery. No wonder shoppers preferred the new stores to outdated markets like his in which the electric lighting was little improvement over the old gas lights they had replaced. He knew for a fact that many of the local residents of Inyo were sneaking off to do their shopping in Reno or Bakersfield, where the selection was not only greater, but the prices better.

He closed his eyes and pictured a brightly lit sign above a store the size of a city block: "Harmon and Son's Supermarket." Then in smaller letters, "Everything You Need Under One Roof." He imagined a sleek office wherein he guided the overall direction of his burgeoning retail empire while Jacob Jr., in an office adjacent, handled the day-to-day operations. There would be an army of secretaries—young, attractive, efficient—busy answering telephones. Of course, there would be the individual store managers: bright young Turks eagerly inspecting goods, tracking orders, overseeing the stores' maintenance and doing everything possible to insure the customers of "Harmon and Son's" had the most pleasurable shopping experience possible.

Jacob slammed his pencil down upon an order form. Who was he kidding? Jacob Harmon sitting behind a desk? If he managed to keep his little market afloat, he would likely end his days behind this counter, wearing the same stained apron around his ever-increasing waistline. To create a supermarket empire on the order he imagined took capital,

capital with a capital "C," and every penny he owned had gone into this miserable excuse for a store in this hot, dusty, nowhere of a town. But, oh, if he had the Capital, what innovations he would bring to the retail business!

With forms waiting to be filled out, he nevertheless gave himself up to the pleasure of dreaming.

In the back of the store, Shoshone Sam sat, trying to read *The Iliad*, but having a hard time staying focused. He was tired of reading about the "stallion-breaking Greeks," and the "stallion-breaking Trojans." The Shoshone Indians knew firsthand about conquering armies, and personally he did not need Homer to remind him of the blood-thirsty ways of men.

It seemed to him that the only thing of value the white man had brought to this continent was the written word. Shoshone Sam was in love with words. Amazing how, with just twenty-six letters, the stories of a myriad of cultures over countless generations could be preserved and retold. As a boy, he loved to listen to his elders recount the legends of his tribe, but grew tired of their repetition and yearned for new stories. Then when he was twelve years of age he, along with other boys of his tribe, were rounded up like cattle by the government and shipped off to a boarding school. Most of his classmates eventually ran away, but Shoshone Sam endured the school's regimen, its strict discipline, its attempt to purge the students of the taint of being Indian, because he fell in love with reading. Reading was, for him, the opening of a great treasure trove. For three years Shoshone Sam read everything he could get his hands on, until, having consumed everything in the school library, he ran off to Los Angeles, ostensibly to seek refuge with an uncle, but, in reality, because Los Angeles had so many libraries.

Nearly everything he had ever learned had come from books. He knew about law, politics, philosophy and art from reading Hobbes, Machiavelli, Aristotle, Hogarth. He had devoured books on the sciences, on economic theory, on religion. On a more practical level, he learned how to repair an automobile from books, how to build a house, to play a musical instrument. Knowledge coupled with his native ability to live off the land had allowed him to live life on his own terms, to do only that amount of work necessary to keep body and soul together so that the remainder of his time could be dedicated to reading.

His big regret was not being able to study at a university. Every year, one or two of the local Inyo youths would to go off to college, for their future prospects, should they remain in Inyo, were slim. Every time one left for school, he unknowingly carried a little bit of Shoshone Sam with him. Shoshone Sam dreamed of what it would be like to walk the halls of academia, to be enlarged by the wisdom of professors, to be prodded, tested, and tried; to be cast upon the flames of knowledge and recast a purer, more noble and wiser human. In his heart of hearts, Shoshone Sam wanted to be a scholar, to not only have the opportunity to continue to expand his knowledge, but to be able to give that knowledge back so that, like the elders of his tribe, he might pass down to future generations the principles for leading a more perfect life.

Shoshone Sam set *The Iliad* face side down on the table before him. Thinking like this, daydreaming really, always upset him. What chance had a Shoshone Indian, whose formal education had ended at the ninth grade, of finding a home amid those hallowed halls of academia?

The bell above the store door rang, and Shoshone Sam turned to see who had entered. It was that crazy Welshman who called himself Jasper. Greetings were exchanged between Jasper and Jacob Harmon. Then Jasper leaned over the counter and said something Shoshone Sam could not hear. Whatever it was caused Jacob to lock the front door and put up the closed sign. Shoshone Sam watched as Jasper strode toward him, a blackened pot dangling from his hand.

Jasper's discovery of gold had left him feeling as if he were not of this earth, as if, were he not careful, he would float off into the heavens. Even now, it seemed as if only the weight of the pot he carried kept him anchored to the ground. Having rescued the coyote's pups and finding gold in his boots, he had combed the hillside and found so much gold that soon his pockets were bursting at the seams. He rushed back to his camp and returned with everything that could hold anything: an empty flour sack, pots, pans, even his winter long johns, knotted at the ankles. All these he filled with gold. Mostly it was bits of gold imbedded in rock–bright, shiny, like tiny rivers of molten sunshine. The weight of it all would have been impossible for Esmeralda to carry, yet there was more gold to be found! It was apparent he had made a major find, for the surface gold was just an indication of much richer veins underground. To get to them, however, would likely require heavy machinery. Then there was the matter of "fines," the minute particles of gold which, once gathered, would likely prove to be as profitable as a gold vein. But separating the fines from rest of the earth would likewise require machinery. Obviously, extracting the gold was a job for more than one man. So, who could he trust to help him? Immediately Jacob Harmon and Shoshone Sam came to mind. He made a cache of all the gold he had gathered, save for the biggest nuggets which he filled his bean pot with. The image had been impossible to resist, for he had found his pot of gold, and then some. With his rainbow's end in one hand and Esmeralda's rein in the other, he headed to town, or rather he floated, as if in a dream.

"So what have you there?" Shoshone Sam said, as Jasper placed his pot upon the table before them. "Are you planning to poison us with some of your beans?"

Jasper kept a hand upon the lid of the pot to prevent Shoshone Sam from peeking underneath. "You might say it is rich stew."

Jacob joined them. "Now what's so important that I should close up my store in the middle of the day?"

Jasper cleared his throat. "I never did suitably thank both of you for the kindness you showed a... how do you Americans say it... a 'babe in the woods'?"

Jacob, uncomfortable with expressions of gratitude, wiped his hands repeatedly on his apron. "I couldn't have called myself a Christian if I had done otherwise."

"So what's this about?" Shoshone Sam said. "You've had Jacob close up his store just so you could thank us?"

Jasper shook his head. "It is about this." He upended the pot and poured its contents onto the table.

It cannot be said that silence creates a sound, for, of course, it could not then be called silence. Yet a certain silence creates its own waves. Therein lies the origin of the phrase, "a wave of silence swept over the room." This is precisely what happened when Shoshone Sam and Mr. Harmon saw all that gold lying upon the table. Who knows how long the silence might have lasted had there not been a knock on the front door of the store.

With lightning speed, Mr. Harmon untied his apron and covered the table with it. "Jasper, don't say a thing until I go chase off whoever's doing that knocking."

While waiting, Jasper whistled "Mademoiselle from Armentières" to the annoyance of Shoshone Sam who wanted to ask questions despite Mr. Harmon's command.

Having gotten rid of the customer, Mr. Harmon went about the store, pulling down shades. "Just a precaution," he explained, upon returning. "If anyone were to see that gold, my store would be overrun by every Inyo resident in less than ten minutes." He folded back the apron, exposing the gold. "Good Lord A' Mighty!"

"And that is just the tip of the iceberg," Jasper said.

Shoshone Sam shook his head in disbelief. "The luck of the Irish."

"Welsh, actually," Jasper said. "But this Welshman will not be able to make the most of his discovery without assistance, which I'm hoping you two gentlemen will be able to provide."

"What do you mean by 'assistance'?" Mr. Harmon said. He pulled out a chair and sat down.

"It seems to me you've enough wealth right here to satisfy any man," Shoshone Sam said, a tinge of anger in his voice.

Jasper sensed a sudden change in the atmosphere. He studied Jacob, who looked upon the gold with bewilderment and perhaps more than a little envy. And Shoshone Sam was making no attempt to mask his irritation. As for himself, the delight he had felt, showing off for his friends, had vanished and left him feeling foolish and somewhat ashamed.

He covered the gold so none of them would have to look at it. "I must apologize. I have acted like a little boy, eager to show off his new toy, without regard for your feelings. But believe me when I say my intention is for us all to profit from my discovery." He held up a hand to stop Jacob, who was about to speak. "Remember the first day I came into your store, Jacob? You took me over to pick out some tools, and I saw all those other things you had on your shelves for the prospector, not that I knew what they were at the time."

"I remember."

"Do you think you can get us the equipment we shall need to develop a mine? We will need machinery to dig up the ore and trucks to transfer the ore to someplace where the gold can be extracted."

Jacob tapped his chest. "You're asking me? All I have are a few odds and ends that have been gathering dust on the shelves. You need to talk to one of those big mining companies."

"I was rather hoping we could do this ourselves."

Jacob shook his head. "You've got it wrong, Jasper. I'm just a lowly grocer. What do I know—"

"Oh, Jacob," Shoshone Sam interrupted, "you sound like a helpless old woman! Don't tell me you couldn't arrange the use of some trucks. And don't you have a brother-in-law in the road building business?"

Jacob ran a hand over his chin. "Well, now that you've mentioned it, I suppose I could come up with a little something. Let me think a moment."

Having achieved some commitment from Jacob, Jasper turned to Shoshone Sam. "That same first day, you asked me all those questions about how I was going to go about prospecting, which made me realize you knew a lot about it."

"Just what I've read in books," Shoshone Sam confessed. "To be honest, I was just trying to take a little wind out of your sails."

Jasper smiled. "Well, you did, a bit. But my present concern is with the legalities of filing a claim. Did your books tell you anything of that? I would not want someone to beat us to the gold."

"Filing a claim should not be a problem. The regulations are pretty clear, and the Bureau of Mining has an office in Carson City." He pointed to the gold. "First we're going to have to go to where this came from and actually stake out a claim, and for that were going to need…" He drummed his fingers upon the table, thinking.

Jasper let both men think while he considered what his next step should be. Until such time as a claim was actually filed, the location of the mine had to be kept secret. If they were all going out to the site of the discovery, they would have to do so in a manner that would not attract attention. In the meantime, it would be best if he hid this gold. He swept up the nuggets and dropped them back in the pot. The motion caught the attention of the other two.

"Are you certain you want our help with this, Jasper?" Jacob said. "After all, you don't owe us a thing."

"Oh, hang that!" Shoshone Sam said. "He's going to need help and who better than us?" He picked up a piece of gold, felt its weight.

Jacob also picked up a piece and stared at it. "Harmon and Son's," he muttered.

"What's that?" Jasper said.

"Oh, I'm just dreaming out loud," Jacob said.

"And I was just thinking about the number of books I could buy with this piece of gold," Shoshone Sam said.

"What about you, Jasper?" Jacob said. "What are you planning to do with your wealth?"

The question surprised Jasper. "I confess I have no answer for you. It has been my dream to find gold. I have little thought what I would do after that." A dark cloud cast a shadow upon his day. What would he dream of now that his dream had come true?

Sarah Petruzelli, Attorney and Baby Sitter

Once engaged in the project, Jacob proved quite resourceful. The journey to the gold discovery site, the last three miles on foot across a long stretch of sand and gravel, proved to him the necessity of first constructing a road to enable them to bring supplies in and to take the ore out. To accomplish this, he leased a Fordson tractor and set Jacob Jr. to dragging a grader along a wash that led from the gold discovery site to an old dirt road. While his son was thus employed, he looked into the possibility of purchasing a used truck for hauling the ore.

While Jacob was solving the problems of transportation, Shoshone Sam and Jasper were busy staking out three claims, one for each of them. This created a dilemma—two, in fact. First was how to determine the "drift," the direction in which the main body of gold was to be found, for each claim was limited to an area six hundred by fifteen hundred feet.

"I read about this in *Roughing It*," Jasper said. "If I recall correctly, a drift of gold was discovered that extended into someone else's claim. But to ensure that that does not happen to us, we need to locate the drift, do we not?"

"Yes, but unless we hire a mining engineer, we'll just have to make an educated guess," Shoshone Sam said. "Let's just hope the drift doesn't run out from under one of our claims." This introduced the second dilemma: what if one of the claims should prove to have riches and the others none?

"You should have first pick of the claims," Shoshone Sam told Jasper. "After all, it was you who made the discovery."

But Jasper was adamant that they share alike in the wealth.

"In that case," Shoshone Sam said, "we'll need to set up a mining corporation."

"And how do we go about doing that?" Jasper said.

"We'll have to talk to a lawyer. We can do that when we go to file our claims in Carson City, which I suggest we do tomorrow."

Leaving Jake Jr. to continue with the road work, the three partners took Jacob Sr.'s delivery van to Carson City the next morning. The clerk at the Bureau of Mining sniffed at seeing the rudimentary map of the claims Shoshone Sam presented him with. "You should really do a proper survey," the clerk said.

"We intend to," Shoshone Sam said. "In the meantime, the boundaries of the claims are clearly marked and notices posted."

The clerk sniffed again and looked down upon Shoshone Sam's map as if it were something loathsome.

Shoshone Sam leaned in until his face was inches from the clerk's. "Is there a problem?"

The clerk drew back, began to sniff, swallowed instead. "No, no problem. Just let me check this against the main survey map." He made a hasty retreat to a back room.

Shoshone Sam shook his head. "Give a man a little power–"

"And he becomes a tyrant," Jacob completed.

Eventually the clerk returned, made them sign a few forms, took their money for the fees, and gave them a copy of the register of the claims.

"Now then," Shoshone Sam said to the clerk, "we need to find a lawyer, one familiar with mining law. Can you recommend one?"

The clerk, having regained some of his poise, sniffed again. "Well, there's Mr. Lawson, and also Mr. Gleason; either one should be able to assist you."

"Lawson, Gleason. Thank you."

Outside on the sidewalk, Shoshone Sam turned to his partners. "Lawson or Gleason, is it? Well, we can discount them. Likely the two of them slipped a little something to that supercilious clerk to get him to direct traffic their way." An older woman was approaching and Shoshone Sam stopped her. "Excuse me, ma'am, we're looking for a lawyer, hopefully an honest one. Perhaps someone new to the trade and eager for business. Would you happen to know someone like that?"

The woman was quick to respond. "Oh, that would be Sarah Petruzelli."

"Sarah?" the three partners said as one.

The woman smiled. "Don't look so surprised, gentlemen. Nowadays women have just as much right to be lawyers as men, and Sarah is as bright as they come. Her office is just around the corner. Here, let me show you. I'm going that way."

The three men followed in her wake. She stopped before a gate leading to what was obviously a residence.

"This doesn't look like a law office," Jacob said.

The woman pointed to a small sign to the right of the door. *Sarah Petruzelli, attorney-at-law.* "Of course, if it's a fancy law office you're after," she said, "then Mr. Gleason's is just down the road."

Shoshone Sam shook his head. "I'm certain Sarah Petruzelli will do just fine. Thank you for taking time out of your day."

As Shoshone Sam began to open the gate, Jasper rested a hand upon his shoulder and waited until the woman was out of earshot. "Are you sure about this Sam? A woman lawyer?"

"And a wop to boot," Jacob chimed in.

"Chalk it up to my liberal spirit," Shoshone Sam said, "but I've a hunch this Petruzelli lady will be just the ticket."

Shoshone Sam rang the bell and was answered with a baby's crying.

"Let's get out of here," Jacob said.

But before they could beat a retreat, the door opened. A young woman, who looked like she had not slept much, stood in the doorway patting the back of a crying infant.

"Are you Mrs. Petruzelli?" Shoshone Sam said.

"*Miss* Petruzelli. Won't you come in, gentlemen?" She turned away from the door.

" 'Miss'?" Jacob said in a whisper, refusing to budge. "An unwed mother?"

Grinning, Shoshone Sam shoved Jacob forward. "This just keeps getting better and better!"

They followed the baby's cries through another doorway and entered a room that looked more the lair of a book-hoarding pack rat than a law office. Piles of books covered the floor and most of the furniture, save a patch which had been cleared to allow a baby's playpen.

Jacob made no attempt at diplomacy. "This place is a mess!"

"Here," Miss Petruzelli said, pushing the baby into Shoshone Sam's arms. As she worked to clear three chairs, Shoshone Sam rocked the baby in his arms and sang to her a song in his native tongue. The baby quieted.

"That's a miracle," Miss Petruzelli said. "She's not given me a moment's peace all morning." She reached for the child. "Teething," she added.

Shoshone Sam showed no willingness to relinquish his charge. "She's fine with me," he said, which was true; with a thumb in her mouth, the infant was nodding off. Shoshone Sam gestured toward a book teetering on the edge of a scratched desk. "You're reading *The Iliad*."

"Yes."

"And how are you enjoying it?"

"A little too bellicose for my taste, although I often think our judicial system would be greatly improved if sometimes we'd just let the contestants duke it out. Now if you gentlemen would take a seat, we can get down to business."

Shoshone Sam explained about their wish to form a mining corporation and share equally in the proceeds of their three claims.

"I see," Miss Petruzelli said, jotting notes down on a piece of paper. "And what is the name of this mine?"

"Name?" Jasper said.

"All mines have a name," Miss Petruzelli said. She pointed her pencil at Jacob. "Tell me, sir, you who have been sitting so quiet, what name do you suggest for your mine."

Jacob, who this whole time had been sitting like a bomb about to go off, finally exploded. "Now listen here!" He wagged at finger at Miss Petruzelli. "I'll not be having any dealings with an unmarried woman, who…" He pointed a finger at the infant, who had awoken at Jacob's outburst.

Miss Petruzelli laid down her pencil, leaned back in her chair and, for the first time since the arrival of her visitors, she smiled. Hers was not a pretty face, but an interesting one, and when she smiled, she did so also with her eyes, sky-blue eyes which hinted at a great, philosophical mind behind them.

"I understand your concern, Mr. …"

"Harmon," Jacob said.

"Mr. Harmon, the child you so rudely jabbed a finger at is not my child, but belongs to my sister, who, unfortunately, is too ill to care for her. She already has three other children, and since her husband has enough on his plate trying to provide for a family and a sick wife, I have volunteered to care for Sarah, my namesake, until such a time as her mother recovers."

Jacob, who knew firsthand the tribulations of caring for a sick wife, was rendered contrite. "I beg your pardon, Miss Petruzelli. Please forgive my rudeness. Is there anything I can do for you and the child? Anything at all?"

"Well, your business would be appreciated. I'm just getting started in my chosen profession, and things have been rather slow." She picked up her pencil. "Now, I will need the full legal names of each member of this mining corporation."

Each man spoke his name, spelling it out when necessary.

"And the name of this mine?"

The three looked at each other. "We have not thought of a name," Jasper said.

Shoshone Sam, who, along with Jacob, knew how the discovery of the gold had come about, spoke up, "There can only be one name for this mine: The Three-Legged Dog."

"The what?" Miss Petruzelli said.

Jasper explained about rescuing the pups of the three-legged coyote then finding gold in his boots.

Hearing this, Miss Petruzelli burst out laughing. Baby Sarah stared wide-eyed then began to laugh also.

"Oh, that is a splendid story!" Miss Petruzelli said, wiping a tear out of the corner of her eye. "A man comes to the aid of a helpless creature and is rewarded with gold! It is a story that might have come straight out of the pages of *The Arabian Nights*. Oh, I can tell I'm going to enjoy working for you! Now, do you have a claim filed?"

Shoshone Sam gave her the necessary paperwork.

"Good!" she said, aligning the pages on her desk. "Now, if you gentlemen would give me a few hours and barring any interruptions..." She looked at baby Sarah, once again nodding off in Shoshone Sam's arms. "You really have a way with babies. Sometime you must teach me that song of yours."

She stood and led the men toward the door. With some reluctance, Shoshone Sam parted with baby Sarah. He lingered in the doorway surveying all the books. "Sometime, if you would be willing, I would like to return and discuss books with you."

"Nothing would give me more pleasure," she said, smiling up into his face.

Out on the main sidewalk, Jasper and Jacob waited for Shoshone Sam.

"Well, she appears quite capable," Jasper said.

"She's certainly different," Jacob said.

Shoshone Sam, skipping down the stairs, announced, "She's perfect!"

Assaying the Ore

Jacob got the idea from the conveyor belt in the cafeteria where the three partners went to have lunch. He had been wrestling with the problem of how they were going to excavate the ore, and still had not come up with a solution. But as to the problem of getting the ore loaded into the trucks, he drew inspiration from the conveyor belt.

"Look at that contraption," he said, pointing with a fork.

At that moment one of the cafeteria patrons placed his food tray and dirty dishes upon the conveyor; the dishes glided away and disappeared through an opening in the back wall.

"Very clever," Shoshone Sam said. "It saves on having to pay a busboy."

"We're going to need something like that to shift the ore into a truck."

"Well, I know where we can get one. Some miners dumped one on tribal land. They're always dumping their junk on our land."

"Do you suppose it could be made to work?" Jacob said.

Shoshone Sam thought a moment. "I think the parts are there. Lots of rust, though. But even if I were to get it to work, how will we power it?"

"I've been thinking about that. We're going to be needing a truck to haul ore. We can rig up something to run off its power train."

Shoshone Sam shook his head. "It'd be better to use the Fordson tractor along with an industrial belt. Here, look." He took out a pencil and began to draw on a paper napkin.

Jasper was content to just sit and watch as the two men studied Shoshone Sam's drawing and made alterations. It pleased him that they had taken this gold mining enterprise to heart. In recent days, Jacob had swapped his shopkeeper's pasty complexion for a newly acquired tan. But more than that he glowed with an inner fire sparked by a challenge. There was something in Jacob beyond just basic decency and a resourcefulness. Jasper thought that, given the chance, Jacob might prove himself another Ford or Edison. Perhaps this mining venture would provide him that chance.

As for Shoshone Sam, fewer and fewer of his comments were laced with sarcasm. To Jasper, Shoshone Sam seemed like a man who once had set his sight upon a distant shore, but somehow missed the boat, leaving him to live out his life in books. Well, if this mine turned out as Jasper hoped, Shoshone Sam could have all the books he wanted.

After lunch, they walked around the State Capitol building, admiring the stonework until they decided they had given Sarah Petruzelli sufficient time to do her work. They found her just finishing up. She explained about Nevada's law concerning incorporation and alerted them to the fact that their claims allowed them an additional plot of land to use for the purpose of processing ore. "And should your mining venture turn into another Comstock Lode, keep in mind that each of you could claim an allotment within a town site."

"I think you're getting a little ahead of things," Jacob said.

"As your attorney, I just want to alert you to the possibilities. Now if each of you gentlemen will sign here, here, and here, I can then go ahead and file these documents at the courthouse."

The partners insisted that Jasper sign first. "And how much do we owe you for your services?" he said, after appending his name to the documents.

Sarah quoted a fee that seemed quite reasonable, and each man anted up his share. To this, Jacob added a twenty-dollar bill.

"What's this?" Sarah said.

Jacob motioned toward baby Sarah, busy gnawing on the rail of her playpen. "It's for the little one."

Sarah pushed the twenty back across her desk. "I don't need charity, Mr. Harmon."

"Pshaw!" Jacob exclaimed, pushing back the bill. "Sometimes we all could do with a bit of charity. But if you don't wish to take charity, think of the money as a retainer for future services, which I'm certain we're going to need."

Sarah smiled. "Well, in that case, I thank you and wish you all success in your venture."

Driving back to the Three-Legged Dog site, now simply referred to as the "Three Dog," they discussed what Sarah had said about a township.

"Do you believe it might come to that?" Jasper said. "A town growing up around the Three Dog?"

"Wouldn't be the first time," Shoshone Sam said. He recited a list of boomtowns: Skidoo, Calico, Wild Rose, Rhyolite, Beatty, Bullfrog.

"Well, nobody better come poking around our mine until such time as we've taken some gold out of it," Jacob said.

The next days were busy ones. Jasper, Shoshone Sam, and Jake Jr. took a trip to the Shoshone reservation, disassembled the conveyor contraption and hauled it back to the Three Dog. While they were doing that, Jacob searched junk yards for parts to adapt the conveyor to run off the Fordson tractor. The mechanics of the conveyor were straight forward, and the first time they got it put together and running, it worked well–for about thirty seconds. Then the belt attaching the drive wheel of the tractor to the conveyor went flying off, which was just as well, for this prevented the conveyor, rocked by vibrations, from tipping over.

"The whole thing needs to be bolted down on a concrete foundation," Shoshone Sam said. "And the tractor has to sit on a more level spot." He drew out a plan, made a list of materials and went off in the delivery van with Jacob to get the necessary supplies. In the meantime, Jake Jr. leveled out a spot with the tractor then continued to make improvements on his road. This left Jasper with little to do. He spent some time with Esmeralda, who lately had been ignored. As an apology, Jasper gave her two pieces of hard candy then loaded her with two small barrels he had purchased to haul water from the nearby spring. Men, working in the hot sun, needed water, but the time spent hauling it could have been better spent in other endeavors. Inspired by the resourcefulness of his partners, Jasper took along a pick and shovel with the idea of digging a small ditch to channel the water from the spring to the Three Dog. But the ground proved too porous, and any water he diverted immediately soaked into the sandy soil. Still, the idea was a good one; it just needed metal pipe to make it work.

When Jacob and Shoshone Sam returned with timber and bags of concrete, they all set to work. They dug holes, formed up piers, and mixed concrete, the latter task requiring repeated trips to the spring for water. Jasper told them of his plan to pipe the water, and his partners agreed it was a good idea and one to instigate in the future.

When the conveyor was bolted to its new foundation and the tractor placed on its level pad, they reconnected the belts and wheels. This time the apparatus worked well; no belts went flying off and the conveyor stayed put, although the racket it made sent jack rabbits scurrying from their hiding places.

Jacob yelled to be heard over the din. "If there are any dead people buried around here, they'll soon be waking up!" He shut down the tractor and blessed silence returned. "So, we've got ourselves a way to load the ore. Now we need a way to dig it up. I've been trying to find us a steam shovel, but the ones I've found are either too beat up or too expensive."

Shoshone Sam shook his head. "We're getting way ahead of ourselves. First we need an ore sample to take to the assay office."

"How big a sample?" Jasper said.

"Five pounds."

"What!" Jacob exclaimed. "I thought we were going to be needing a whole truck load of ore."

"Just five pounds," Shoshone Sam said, "but it needs to be a representative sample."

"And how do we achieve a 'representative sample'?" Jasper said.

"Through a careful examination of the pay dirt."

"Meaning?" Jacob said.

Shoshone Sam grinned. "We start digging."

"Then we're going to need more picks and shovels," Jacob said. "Wheelbarrows, too. I've got them at the store. Why don't me and Jake Jr. go pick up the tools. That way I can also check up on that lazy cousin of mine and see if he's managed not to burn down the store in my absence."

"Then come tomorrow we'll start the process of becoming wealthy men," Shoshone Sam said.

The Harmons spent the night in Inyo. When they returned the next morning, they were driving a military surplus truck.

"You got a lot of faith we're going to strike it rich," Shoshone Sam told Jacob, as he walked around the truck.

" 'In for a penny, in for a pound,' " Jacob replied.

The four of them unloaded the tools and set to work. Once they were through the loose scree, they found the ground very hard, but Jasper, with his strong arms, was able to drive his pick deep and to break the ground into fragments. Though the work was backbreaking, and the heat like a brick oven, they ignored their physical discomfort, for the dirt they were digging up fairly glittered with gold fines.

"Sam, how much do you think this dirt is going to assay out at?" Jacob said, when they stopped to take a break.

Shoshone Sam picked up a broken rock which showed a streak of gold running through it. "I wouldn't be surprised if this ore came in at three thousand dollars a ton."

"Three thousand dollars!" the others sang in unison.

Jacob did some calculating. "That truck will hold about seven tons. So, that's seven times three thousand…my god, that's over twenty thousand dollars!"

This knowledge inspired them to greater efforts. After three grueling days of work, they felt they had dug enough ore to produce a truly representative sample.

"Jasper," Jacob said, "you started this whole thing, you should have the honor of taking the sample to the assay office."

Jasper shook his head. Shoshone Sam had already told them that assaying the sample would take three days, and to be anxiously waiting around doing nothing for three days would drive him stir crazy. "Be merciful and let me occupy the time slaving away in the hot sun."

It was decided that Jacob and Jake Jr. would deliver the sample. The next morning, even before the stars had disappeared from the sky, the two were headed down the road Jake Jr. had graded, taking with them a five-pound ore sample and a truck load of dreams.

It was a delusion for Jasper to think work would keep his mind off the results of the assay. Yet it was not the anticipation of riches that most concerned him, but whether the ore should prove to be of little worth, for he knew just how much of themselves his friends had put into this venture, and he did not know how he could live with himself if all their efforts were for nothing.

Time on that third day following the Harmons' departure slowed to a seeming standstill. Every few minutes, Jasper looked to the sky to judge the time by the position of the sun. "I do believe the earth has stopped turning," he told Shoshone Sam.

It was not until well after the sun had finally set, that they heard the growl of a truck making its way up the graded road. Jasper and Shoshone Sam ran to meet it. Jacob Sr. was first out of the truck. His face was grim. Jake Jr. did not look much happier.

"So," Jasper said, "tell us the news. Did you get an assay on the ore?"

Jacob nodded. By the look on his face, Jasper knew the news was not good.

"No three thousand dollars a ton, eh?"

Jacob shook his head sadly.

It was Jake Jr. who could no longer keep up the act. He burst out laughing and started to dance a jig.

Jacob smiled the biggest smile Jasper had ever seen on a man's face. "Not three thousand dollars a ton, Jasper. Eight thousand!"

They all came together in a circle dance, joining hands and kicking up their heels. "We're rich!"

Desert Rose

No matter how much the partners would have liked to have kept secret the whereabouts of the Three Dog, there was no way that word of ore valued at eight thousand dollars a ton would not get out. As a consequence, Shoshone Sam noticed a car following after he and Jake Jr. delivered the first load of ore to the stamp mill. Having anticipated this, Shoshone Sam had made preparations. When they left the highway, they did so onto Shoshone land. The car followed as the truck negotiated a narrow canyon. Suddenly, a large boulder came rolling down a bank just after the truck passed, blocking the roadway, and preventing the car from going any further.

Shoshone Sam grinned as he looked back. "Looks like I owe my cousin Walter a big favor," he told Jake Jr.

But even subterfuge could only postpone the inevitable. A few days later, as they were busy loading ore onto the truck, they heard the sound of an engine, audible even above the rattle of the conveyor belt. They looked up to see an airplane flying directly overhead.

"Well, that's it then," Shoshone Sam said, waving to the pilot who dipped the wings of his airplane in reply. "I suspect we'll soon have company."

The next morning, a man not much taller than the donkey that accompanied him, came wandering up the wash.

"Howdy," he said, dropping the reins of his donkey then wiping his face with a bandana. "Hot, ain't it?"

The partners of the Three Dog agreed that it was.

"Name's Shorty Harris. Mind if I look around?"

"Not much we can do about it, if we did," Jacob said.

Shorty acknowledged this with a smile. Then they all turned at the sound of an engine in the distance. Shorty immediately sprang into action. He did a quick survey, noting the stakes marking the boundaries of the claims Shoshone Sam and Jasper had laid out, then began to stake out his own claim. With an efficiency born of practice, he had nearly staked his claim before a Model-T Ford, which had been cut down to make a flatbed truck, came into sight. The Ford was so loaded with men, it scraped the ground. No sooner had the Ford stopped than the men sprang to work, and without bothering with introductions, began to stake out their own claims. Another truck arrived shortly thereafter, followed by another, and it went on like that all day. The partners could only look on in amazement as, antlike, men swarmed over the nearby hills and valleys, staking out claims and posting notices.

"Well, so much for the quiet life," Shoshone Sam observed.

Near sunset, a man pulled up in a wagon drawn by two mules. He did not move to set out a claim, but rested with reins held lightly in his hands as he took in the lay of the land.

Jasper approached the newcomer. "Good evening."

The man stepped down off the buckboard. The lightened wagon rose half a foot, for he was a big man, as tall as Jasper, but gone to fat. The man leaned back to stretch the kinks out of his back before speaking. "You the fellows responsible for this calamity?"

Jacob answered for them. "Calamity is the word for it. And who might you be?"

"The name's Ezra Harris." He extended a hand in greeting. The partners promptly shook his hand, for there was something immediately likeable about Ezra Harris. With his girth, his white beard, his rosy cheeks, he looked like Santa Claus, albeit attired in bib overalls rather than red flannel. "Maybe you've seen my cousin–short little fellow, stands about so high." He brought his hand up to chest height then lowered it a few inches.

"We've seen him," Shoshone Sam said, "Shorty was the first to stake out a claim after us." He looked Ezra up and down. "Hard to imagine you two are related."

Ezra grinned. "Shorty was the runt of the litter. But what he lacks in height he makes up for in being clever, so I'm not surprised he sniffed out your discovery ahead of the others." Ezra again took in the surroundings, all the little ants combing the hillside for as far as one could see.

"You best hurry if you figure on staking out a claim before dark," Jacob said.

Ezra shook his head. "Don't mean to stake out a claim." He continued to look around.

"May I ask what it is you are looking for?" Jasper said.

"I'm looking for a place to set up business. Looks to me nobody's laid claim to that flat area up there." He pointed to a level stretch of ground atop a wash.

"And what might your business be?" Jacob said.

In response, Ezra lifted a small barrel off his wagon. It had a bung hole stopped with a cork. Holding the barrel over his head, he unstopped the barrel and poured a stream of amber liquid directly into his mouth. Thirst satisfied, he corked the barrel. "Whiskey's my business," he said, wiping his mouth with the back of his hand. "Care for a sample?"

None of the partners responded to this offer save Jake Jr., who stepped forward and was pushed back by his father.

Ezra looked crestfallen. "Not a bunch of teetotalers, are you? I was hoping to make you fellows a trade: whiskey for helping me unload my wagon."

"Last time I drank whiskey, the earth responded by nearly knocking me off my feet," Jasper said. "That said, I shall be glad to help you." He lifted a whiskey barrel out of the wagon and began to carry it up the bank. The others joined in, helping carry barrels. While they were thus occupied, Ezra measured out an area roughly sixteen feet by twenty and hammered into the corners four short sections of pipe. Over these he slipped four poles and attached to these a faded blue canvas, creating a sunshade. A wide board placed atop two barrels made for a counter top. All that remained was for Ezra to hang his sign: Whiskey—four bits a shot!

"There now," Ezra said, looking with satisfaction at his makeshift saloon. "I've just established the very first business in the town of..." He turned to his helpers. "Say, you boys got a name for this place?"

"We weren't expecting to have a town," Jacob said, "so a name has never crossed our minds."

"Well, every town has got to have a name," Ezra said, pouring himself a drink. "Sure you won't join me?"

"Well, maybe just one," Jacob said.

"And that goes for me!" came a voice behind them.

They all turned to see a tall man, digging into the pocket of his jeans.

"Why, Tom Wilson!" Ezra exclaimed. "They ain't lynched you yet?"

Tom tossed a fifty-cent piece onto the counter. "I've always been too fast for 'em."

Introductions were made, then more introductions as others wandered over. As it was getting on toward dark, Ezra lit a kerosene lantern, which attracted a few moths along with more customers. They were a friendly bunch, mostly the veterans of dozens of boomtowns. Good-natured ribbing blended with a lot of reminiscing about "the good old days," as the whiskey continued to flow.

During a pause in business, Ezra called attention by banging a rock upon one of the metal poles.

"Gentlemen, while some of you are still sober enough to think straight, there is a problem we must address. But first, for those of you who have not met the men responsible for our being here this evening, let me make introductions."

Jasper, Shoshone Sam, Jacob and Jake Jr. were presented.

A whiskered man with a dilapidated hat held up a rock streaked with gold. "How'd you fellas come to find gold here?"

"That's Al James asking the question, by the way" Ezra said, acting the part of master of ceremony.

"And I'm Gus Eisen," another man said, "and I swear I've been all through here and nary did see anything fit to call my attention."

Jacob cleared his throat. "We best let Jasper answer, since he's the one who made the discovery."

Jasper was a head taller than most of the men, so they had to look up as he addressed them. "Gentlemen, you will gather by the way I speak that I am not from these parts. I am new to this country and have no great knowledge of prospecting. I lack the experience of Mr. James and Mr. Eisen. My discovering of gold was just a matter of luck, the result, you might say, of an act of kindness."

Mesmerized by the lilt of Jasper's Welsh tongue, the men hung upon Jasper's words as he related the story of the three-legged coyote and how the rescue of her pups led to the discovery of gold. Though the manner of Jasper's discovering the gold seemed the stuff of fairy tales, still there was the ring of truth to it, for many, if not most, of the big gold discoveries were not the result of careful calculation, but sheer dumb luck.

"So there you have it," Ezra said. "Jasper discovered gold, and I gather from bits of conversation I've been hearing tonight there's a lot of it here, and you know what that means: there's going to be a whole lot more folks moving in. Businesses will be established, houses built, a school, a post office, who knows, maybe even an opera house. Before you know it, there's going to be a town right here where we're standing, which brings me back to the problem I alluded to earlier. What are we going to name this here town?"

"How about 'Jasper,'" someone said, "since Jasper is the one who made the discovery."

This suggestion was received with general acclaim, but Jasper did not want a town named after him. He had come to the desert looking for gold; miraculously, he had found it. But more than that, he had found something of greater value: peace. Add to that solitude. Both of which were at odds with notoriety.

"I thank you for the offer," he said, "but excuse me if I decline. It would be just as well to name the town after the three-legged coyote."

The name "Three-Legged Coyote" was not well received. For one thing, it was a mouthful. Also, many had low opinions of the coyotes, even abbreviated ones. General consensus was that they were "varmints."

"So, 'Jasper' is out," Ezra said. " 'Three-Legged Coyote' is out. Any more suggestions?"

There were plenty. Most reflected personal sentiments and bore little in common with their current surroundings: Dixie, Brooklyn, Victoria (after the late queen), Armistice, True Blue, Jefferson, Bohemia. Then there were names suggested by harsh conditions in the desert: Hellfire, Pitchfork, Purgatory, Boneyard.

A couple of suggestions, which to a few whiskey-soaked brains seemed humorous, drew an angry comment from Ezra.

"It won't do, gentlemen!" he exclaimed. "It just won't do! We can't have our new town being called 'Dog Bottom.' A name must reflect our highest aspirations. It should inspire the kind of town we'd like to see here. What kind of town are we going to have if we name it 'Buzzard Guts'?"

"Well if you don't like our names, Ezra," exclaimed Tusker Oddie, an old-timer, irritated at having his suggestion of 'Buzzard Guts' rejected, "what do you got that's better?"

"I don't know, Tusker. I'm not good at naming things. I just think the name of our town should have some beauty to it."

Of course, the idea of 'beauty' brought to mind every sweetheart the miners had ever known. As such a topic was close to heart, the discussion over the prettiest name quickly grew heated. While the debate raged, Jasper stepped away, beyond the lantern's light. A pale glow lingered in the west, enough to outline a range of mountains. Overhead the sky was blue-black with a scattering of stars. Though the earth continued to give back the day's heat, a bit of breeze hinted at the coolness that would follow and also brought with it that "bread-baking" smell that Jasper loved about the desert.

Esmeralda, who had shied away from the crowd, made her way to him. As Jasper scratched the back of her neck, he reflected upon the suggested names of past sweethearts. To his mind, those names missed the mark, for, though undoubtedly pretty, they were not pretty in a way that reflected the true beauty of the desert. Jasper was not a great one with names either, but the name "Desert Rose" came to mind. The pink-blossomed desert rose did not grow widely, being limited to higher elevations where greater rainfall occurred. But that made the name all the more appropriate, for it is through scarcity that the true beauty of the desert is revealed. Moreover, "Desert Rose" was the name given to a particular mineral that Jasper had come upon a time or two, a form of the mineral barite, which, under certain conditions, developed sparkling clusters of rose-like petals.

Jasper turned and strode back into the light. "Desert Rose!" he declared.

This suggestion was met by a moment of silence as the men considered. This was quickly followed by a nodding of heads and comments voicing approval.

" 'Desert Rose,' now, that's the ticket!"

"Can't say I can think of a prettier name!"

"Reminds me of a girl I knew over in Tonopah."

Ezra banged with his rock to get attention. "All those in favor of calling our new town 'Desert Rose', say aye!"

"Aye!" rang out the voices in unison. Then they swarmed Jasper, praising his genius in coming up with the name.

"My first thought was to suggest the name 'Esmeralda,' " Jasper confessed to a well-wisher.

"Is that the name of your sweetheart back in England, son?"

"Wales. No, it is the name of my donkey."

The Miners' Ball

The partners of the Three Dog eventually received their first pay out from their ore, the gold having been extracted, refined and formed into bars securely housed in a bank's vault. The value of that bullion was then available to be drawn upon by the partners as needed. What the partners decided they needed was a means of excavating the ore that did not leave them bent over like decrepit old men after each day's work. Jacob disappeared for a few days, and when he returned, he brought with him a new steam shovel. It was so large, it had to be hauled in three trucks then assembled on the spot, all of which was an expensive proposition. But the steam shovel quickly proved its worth, for it could dig more ore in one hour than the partners, digging by hand, could in three days. Of course, the old conveyor had to go, pushed over to one side and replaced by a much larger one with its own engine. Then there was the matter of transport. With so much ore being dug, one truck was insufficient. Jacob contracted with a trucking firm to do the hauling.

The partners worried that with so much money going out there would be little left for themselves, but, in fact, the ore from the Three Dog proved so rich that their expenditures were but a pittance compared to the ever-growing stacks of bullion filling the bank's vault.

In truth, they were rich! Rich beyond imagining. Rich beyond any person's right to be. Fantastic offers were made to buy them out and quickly refused. They joked about changing the name of their mine to the Golden Goose, for there appeared no end to the golden eggs it produced.

With money to spare, they could now leave the daily operation of the mine to others, albeit under the watchful eye of Jake Jr., who was proving himself capable beyond his years. This left the partners free to pursue other ventures. Jacob, analyzing the current haphazard means by which the miners were receiving necessary goods, rushed to build Desert Rose's first general store. He purchased two additional town lots, hired a crew of carpenters, and within three months of Desert Rose's founding opened the largest general store in northern Nevada.

Not to be outdone, Shoshone Sam also put up a building; not a hastily constructed board and batten affair, but a two-story edifice built of stone with hardwood floors and rich interior paneling. The downstairs was divided into office space, and the upstairs into rooms for lodging, which Shoshone Sam immediately rented out at exorbitant rates. Then he made a trip to Carson City and attempted to convince Sarah Petruzelli that her business would thrive better in Desert Rose. In making his arguments, Shoshone Sam pointed to the number of boundary disputes and accusations of claim jumping. Then there was the matter of stock speculation, that malady which invariably cropped up after a major gold discovery and often earned speculators more money than the honest miner could boast by his hard labor. To issue stocks required that at least some patina of legal formality be observed.

Sarah agreed that moving to Desert Rose might prove a godsend to a struggling lawyer. Her concern, however, was for her newly adopted daughter, for, sadly, little Sarah's mother had died, and it was decided that Aunt Sarah could best care for her namesake. Sarah also had no illusions about the nature of boomtowns like Desert Rose. Invariably they were shameless Gomorrahs, where miners squandered their newly acquired wealth upon cribs, cards and cheap whiskey. Such devil's playgrounds, Sarah declared, were unsuited to the upbringing of a child, and unless Shoshone Sam could guarantee respectable conditions for her and her daughter, she would have to refuse his offer, kindly though it was made.

Of course, Shoshone Sam could make no such guarantees, so he went from Carson City with a heavy heart, for he had fallen in love with Sarah Petruzelli and knew she not only harbored reciprocal feelings, but, being of a liberal mind, was able to set aside their racial differences. To assuage his sadness, Shoshone Sam turned to his usual painkiller: books. He turned one of the rooms in his new building into a library and reading room with the thought of creating a lending library. He envisioned debates and lectures and his reading room becoming the intellectual center of Desert Rose.

But all that would have to come later. For now, Shoshone Sam simply holed up with his books and wrote about what he read and shared these ruminations in long letters to Sarah Petruzelli.

Jasper, for his part, found himself at loose ends. His passion was for finding gold, and he had done that. Unlike Jacob, he had little aptitude for business, and when a plague of penniless entrepreneurs assured him they could multiply his wealth without his having to lift a finger, he took to roaming the desert with Esmeralda in order to avoid these pestilent promoters.

One issue, however, did interest him, that of water scarcity, for he recalled his long days spent hauling water from the nearby spring. Out of his own pocket he hired an engineer to study the feasibility of piping water directly from the spring to Desert Rose. Little did he realize he was putting the poor engineer in harm's way, for several teamsters had been making a business of hauling the spring water and selling it to the citizens of Desert Rose at three dollars a barrel. When the teamsters ascertained the reason for the engineer's visit, they made it known that his continued presence was unwelcome and punctuated their demands that he leave by firing several shots above his head. Still, the engineer had seen enough to realize that the flow from the spring was insufficient to meet the needs of a growing town. He recommended piping water from the more productive Terry Springs. Unfortunately, Terry Springs was a good twenty miles from Desert Rose with a sizeable mountain range between.

His recommendation put Jasper in a funk, for what he thought was going be a straight forward bit of engineering was now looking to be something else altogether. He took his troubles to Ezra Harris, newly elected mayor of Desert Rose, who cheered him with a shot of whiskey along with wisdom garnered from years of experience with boomtowns. He advised Jasper to organize a Citizens' Action Committee for the purpose of supplying water to Desert Rose and offered his recently erected Palace Saloon as a place for the committee's first meeting.

The meeting drew a large crowd, not only because of water scarcity being of general concern, but also because Mayor Harris offered half-price drinks to attendees. It soon became apparent that the will to tap into Terry Springs was there, but the financial means for doing so were not. The attendees elected members of a committee, to be headed by Jasper, and charged them with exploring ways to raise the necessary funds. Joining Jasper on the committee were Mayor Harris, Tom Wilson, Frank Mannix, editor of the Desert Rose's first newspaper, the *Flower Press*; and Countess Isabella, proprietor and manager of Desert Rose's most popular brothel.

No one thought to judge the propriety of the Countess' participation in this civic project, and, in point of fact, the Countess, whose real name was Isabelle Hackett, proved the most resourceful member of the committee. It was her idea to levy a "Red Light" tax upon Desert Rose's nightlife district, recognizing that the miners, being "flush," would not mind small surcharges added to the cost of their amusements. She also suggested a box social, where miners could bid on a box lunch prepared by a lady of the night who would also act as dining companion. The Countess assured the committee members that these box socials were to be respectable affairs, picnics with the couples dressed in all their finery, enjoyed on blankets set out on the grounds of the new ballpark where the Knights of the Rose would provide entertainment as they battled the Washoe Wonders from Carson City.

If Jasper had his doubts about the profitability of a box social, he did not reckon upon the generosity of the miners and the limited opportunities for spending their wealth. So frenzied was the bidding on box lunches, one would have thought they were auctioning off the Holy Grail. Of course, the favorite girls received the highest bids. The box lunch of Tessie Alfred netted the Citizens' Action Committee one thousand dollars. Little Fay's box lunch took in twelve hundred. And the opportunity to share a picnic with Skidoo Babe cost the bidder fifteen hundred dollars! The only limiting factor was the finite number of girls. But when the miners ran out of box lunches to bid on, they bid on each other, this so that no one would feel left out. Mayor Harris went for one hundred dollars, Tom Wilson for seventy-five. Jasper got the idea of putting up Esmeralda, and the donkey netted ten dollars, which was nine dollars more than what was bid for Tusker Oddie.

All told, the box social was a remarkable success, netting the Citizens' Action Committee over ten thousand dollars. The only damper on the day's festivities was the defeat of the Knights of the Rose in extra innings, but the loss was soon forgotten when a brass band, made up of members of the Miners' Union, Local Number 236, struck up "There'll Be a Hot Time in the Old Time Tonight," and fireworks lit the sky, punctuated by the discharged firearms of tipsy miners. Fortunately, no one was hurt.

But by far the biggest money maker for the Citizens' Action Committee was the Miners' Ball. The price of a ticket was a twenty-dollar gold piece, and so many advance tickets were sold, it soon became apparent that no structure in Desert Rose was large enough to accommodate all those who wished to attend. Thus, it was agreed to hold the event out-of-doors. Trucks hauled in timber to make a dance floor, miners volunteered their labor, and for three days the sound of hammers proclaimed that something special was in the works. A negro gentlemen by the name of Roulette Davies came forward with a suggestion for illuminating this nocturnal affair. Mr. Davies had been doing a brisk business, hauling ice, a commodity valued by the miners almost as much as whiskey. Recently he had decided to build an ice plant and had purchased a gas-powered generator to run his compressor. Mr. Davies offered the use of his generator for the ball. The Citizens' Action Committee dipped into its funds to purchase lights which were strung by volunteers from the Electrical Workers' Union.

Once complete, the dance floor appeared sturdy and functional.

But Countess Isabella pronounced it "about as festive as a fireplug." She enlisted the aid of the ladies who made bows of colorful ribbons and bouquets of silk flowers, which were hung from the electric wiring. The men admitted this was a definite improvement, and once illuminated, the dance pavilion, which is what they were calling it now, was a glittering oasis of light and color. Countess Isabella declared it almost as cheery as a Barnum and Bailey circus.

The day of the ball was hot as usual, yet this did not deter the miners, who lined up behind the restraining ropes hours ahead of time. As the first of the stars appeared the sky, the brass band of the Miners' Union, Local Number 236, augmented with a string section brought in from Carson City, launched into a lively rendition of "Buffalo Gals." This was the signal for the arrival of the ladies. In pairs, they strolled down the main thoroughfare as boys ran alongside, holding torches to light their way. Rarely had any community seen such finery as the gowns worn by the ladies that evening. Acres of satin and lace had gone into the making of their dresses. With each stride, their skirts, supported out by layers of petticoats, swayed back and forth like brightly colored bells. But the splendor did not end with their gowns. Hats of every shape and color adorned their fair heads, some almost as broad as their voluminous skirts, and none that were not decorated with plumes of dyed feathers and sparkling glass gems.

In response, the miners let forth a cheer then joined the band, singing:

> *Buffalo gals won't you come out tonight,*
> *Come out tonight, come out tonight.*
> *Buffalo gals won't you come out tonight,*
> *And dance by the light of the moon.*

The ladies mounted the steps leading up to the dance floor then arranged themselves upon benches that had been placed around the edge. The waiting miners, eager to grab a partner, pushed against the ropes. Tempers rose. Angry words were uttered. But before matters got out of hand, the electric lights went out. By the time the miners had adjusted their eyes to the darkness, a single bulb came back on, illuminating Countess Isabella standing center stage.

"Well, would you get a look at that!" one of the miners exclaimed, pointing.

He need not have pointed, for all eyes were upon the Countess. She was attired in a gown to rival any which the Fairy Godmother might have created for Cinderella. It was re-creation of a gown once worn by Lily Langtry, the Countess' idol, whose portrait the Countess carried with her to every boomtown where she set up business. The gown featured a scooped neckline outlined with a lace ruffle and with a small bouquet of satin roses pinned directly over her heart. From the neckline, the gown descended, skin tight, to the Countess' still slender waist then billowed out in cascades of shimmering white silk, descending nearly to the floor where dainty satin slippers were just visible beneath layers of petticoats. A small satin bustle served to emphasize the Countess' erect posture as she stood as regal as a queen, waiting to receive her worshipful subjects.

Into the spotlight stepped Jasper, but a Jasper heretofore unseen by the denizens of Desert Rose. His red beard and shoulder length hair had succumbed to the barber's shears. Gone was the well-worn denim and flannel to be replaced by a suit that would have been the height of fashion, had the year been 1860. A narrow, string-style cravat was tied about a high, winged color. He wore a shawl-collared vest of a bold pattern with brass buttons, and over this a black frock coat that came nearly to the knees of his high-waist trousers. A gold watch and chain, patent leather shoes and black gloves completed his attire. All told, he looked the equal of any dandy that ever trod the boardwalks of the once gold-rich Virginia City.

Jasper bowed to the Countess. The Countess curtsied to Jasper. The orchestra struck up "The Starlight Waltz," and the couple proceeded to glide across the now fully illuminated dance floor. Jasper later confessed that it had taken hours of practice under the Countess' careful tutelage before he could make his way over the floor without doing injury to his partner's feet. Yet that night he looked as agile as Nijinsky.

"Well, if I had known it was going to be like this," one miner said, "I would've gotten me a new suit myself."

Had the Countess heard this comment, she would have smiled, for it had been her wish, her dream really, that this ball be no crude barroom shindig, with a miner dragging his partner across the rough planks as if she were nothing more than a broom with which to sweep up the sawdust, but rather as refined and genteel a ball as any her darling Lily might have attended on the arm of Prince Edward.

For Jasper's part, this ball was to be the culmination of all the romantic dreams which had lured him to the desert and drove him to strike it rich. Dressed as he was, he might have been a character right out of *Roughing It,* one of those charmed few who went from being a dirt-poor dreamer to a Prince of the Comstock with all the world at his feet. Yet it was more than pride that Jasper felt as all eyes were upon him and his beautiful dance partner. In truth, he was hardly aware of the attention. Though a part of his mind concentrated upon the steps the Countess had taught him, the remainder drifted upon a higher plane than that shared by mere mortals. He felt as if he were dancing upon air under the approving eyes of the smiling gods. It was a feeling oddly exhilarating and sad at the same time.

The miners, mesmerized by the dancers, hardly noticed when Jacob Harmon Jr., looking the dandy himself in his new store-bought suit, untied a section of the rope, making an opening for the miners to enter. "Gentlemen, one at a time, if you please."

There was no rush to get to a partner, for the miners had been subdued by the example set by the Countess and Jasper. With some trepidation, each miner approached a lady, bowed awkwardly, and received a curtsy in turn.

One of the miners, unable to find an available partner, voiced dissatisfaction with the solemnity of the occasion.

"I thought this was supposed to be a dance. Seems more like a wake to me."

Then the waltz ended, and the orchestra launched into "The Champagne Polka," a dance much favored by the dancers, for it allowed them hop about in joyous abandon.

"Now, this is more like it!" exclaimed the disaffected miner, and, lacking a female partner, he grabbed the fellow next to him, and they proceed to cut a tear across the dance floor.

"The Champagne Polka" was also the prearranged signal for bottles of bubbly to be popped. There was a stampede to a table where the drinks had been set up. Harried tenders rushed to pass out glasses of champagne as silver dollars rained down upon the counter. Almost as popular was the ice cream which Roulette Davies had made and donated just for this occasion. The miners soon discovered they could get any flavor they wanted, so long as it was vanilla. There were, however, a variety of toppings; chocolate fudge vied for favorite with a spoonful of brandy.

As "The Champagne Polka" ended, miners made a beeline for the Countess, but Mayor Harris beat them to her. "I may not cut a figure like our friend Jasper here," the mayor declared, "but judging by the hordes of your admirers, Countess, this may be the only chance I'll get to dance with you tonight."

"Mayor, you have arrived just in time to spare the Countess any more abuse from my big feet," Jasper said.

"Nonsense," the Countess said, tapping him with her fan, "you dance superbly."

Jasper smiled. "Well, if I manage to get around the dance floor without causing too much damage, it is because I had a good teacher."

The orchestra again began to play. Jasper looked for another partner, but saw all the ladies had been scooped up. Jake Jr. with a look of fright, was being swung about like a rag doll by a woman twice his size. Jasper wandered over to the drinks table where he found Jacob Sr. busy popping the corks of the champagne he had donated.

Smiling, Jacob said to Jasper, "I'd ask you to help, but I'm afraid you'd spill champagne on that fancy suit of yours." Jacob looked out at the dance floor where Jake Jr. was being lifted clear off his feet by his partner. "I do hope Miss La Belle doesn't break any of Jake's bones. I need him to work tomorrow."

"I do not see Sam anywhere," Jasper said.

Jacob shook his head. "I fear our Indian friend would not be welcome. Besides, I'm sure he'd rather keep company with his books."

"Then I shall seek him out and bring him a dish of ice cream," Jasper said.

He ambled over to Shoshone Sam's reading room where he found Shoshone Sam with more company than just his books. "Why, Miss Petruzelli, what a pleasure to see you. Here, take this ice cream, and I shall get some more for Sam."

"I don't want any ice cream," Shoshone Sam said, holding a sleepy-eyed baby Sarah on his lap. "Besides you can see my hands are full. Take a seat and join us."

Jasper slid out a chair. "Miss Petruzelli, what brings you to our little corner of the world?"

"My, aren't you being formal. It must be that lovely suit you're wearing. Call me Sarah, please. But to answer your question, Sam has been after me to visit, so I thought I would surprise him. I did not realize it was to be a night of festivities."

"You are more than welcome to join in," Jasper said, "though I must warn you that you might be danced off your feet by men lonesome for female companionship."

Sarah smiled. "I thank you for the invitation, but I've never been fond of crowds. Unless, of course, it's crowds of books." She swept her arm out toward the shelves of books lining the walls of the room. "Isn't this wonderful? When Sam told me he was building a library, I never imagined it would be like this."

"And I am not done yet," Shoshone Sam said. "I've plenty of more books coming."

"Where will you put them? Your shelves are already full."

Shoshone Sam smiled. "Then I guess I'll just have to build a bigger library." His smile was replaced with a thoughtful expression.

"What?" Sarah said.

"The idea of a bigger library just got me to thinking. But never mind. Your ice cream is melting, Sarah."

As Sarah began to spoon up her ice cream, Jasper rose from his chair. "I suppose I should return to the ball. There is to be a raffle for a case of whiskey, and I am to see no one breaks into the prize ahead of time. Will we be seeing more of you, Sarah? Are you planning to stay long?"

"I really should leave tomorrow so I can be back in the office on Monday, though it is tempting to stay right here in this cozy room and just sit and read."

"Then let me tempt you further," Shoshone Sam said, placing a book upon the table. "It's a new book I got just today, about a detective named Hercules Poirot."

Sarah took up the book and examined the cover. "Is it any good, you think?"

"Stay and find out."

"Sam!"

Shoshone Sam grinned. "All right, take the book with you. I suspect this Hercules Poirot will turn out to be another one of those ridiculous dime-novel heroes like Nick Carter."

"I'll have you know I grew up reading dime novels. There's nothing wrong with good entertainment."

"Agreed, so long as it serves a higher purpose. Shakespeare is good entertainment, but his plays have lasted because the entertainment serves to draw us toward something richer and more profound."

"Listen, Sam, not everything needs to be profound. Take this Nick Carter you've been ridiculing…"

Jasper tiptoed out, leaving Sarah and Shoshone Sam to their literary debate. The desert air had begun to cool, which was a relief from the heat of Shoshone Sam's library. The brilliant lights of the ball backlit the dark and deserted buildings, casting long shadows that stretched far out into the desert. Jasper returned to the ball and found the orchestra taking a break. In the interim, entertainment was provided by two Irish miners who danced a frantic jig in time to fiddle and penny whistle. This was followed by a pretty girl singing a sentimental song accompanied on guitar by a young man who, judging by similar features, was her brother. Jasper had not seen the two before, but as the population of Desert Rose had been growing daily, this was not surprising.

The girl had a sweet, pure voice, well suited for the song, which had been popular before the war.

> *Just a wearyin' for you,*
> *All the time a feelin' blue;*
> *Wishin' for you, wonderin' when*
> *You'll be coming home again.*
> *Restless, don't know what to do,*
> *Just a wearyin' for you.*

Though her voice was not strong, she held the miners spellbound.

> *Evening comes I miss you more,*
> *When the dark gloom's round the door;*
> *Seems just like you ought to be*
> *Here to open it for me.*
> *Latch goes tinkling, thrills me through,*
> *Sets me wearyin' for you.*

The song made Jasper feel a sudden need to get off by himself, and as he wandered away, certain lines played over in his mind.

> *Restless, don't know what to do.*

How that line summed up his feelings of late. He had enjoyed working on the Citizens' Action Committee, for it had given him something to while away the hours until such time as he figured out what he was going to do with the remainder of his life.

Wishin' for you, wonderin' when
You'll be coming home again.

Briefly he had entertained the idea of returning to Wales, but the truth was he had not anyone back in Wales wondering when he'll be home again. No one, that is, except for Delwyn, his half-brother, many years his junior. Delwyn was a sweet and clever child, who would go far given the chance, and now that Jasper had the means, he intended for Delwyn to have that chance, provided he could be assured Delwyn's rapacious mother would not pilfer the money meant for Delwyn's education. It was something he needed to talk to Sarah Petruzelli about.

Jasper found himself at the edge of town, standing before the darkened Palace Saloon. Though Ezra had closed his saloon on account of the Miners' Ball, the windows glimmered with light. Curious, Jasper went to investigate and found a small building near to the saloon engulfed in flames. Sparks from the fire shot up into the sky and drifted down onto the roof of the Palace Saloon and another building nearby.

Jasper's first thought was to try and extinguish the fire himself, but the fire was far too advanced for him to tackle alone. He raced back toward the Miners' Ball to get help. Yet even as he ran, he wondered what good help would do. The fire station was only half built, and even if it were complete, there was no water to fill the pumps. There was no water anywhere save that in barrels scattered about town.

Jasper reached the edge of the crowd and immediately commenced hollering. A few men turned toward him, but generally he was ignored. Jasper pushed his way through the crowd until he stood in the center of the dance floor.

"Fire! Fire!" he yelled.

The dancers continued to sweep across the floor in time to the music. Jasper ran to the music conductor and wrested the baton from his hand. This caused the musicians to cease playing. Now he had the dancers' attention.

"Fire!" Jasper yelled, pointing with the baton. "There's a building on fire!" It took a moment for his words to soak in then everyone was running at once. Jasper plowed his way through the rush of bodies to the drinks table where he grabbed a case of champagne and thrust it into the arms of a passing miner. "Take this!" He grabbed another case and gave instructions to anyone who would listen. "Bring them all!" With a case of champagne tucked under each arm, he ran to get ahead of the others. Yet there was already a crowd when he got to the burning building. The miners just stood there, watching, doing nothing. Then again, what could they do? There was no water!

Jasper dropped the cases of champagne and began to peel off his frock coat. There was no hope of saving the burning building, but maybe, just maybe, they could save the town. Jasper dropped his coat upon the ground and was in the process of soaking it with champagne, when a miner, more resourceful than the others appeared with a barrel of water in his arms. Jasper grabbed the barrel just as the man was about to fling the water upon the fire.

"What's the idea!" yelled the miner, more surprised than angry.

"That will not do any good," Jasper yelled back. "The building is gone!" He dunked his coat into the water. "Take this!" he cried, thrusting his dripping coat into the arms of the miner whose barrel he stole. "Try to keep the fire from spreading to the other buildings!" Jasper pointed to a nearby building where sparks rained down upon its roof.

"I'm going to need a ladder," the miner said. "Hey! somebody get some ladders!"

"And buckets!" Jasper cried.

"Buckets?" cried Mayor Harris, who stood helpless as embers rained down upon his saloon. "What good are buckets?"

Jasper ignored him. "I need some more coats!" he shouted. "Coats, blankets, anything we can soak with water. And more barrels of water!"

Ezra Harris grabbed Jasper by the arm. "What good are buckets?"

Jasper pointed to the tailings of the nearby mines. "We can form a bucket brigade, put out the fire with dirt! But we've got to have buckets."

Ezra nodded. "Right! Buckets, we got! We may not have a fire station yet, but, by God, we got buckets." He turned. "You men there, follow—"

The mayor words were drowned out by roar of a nearby miner's shack, which, sided with only black tar paper, exploded into flames.

"Good God!" the mayor cried. "This whole town is covered with tar paper. What'll we do?"

Sarah, who had appeared, cradling little Sarah in her arms, answered. "We tear it all off. It's something we ladies can do." She turned to hand baby Sarah to Shoshone Sam, but he had grabbed a wet garment out of the hands of a man who stood there, doing nothing, then flung it onto the roof of a nearby building. With the agility of a gymnast, Shoshone Sam leaped up, grabbed the edge of the roof and pulled himself up. Picking up the wet garment, he began to beat at the burning embers raining down upon the roof.

"Oh, Sam! Do be careful!" Sarah cried. She turned toward a girl standing next to her, the same one who had sung earlier. "Here," she said, placing baby Sarah in her arms, "I want you to take her far away from the flames, someplace she'll be safe. Can you do that?"

"I have five brothers and sisters, all younger than me," the girl replied. "I'll have no trouble with this one." And crooning a song to baby Sarah, she hurried off toward the mines.

"Now then, ladies," Sarah said, addressing an on-looking crowd of women attired in their finery, "first, off with the petticoats. Then we've got to go ahead of the fire and tear tar paper off the buildings."

As the ladies made a pile of their petticoats, someone appeared with an armful of blankets, price tags still on them, taken from Jacob's store. Jacob himself brought a load of shovels. "Take a shovel, somebody!" he ordered. "Fling dirt on any fire you see."

A group of men, led by mayor Harris arrived with buckets. "Form a bucket brigade!" the mayor commanded. "Make a line from here to the tailings. Fill the buckets with dirt and fling the dirt on the fire."

The building where the fire had started was now a tower of flames, shooting up sparks which were carried out over the town by a breeze. One of its wall toppled over, smashing against the back of the saloon, immediately igniting its dry clapboard siding.

"Hurry men!" the mayor shouted. "If the Palace goes, the whole town will go!"

Fearing the loss of the town, the men and women worked as if their fortunes were at stake, which, for most of them, it was. No one worked more valiantly than Shoshone Sam. He leaped from rooftop to rooftop, beating at the falling embers. Ladders having been located, other men joined him. But no sooner did they get one hotspot put out then another erupted. So many of the roofs were covered with nothing but inflammable tar paper!

Meanwhile, the bucket brigade was doing its best, flinging buckets full of dirt upon the back wall of the mayor's saloon. But the heat from fire was so intense they could only work from the edges.

"We're losing her!" The mayor cried as he watched flames travel up the wall. He turned to see numerous roofs alight with flames. "We're going to lose the whole town!"

"No, we're not!" Jasper declared. Jasper was no stranger to a fight, and though this was a different kind of battle than those he fought while serving King and Country, it was a battle nonetheless. And just like on the battlefield, when all hope was lost and defeat certain, he and his comrades had found the will to fight harder and turn back the tide.

Jasper grabbed a ladder and climbed onto the roof of the saloon. Back lit by the fire he was visible to all. "More water! More blankets! More dirt!" he yelled.

Later when the town was saved someone made a banner with those very words and strung it across Main Street as a reminder of what can be achieved if one has the will to do it.

With a shout, men rushed up the ladder to join Jasper. With wet blankets, they fought the saloon fire from topside.

The Palace Saloon was the tallest building in Desert Rose and Jasper could look out over the entire town. Shoshone Sam and others were doing a notable job, beating out the flames atop the roofs, but

Jasper could see they were not organized. Some stood, not knowing what to do, while small fires broke out on unattended rooftops. Jasper shouted down to the men working beneath him.

"Get a ladder on Jacob's store!" he ordered. "Get men up there and work outward from there!" Jacob's store was central to all the other buildings, the very place from which to best direct their efforts.

The men rushed to obey. Soon there were men atop Jacob's store and others passing up buckets of dirt to them. In lines radiating out from Jacob's store men dumped buckets of dirt on the spots Jasper directed them from atop the saloon. Others followed the bucket brigade with wet blankets, mopping up the flames smothered by the dirt.

In the meantime, the women had succeeded in tearing large sections of tar paper off miners' shacks and carrying the inflammable material far from the flames. This left many of the shacks looking like skeletons, but far less likely to ignite.

The men fighting the saloon fire managed to contain the blaze to the back wall. The fire broke through in one area, sending burning shards onto the plank flooring inside, but men, working from within, quickly squelched the flames.

The sky began to grow light in the east, but no one took note as they fought to save a town that seemed beyond saving. Yet there came a time, though no one realized it, so caught up were they in the fight, that they broke the back of that monster fire. Jasper, standing atop the saloon saw fewer and fewer hotspots to direct the men to. As the sun rose red through the smoke, exhausted men dropped where they stood and sat with heads between their knees. Mayor Harris, as black as a chimney sweep, managed to climb to the roof of his saloon while carrying two bottles of champagne. "Here," he said, handing one of the bottles to Jasper. "These are the last. All the rest went to fight the fire."

Jasper and the mayor sat with legs dangling over the edge of the roof and uncorked their bottles. Smoke lingered in the air, but all the fires appeared to be out. As they surveyed the damage wrought by the fire, there were clear signs of hope. Though there was hardly a building whose roof did not suffer some damage, nor siding that was not charred, the basic structures still stood.

"It could have been a lot worse, Jasper." The mayor sipped champagne and immediately spat it out. "Good Lord A' mighty! Is there nothing that don't taste of smoke?"

Jasper swished some champagne around in his mouth and spat it over the side. He then took a long drink from the bottle, wiped his mouth with the back of his shirt sleeve, smearing his face with more soot.

The mayor laughed. "You look like you walked through the fires of Hell, son. So much for your nice new clothes."

Jasper stood so he could better examine himself. His suit, his beautiful suit made in imitation of those worn by Comstock tycoons, was ruined. God only knew where his frock coat had ended up, likely consumed by the fire. What remained of his attire was either torn, shot full of burn holes, or so black with soot as to never come clean. Jasper dug out his handkerchief, still comparatively untouched, and with great elaboration, proceeded to wipe off his patent leather shoes, now completely devoid of shine.

"What on earth are you doing?" Mayor Harris said.

"My father had a wealth of sayings, especially about appearances. He used to say to me, 'Son, you can judge a man by how well he takes care of his shoes.'" Jasper gave his shoes a final dusting. "There, that ought to put everything to rights."

"Everything to…" The mayor threw back his head and roared with laughter. Jasper joined in, and together they laughed the laugh of men made senseless by exhaustion. Yet there is something clarifying about senselessness; it washes the mind of unwanted clutter.

"Oh that's rich!" the mayor said, when he could draw breath. "So what do your nice clean shoes say about you?"

"I think," Jasper said, giving his handkerchief a shake, "I think they are saying either I am not the man for these shoes, or these are not the shoes for this man."

"Now, what on earth does that mean?"

"It means I doubt I am a man cut out for fancy clothes and shiny shoes."

"Why ever not? You're a handsome young man. Not only that, you're rich. Why shouldn't you play the part of a rich man?"

Jasper shook his head. "Life is for living, not playacting." He held up his handkerchief and watched it flutter in the breeze. Strange that it took the burning of a town to clarify his thoughts, to make clear the true path before him. A little over a year ago, he had dreamed of a path, one paved with gold. Now he saw that despite having found the gold, such a path never was, and never would be, the right one for him. His true path was not made of gold, but plain rock and sand, and it meandered amidst rabbit brush and mesquite and cacti. He did not know to what end this path would take him, but what did that matter as long as it led him through his beloved desert.

He made a ball of his handkerchief with his fist. "I came to this country, hoping to be a prospector," he said, but so softly, mayor Harris took no notice. Jasper realized he wished to be a prospector still; finding gold had not changed that. Knowing this, he felt a great urge to find Esmeralda and head out into the desert this very moment.

Yet he could not just walk off and desert his partners. He would have to wait until some normality returned to Desert Rose then tell them of his decision and figure out a way to extricate himself from the partnership. With any luck, Sarah Petruzelli would find a solution satisfactory to all concerned.

Having reached this decision, Jasper stepped to the edge of the roof, flung his handkerchief over the side and watched as the breeze carried it away.

Love Letters

Jasper, Jacob and Shoshone Sam sat in a half circle before the desk of Sarah Petruzelli, attorney-at-law.

"Are you sure you wish to do this?" Sarah said. "From what I understand, the Three-Legged Dog Mine is still producing quite well."

"Which is a good reason for us to sell now while we can get a good price for it," Jacob said.

Jasper nodded in agreement. He had been surprised at the alacrity with which his partners had agreed to the selling of the Three Dog and to the dissolution of their partnership. Perhaps he should not have been, for the signs had been there all along, what with Jacob spending most of his time in his store and Shoshone Sam in his library.

Shoshone Sam voiced Jasper's thoughts. "We've made our fortunes already and have other things we'd rather be doing. Selling the mine will just be more icing on the cake."

Sarah smiled. "A rather rich icing, I should think." She shuffled some papers. "Who have you gotten as your legal representative for the sale?"

The partners spoke as one. "You!" They all laughed.

"You've done well by us so far, Sarah," Jacob said. "No use switching horses in the middle of a stream."

"In that case, I shall need to see your financial records. It would be wise to settle all outstanding debts before the sale; it'll make things easier."

Jacob handed her a sheaf of papers. "Everything is right here. Outside of a few trifling debts and the current payroll, everything is free and clear."

"Good," she said. "Once the sale is finalized, it will just be a matter of signing a few papers to end the partnership. I'll get to work right away unless you have other business for me."

Jacob rose from his chair. "No, that should about do it."

"Not so fast, Jacob," Shoshone Sam said. "Jasper and I have business with Sarah that concerns you."

"Eh?" Jacob said, sitting back down. "What business might that be?"

"You tell him, Jasper. It was your idea."

Jasper cleared his throat. "Once the mine is sold, Sam and I would like to invest our shares of the proceeds, providing you would be willing, of course."

"Invest in what?"

"In you," Shoshone Sam said.

"Me?"

Jasper leaned forward. "Sam and I feel we could do no better than to invest our money in the stores you are planning to build."

"Stores? Who said anything about stores?"

"Oh, come on, Jacob," Shoshone Sam said. "It's no secret you have been planning to open a chain of markets. Haven't we seen you poring over plans and writing up lists?"

"But it's all just scribbling on paper. What if I fail? I'd never forgive myself if I lost your money."

"If any man were to succeed, Jacob, it would be you," Jasper said. "Where would we be if it had not been for your ingenuity and industriousness? Yet if by some unforeseen circumstance matters were to go awry, we would never fault you the loss of our money."

"Because it's all just icing anyway," Shoshone Sam said, then laughed.

Jacob eyes watered. "I am moved by your faith in me, and I confess that having further capital will increase the likelihood of my success."

"Then we've as good as made our fortunes," Jasper said.

"Our second fortunes," Shoshone Sam said.

Jacob turned to Sarah. "I guess we have some more business for you after all, Sarah. You'll need to make out some sort of legal paper so my friends will know I'm not cheating them out of their money."

"I already have," Sarah said. "Your partners came to me earlier. I'm afraid they have been plotting behind your back."

"You scoundrels!" Jacob said, laughing.

"We just know a good investment when we see one," Jasper said.

Sarah took up her pen. "There is one thing I shall need, Jacob. Have you given thought to a name for your enterprise, these markets of yours?"

"Yes, I have," Jacob said. "A name was one of the first things I'd thought of, even back before Jasper discovered the gold. I want all my supermarkets to be called 'Harmon and Son's.' "

Sarah wrote this down then set her pen aside. "Well, you gentlemen have given me a lot to work on. Anything else?"

"There's one more thing," Jasper said, "but I need not keep my friends waiting, as it is of a personal nature." Jasper waited for his partners to say their good-byes before explaining to Sarah his desire to provide for his stepbrother Delwyn living back in Wales. "I wish to set up a fund strictly for his education, something his mother cannot get her hands on. Is that something you can do for me?"

"As your stepbrother is a resident of the United Kingdom, it will take me a while to sort out the differences in law concerning trusts," Sarah said. "I doubt the problem would be insurmountable. I'll just need time to look into the matter."

"Take all the time you need," Jasper said. "This can certainly wait until you have dealt with the other demands we have placed upon you."

"I appreciate that," Sarah said.

Jasper sat back in his chair, looking thoughtful.

"Is there something else?" Sarah said.

Jasper nodded. "Please do not ask the reason for what I am about to ask of you. Let us just say that I have reached a crossroads in my life, and I need you to help me move through it."

"I'll help, if I can."

Jasper took in a deep breath then slowly let it out. "I want you to take charge of all the money I have made in the Three Dog."

"What?"

"I know it is a lot to ask, but if you could do this for me, you would be relieving a poor soul of a great burden."

"But, Jasper, I am not a financial advisor. I am sure there are others who would do much better by you."

"But no one I trust more than you, Sarah. I am not asking you to achieve great gains with my fortune, just to preserve it for me until such time as I have decided what to do with it. My only stipulation is that a small amount of money be always available to cover my simple needs."

Sarah leaned back in her chair and placed her hands in her lap. "I don't know what to tell you. It is a great responsibility."

"Perhaps you need time to think about it."

"Yes, that would be good."

Jasper rose from his chair. "As I said before, take all the time you need. My money is certainly not going anywhere."

Outside of Sarah's office, Jasper found his partners waiting for him.

"What was that all about?" Jacob said.

"I have a stepbrother I would like to see have a good education. Sarah is going to help me set up a fund for him."

"I could've used a brother like you," Shoshone Sam said. "Anyway, I'm hungry. Where shall we eat?"

"I am going to skip lunch," Jasper said. "I have a couple of friends I wish to look in on. As it may take a while, I'll find my own way back to Desert Rose."

Jasper walked to the State Library where he found Margaret Rutherford bent over a reference book.

"Excuse me," Jasper said, "do you have any books on archeology?"

Margaret looked up, saw who it was, and smiled. "So you're now planning to make a fortune in antiquities?"

"Yes, I foresee a large market for dinosaur bones."

Margaret laughed. "I'm sure you do. So, tell me, how's the big mining tycoon?"

Jasper grinned. "All the better for seeing you. I thought to pay Eros a visit and wondered if you might find time to join me."

"Your timing could not have been better. I had planned to go see him this afternoon. I am afraid Eros is not faring well. I fear his years have finally caught up with him."

"Then I will tag along, if you do not mind."

Eros' cottage was nestled in a wooded canyon next to a perennial stream tumbling out of the Sierras. Jasper had visited there several times before. No electric or telephone lines serviced Eros' remote cottage, which was fine with Eros, who counted such modern innovations intrusions upon his solitude.

Margaret's knock upon the cottage door drew no response. She knocked louder, and they heard the shuffling of house slippers over wood floors. The door opened and, seeing his visitors, Eros' face lit up. "Maggie!" he said. "And Jasper too! Come in, come in."

They followed Eros as he shuffled back to his chair beside a woodstove. The air inside the cottage was stifling.

"I'm so glad you've come," Eros said, lowering himself into his chair. "Pull up a chair and make yourself at home."

"We will, if you don't roast us out," Margaret said. "It must be a hundred degrees in here."

"What do you expect for an old desert rat? But you can crack a window if you want."

Margaret did just that.

"I was meaning to contact you, Maggie, hoping for advice on a little problem I have."

"And what is that?" she said, sitting down.

"Jasper," Eros said, "hand me that letter on the table there next to you. It's something sent from some fellow who claims to be a lawyer." He handed the letter to Margaret. "Read it aloud, Maggie."

Margaret opened the letter. " 'Dear Mr. Slaughter–' "

" 'On behalf of Mrs. Phyllis Fischer Walters, I have been instructed to contact you concerning personal letters written by you to her late grandmother, Mrs. Esmeralda Stover Fischer. Only recently has Mrs. Walters come in possession of these letters, and she wishes to see that they are returned to you. Unfortunately, Mrs. Walters can ill afford the costs she has incurred in trying to locate you, and she only asks that you reimburse her for expenses. The amount of two hundred dollars would be sufficient.'"

Margaret lowered the letter. "Two hundred dollars! For just a bunch of old letters? Sounds specious to me."

Eros waved his hand. "Read on."

"'As her attorney, I assure you that everything written in these letters will be held in strict confidence, and they will be shown to no one unless, of course, you show no interest in them. A check made to Phyllis Walters may be sent to the above address. The letters will immediately be released to you upon receipt of this money. Sincerely, Otis Pepperidge, attorney-at-law.'"

Margaret set the letter aside. "Why, this is outrageous. It's absolute blackmail. That shyster is implying there is something in the letters you do not wish known. That is absurd."

Eros avoided looking at Margaret.

"It is absurd, isn't it, Eros?"

Eros groaned. "How did they find me? What made them think I was still alive?"

"I have read about people like these," Jasper said. "They call them scam artists. In particular, they prey upon the elderly."

Margaret leaned forward. "You've not answered my question, Eros. What's so all-fired important about these letters? Is this the same Esmeralda you told us about before, the girl you wished to marry at one time?"

Eros nodded.

"I thought you said she went off and married some rich man and moved to San Francisco."

"She did! She did!"

"But you continued to write to her? Love letters, I presume?"

Eros leaned his head back against the chair. "It wasn't like that. She was the one who wrote me first. She said she had no one else to turn to, that her marriage had become a nightmare. Believe me, Margaret, I would never have violated the sanctity of that marriage had there been a glimmer of happiness in it."

"Violated?"

Eros sighed. "There was a child."

"Eros!"

"Don't look at me like that, Margaret! You can't understand what it was like for her, living with that drunkard. I wrote back, agreeing to meet her in San Francisco. When I saw her, I could not believe how she had changed, how the flower of her youth had been crushed under the heel of that brute."

"So why didn't she divorce him?"

"Believe me, I wanted her to. I begged her to! But she was Catholic, and you know how those Catholics are. She feared damnation should she divorce him. And later on, there was another problem."

"That being the child, I take it."

Eros closed his eyes. "The first time we met it was all very respectable, just a couple of old friends having tea in a public place." Eros looked away. "Later on, we met for more than just tea."

Margaret shook her head. "Adultery is fine, but divorce is not. Not much of a Catholic, if you ask me."

Eros glared at Margaret. "Don't judge us, Maggie! If there is one thing I have learned in all my years, it's that life offers little happiness. God knows Esmeralda had none to speak of, and I…" He shook his head. "We both craved affection, Maggie, and as it turned out our meetings were the salvation of her."

"How so?"

"She and her husband had never succeeded in having a child. When Esmeralda got pregnant, her husband, thinking the child his, became a different man. He stopped drinking–mostly, anyway. And he started to show Esmeralda some respect. Life became bearable for her."

Margaret picked up the letter again. "So, what about this? Are you going to pay the extortion money?"

Eros smiled. "It surprises me that Esmeralda kept those letters. It took courage on her part, for Lord knows what would have happened had her husband found them."

"You've not answered my question."

"Damn the letters! I don't give a fig about the letters. They were written a long time ago. They can go ahead and publish the letters on the front page of the *Chronicle* for all I care."

"I see," Margaret said. "So what's this problem you want help with?"

Eros pointed to the letter. "It said, 'on behalf of Mrs. Phyllis Fischer Walters.' She would be my granddaughter, Maggie. What do I know of her? What if she has fallen upon hard times, and that is the reason she needs the two hundred dollars? I've got a little saved by. I'd like to see her have it."

"And what if this is all just a big hoax?" Margaret said.

Jasper, who had been silent during this exchange, now spoke up. "Perhaps I could go to San Francisco, make some enquiries, see if everything is really on the up and up?"

Eros' face lit up. "You would do that for me, Jasper?"

"I would think it a privilege."

Eros pushed himself up out of his chair. "I still have a few of the letters Esmeralda wrote me." He opened a drawer in an old desk and removed a faded letter. "At the time, she was living in a big old house on California Street. Of course, I could never write to her there, but I remember the address because the house number was the same as the year my father was born: 1817."

Eros handed Jasper the letter. "Take this. It will act as proof in case they want some assurance that you are who you say you are."

"And who am I supposed to be?" Jasper said.

"Why, my representative, of course. Tell this Pepperidge fellow that I sent you. In fact, I'll give you a letter of authorization. Then give him the money for the letters, but only in exchange for the address of my granddaughter. Then go and see her and…" Eros stared off into space.

"And what?" Margaret said.

"Do you think I should let her know I'm her grandfather, Maggie?"

"Not if you don't want her to soak you for every penny you've got. There is still something about all this that smells fishy to me."

"It's not the money, Maggie. It's whether she wants to know. How would you feel if you learned that your mother's father was somebody other than the person you thought he was?"

"Perhaps it would be best to take one step at a time," Jasper said. "I will go to San Francisco, meet with the lawyer, learn of your granddaughter's whereabouts and see how matters fare with her. I can then send you a telegram, relating what I have discovered, and you can instruct me how to proceed."

"That is a good plan," Margaret said. "But may I make a suggestion? See if you can get the address of this Mrs. Walters before you go and meet with this lawyer. It might save Eros his two hundred dollars. I'm sure you could probably locate her through tax records or something."

"You're so suspicious, Maggie," Eros said.

"My father did not raise me to be a fool, Eros. Moreover, he taught me the value of thrift."

"I will attempt to satisfy both your wishes." Jasper said. "I will first try to locate Mrs. Walters on my own, but should I not succeed in a timely manner, I will repair to the lawyer's office and present myself as Eros' representative."

The next day, Jasper took the train from Reno to Sacramento and from there a ferry to San Francisco. He stepped from the ferry into a fog little dispelled by street lights. He was tired, having been up since before dawn, and all he wanted was a nice bed out of the chill night air. He flagged down a taxi and asked the driver what was a good hotel.

The driver sized up Jasper: his rough clothes, his unkempt beard, the absence of luggage. "Why the Palace, of course," he said, with a grin.

Jasper ordered him to take him there.

"But…" The driver thought his passenger knew he had spoken in jest. The Palace was the finest hotel in San Francisco. The taxi driver decided to keep his mouth shut, however, and since his passenger was obviously an innocent, he took a roundabout route to the Palace, thereby earning himself a larger fare.

The Palace doorman immediately opened the door of the taxi. As Jasper counted out money for the taxi driver, the doorman asked about luggage. Jasper told him he had none and proceeded to enter the hotel before the doorman could open the door for him. Upon entering, Jasper could see why the hotel was named the Palace, for if someone had told him he had walked into the palace of a French king, he would not have been more surprised. Crystal chandeliers beamed with dazzling light. The vaulted glass ceiling was supported by marble columns reflected in the spotless terrazzo floor. The bright lights, the glitter, it was all too much for Jasper's tired brain, still woozy from his taxi ride up and down over the San Francisco hills. Due to the lateness of the hour, Jasper saw only two other people: the night desk clerk and a man ensconced in a wing-backed chair and hidden behind a newspaper.

The night clerk cleared his throat. "May I help you… sir," he said, reluctant to award Jasper the title.

Given this chilly reception, Jasper was tempted to seek shelter elsewhere. But he was tired and a little angry, for who was this dandified clerk with his pomaded hair and trim little mustache to look down upon him? Had not he fought in the Great War to make the world safe for people like him?

Jasper marched toward the counter with such determination that the clerk involuntarily took a step back.

"I wish a room for the night," Jasper said.

The clerk quickly recovered and began to leaf through his register. "I am afraid we have no available rooms at present."

"What?" Jasper exclaimed. "Why, this place must have a thousand rooms. Surely they cannot all be taken?"

The clerk slammed his register shut. "Sorry, we are full. Now, I must ask you to leave."

This exchange had caught the attention of the man in the chair who had set aside his newspaper. "Jasper?" he said, getting to his feet. "Jasper Owen, is that you?"

Jasper turned to see Charles Schwab, a wealthy steel manufacturer who had been actively trying to purchase the Three-Legged Dog mine. They shook hands.

"Do you know this man, Mr. Schwab?" the clerk said.

"Of course, I do, you little termite. He's a friend, who also happens to be one of the richest men in America. What's this I hear about you not having a room?"

The clerk quickly opened his register. "Ah, I see we've had a cancellation, a regular room with a small bath."

Schwab slammed shut the register on the clerk's fingers. "Listen you little rodent, you'll find my friend a nice suite. And…" he pushed down on the register, crushing the clerk's fingers, "… you will charge him the rate for a regular room or, by God, come tomorrow you'll find yourself out on the street with the rest of the bums. Is that understood?"

The clerk, tears filling his eyes, managed to extricate his fingers. "Of course, Mr. Schwab. When the gentleman asked for a room, I had no idea he wished for a suite." He turned the register around. "If you just would sign here, sir?"

Jasper added his name to the register.

"Will you be staying in town long, Jasper?" Schwab said.

"I am not sure. I am on a mission for a friend, yet I do not think it will take more than a couple of days."

"Well, plan to have dinner with me while you're here. I'd like to twist your arm a bit. Get you to convince those partners of yours to sell that mine to me."

Schwab and Jasper shook hands again then Schwab headed toward the elevator, but not before firing off a final look of warning at the night clerk. Jasper waited until the operator had closed the elevator door before placing a twenty-dollar gold piece on the counter.

The clerk looked at the gold piece. "You need not pay until you're ready to depart, sir."

"That is for you by way of apology for Mr. Schwab's conduct," Jasper said. "My experiences with him have been likewise unfavorable, though not quite as painful. I doubt my partners and I shall be selling our mine to him."

The clerk picked up the gold piece and studied it. He was obviously moved. "Thank you, sir. I…" He smiled. "When would you like breakfast? The Palace has an excellent breakfast. I'll have it sent to your room any time you wish–compliments of the house, of course."

"There is no call for that," Jasper said, "and to be honest, I would be more comfortable in a regular room than a suite."

"Very good, sir. I will put you in room 411. It has an excellent view."

"And would you wake me at seven? And maybe breakfast around seven-thirty?"

"Consider it done," the clerk said, and rang a bell. As if by magic a bellhop appeared. "Take Mr. Owen to room 411."

The Palace indeed had an excellent breakfast, served on fine china accompanied with a large silver pot of piping hot coffee. As Jasper tucked into this fare, he mentally made plans for the day. He had promised Margaret he would first attempt to locate Mrs. Phyllis Fischer Walters. Margaret mentioned tax records. Jasper had little stomach for combing through old records and wondered if there were not an easier way to locate Mrs. Walters.

He picked up the in-room telephone and dialed the main desk. The desk clerk immediately answered.

"Good morning," Jasper said. "Tell me, do you have a house detective?"

"Oh, sir," the desk clerk said, "has something gone missing?"

"No, not at all. I only wish to speak with him."

"Very good. I shall let him know."

A few minutes later, there was a knock on the door. Jasper opened the door to a burly man, dressed in a well-worn, three-piece suit, sporting a bowler atop graying hair.

"You asked for the house detective," he said, removing his hat. "How can I be of service?"

Jasper motioned for him to take one of the two chairs. Then he explained his reason for coming to the city. The detective listened without comment, occasionally rotating his bowler hat, which he balanced upon his knee. When Jasper finished, the detective did not speak for a while, appearing to order his thoughts.

"So, you think this might just be a big scam, and you would like to find out whether this Walters lady is on the up and up?" the detective said.

"Yes. Do you know of someone I could hire to investigate her for me?"

The detective nodded. "I know just the person, my brother-in-law Rupert. Rupert runs a private detective agency. If anyone can get the goods on this Walters person, it's Rupert." The detective stood up.

"How can I contact this gentleman? I would like for him to start as soon as possible."

"I'll contact him myself, let him know what you want done. Something like this should take Rupert no time at all. I expect I should have something for you by the end of the day."

Jasper thanked the detective and saw him out. He then realized that, relieved of duty, he had the whole day before him with nothing to do. He first took a long hot bath. Feeling refreshed, he set out to explore the town, but upon exiting the hotel, he was immediately enshrouded in fog, which set him to shivering. He asked the door man where he might buy a coat and was directed to a department store a few blocks away. He purchased a coat not all that different from one he had worn while in the army. After paying for the coat, he had a sudden inspiration.

"Tell me," he said to the sales clerk who had waited upon him, "do you know how I might get to 1817 California Street?"

"It's easy," the clerk said. "Just take the Powell Street cable car up the hill and get off around Nob Hill." He led Jasper out of the store and pointed out where he could catch the cable car. The hill the cable car ascended was, to Jasper's mind, too steep to have buildings upon it, yet there they were, stacked one above the other like a stairway leading to the sky. He also began to worry what would happen should the cable break, yet soon forgot his anxiety as the cable car rose above the fog and warm sunlight filled its interior. By the time he exited the cable car, he had his coat unbuttoned and was considering taking it off.

It had been a whim, his deciding to seek out the one-time residence of the late Esmeralda Stover Fischer, yet now he was glad he did, for standing atop Nob Hill he had a taste of what it must have been like for Esmeralda to have married a rich man. An island of sunshine in a sea of fog, Nob Hill was a place of opulent houses owned by those whose wealth had allowed them to rise above those of the common lot. The house at 1817 California Street bordered a small park of perhaps two acres, crisscrossed with walkways, creating triangles of lawn upon which well-dressed children cavorted under the watchful eyes of nannies ensconced on park benches. The house was not quite as grand as those surrounding it, yet had the advantage of a side garden the others lacked. Jasper interrupted a gardener, kneeling down, planting out flowers.

"Excuse me, might I ask you a question?"

The gardener stood up, checked the side window of the house perhaps to see if anyone were watching. "I suppose so."

"I believe this was once the home of an Esmeralda Stover Fischer. Am I right?"

"Fischer?" the gardener said, rubbing his chin. "Don't ring a bell, but then I've only been working here a couple of years. Old Mrs. Ainsworth is the owner now."

"Is there someone else whom I might ask?"

The gardener looked Jasper over and appeared to decide he was no threat. "I guess we could ask Lizzie, the cook. She's worked here a lot longer." He led Jasper along a walkway to the back of the house.

A woman of perhaps thirty years answered the gardener's knock upon the back door. "What is it?" she said, wiping her hands on a stained apron. "Can't you see I'm busy?"

"Sorry, Liz," the gardener said, "but this gentleman here wants to ask you a question."

Liz looked at Jasper with disapproval. "Well, make it quick. The old lady is in a snit this morning as usual."

"Please pardon my interruption," Jasper said, "but I wonder if the name Esmeralda Stover Fischer means anything to you? I believe she and her husband once owned this house."

Jasper thought he saw a flicker of change in the cook's otherwise sour expression. A momentary look of alarm.

"Never heard of her," she answered. "Now be gone! I'm busy." She slammed the door.

The gardener shrugged his shoulders. "Well, there you have it. You might try asking the local estate agent. He might be able to help you."

Jasper thanked the gardener, returned to the front of the house, crossed the street and entered the park. The encounter with the cook had lessened his joy of the day, for it was not pleasant to be spoken rudely to. He removed his coat and laid it across the back of a park bench and sat down.

"My son had a coat very much like that," a small voice said.

Jasper, lost in thought, had little noticed the old woman who shared the bench.

"He wore it when he came home on leave from the service," she said.

"Yes," Jasper said, "it is very much like the one issued to me, though I think the quality better. I do believe the army makes a point of selecting material destined to send a soldier scratching like a dog with fleas."

"You were in the recent war then?"

"I had that misfortune, yes."

The lady nodded. "War is a horrible thing."

Jasper turned to better see the woman. She wore a thick sweater about a high-collared dress and a lap robe tucked around her legs. The skin of her hands and face had a translucent quality sometimes seen in old people, revealing blue veins beneath the surface. Jasper imagined she once had been as lovely as a beauty queen, and she still exuded a regal air.

"Yes, it is," he said. "I would not wish it on anyone. Was your son also in the war?"

A sad smile appeared on her face. "Oh, no. At least, not in this last one. Marcus rode with Teddy Roosevelt up San Juan Hill. Alas, he did not ride back down again."

"I am sorry," Jasper said. "War is, indeed, a horrible thing."

The lady nodded slightly, stared off into the distance, the small smile gone. "One must wonder what it was all for. I cannot see that defeating the Spanish changed anything, or, for that matter, defeating the Germans either."

Jasper had to agree. Five years of war, and what had changed, really? Nothing that he could see, other than countless young men had not returned home to their loved ones.

"I am glad you made it back," she said.

"Thank you."

A black limousine pulled to the curb in front of them, its side lettered in copperplate: "The Fairmont Hotel."

"Oh, here is Robertson," she said, "and it seems as if he only just dropped me off. Well, it is like that when you get old. Time rushes on like an ever-faster-moving train."

Robertson, a tall black man with short gray hair, took the lap robe from her, draped it over one arm, then helped her to stand.

"Thank you, Robertson," she said.

Jasper watched the limousine pull away then went to catch the cable car. He rode it down to the wharf where he spent a couple of pleasant hours watching large cargo ships being unloaded. He followed this with a delicious lunch in China Town, where he also purchased a hand-painted vase he thought Margaret would like. A nap back in his room back at the Palace was interrupted by the house detective, brother-in-law in tow.

Jasper bid both gentlemen to make themselves comfortable in the chairs while he sat on the edge of the bed.

"Tell Mr. Owen what you found, Rupert," the detective said.

Rupert crossed one leg over the other before speaking. "First off, I went to see this lawyer fellow, Otis Pepperidge, but the address you gave us turned out to be a rundown boardinghouse. So, I took another tack, but could find no mention of a Mrs. Phyllis Fischer Walters in the public records."

"Oh, I see," Jasper said, disappointed.

"I did, however, come across the name of a Miss Phyllis *Elizabeth* Walters, a cook, currently employed by a Mrs. Augusta Ainsworth residing at 1817 California Street."

Jasper sat tall. "That is the same address where Esmeralda Fischer once lived. I believe I met this cook this morning."

Rupert nodded. "She told me you'd been around."

"You went to see her?" Jasper said.

"I did indeed. I told her I knew the whole thing was just a swindle and got her to confess she found the letters, written by Eros Slaughter to Esmeralda Fischer, in a box in the attic of the house of the lady she works for. Being dirt poor–I gather the old lady pays slave wages–she thought she might try improving her situation by selling the letters back to your friend, Mr. Slaughter. Not content with just a finder's fee, she dreamed up this scheme implying your Mr. Slaughter would not want the letters circulated. She then got some clever friend of hers, likely residing at the boardinghouse, to help her write a letter, making appear as if it was written by a lawyer."

"Eros is not interested in the letters," Jasper said. "His concern is for Phyllis Fischer Walters, who he thought to be his granddaughter."

"Well, you can tell Mr. Slaughter that the only way he's related to this Phyllis Elizabeth Walters is by way of Eve."

Jasper wondered whether this was good news or bad. Had Eros hoped to discover he had a granddaughter and perhaps establish a rapport with her?

Rupert and the detective rose from their chairs. "I suggest you take this information to the police," Rupert said.

"Perhaps I shall," Jasper replied. "Let me think on it."

"It's no good letting crooks get away with extortion," Rupert warned, then presented Jasper with a bill, which Jasper paid along with a generous tip to the house detective.

After the detectives departed, Jasper sat down and tried to order his thoughts. It was nearly dark by the time he sent a telegram to Margaret telling her all that had transpired. Then he went to the theatre and saw Ina Claire perform in *The Gold Diggers*, a play about a chorus girl bent on catching a wealthy husband. It was a thoroughly delightful bit of nonsense, yet got him to thinking about those who must make their way in this world by any means they can.

The next morning, he was at the local bank as soon as it opened. He then rode the cable car back up Nob Hill. The gardener was absent from the house on California Street, but Jasper already knew the way to the back door. Prepared to be rebuffed, he had his foot in the door before Lizzie could close it.

"I only wish to pay you for the letters," he said, biting back the pain in his foot.

"Pay for the letters?" Tentatively, Lizzie opened the door.

"Yes," Jasper said. "May I come in?"

Lizzie did not reply, but left the door open. Jasper entered the kitchen where there was a pleasant smell of bread baking. He placed an envelope on the table. "There are two hundred dollars in that envelope, in exchange for the letters."

Lizzie wiped her hands on her apron as she studied the envelope. "Why are you doing this? I already promised that detective I would send the letters on to Mr. Slaughter."

"I thought it–" Jasper's explanation was interrupted by the sound of a buzzer.

"Oh, what does the old bat want now?" Lizzie rushed from the kitchen, returning a short time later. "More coffee," she explained. "She only wants it to hide the fact that she laces it with whiskey, as if I don't know." She poured coffee into a fine china cup, placed it and a saucer on a silver tray. "I'll be right back."

When she returned, she offered Jasper a seat at the table then poured them both a cup of coffee before sitting down herself.

"You sound English," she said. "I suppose you'd rather have a cup of tea?"

Jasper smiled. "Welsh. Since coming to America, I have acquired a taste for coffee." He took a sip. "Very good, thank you."

"So, answer me. Why are you wanting to pay me now when I already told that detective I'd send the letters?"

Jasper wondered how to explain. Partly it had to do with the play he had seen last night, how the chorus girls depicted in that play had only their small talent to keep them off the streets. And part of it had to do with what he had noticed about Lizzie the first time he saw her: her anxiousness, her irritability, the bags under her eyes from lack of sleep; all signs of being overworked.

Jasper rarely delved too deeply into thoughts concerning the vicissitudes of life. He knew that many people lived on the edge. That is just the way things were. Yet here was an opportunity to do a little something about it.

"The detective and I thought a finder's fee might be in order."

Lizzie was not fooled. "I don't think that detective thought any such thing." She picked up the envelope, peered inside. Her eyes went wide, seeing all the twenty dollar bills. "And you're not going to sic the police on me? That detective said you might."

"I have no wish to sic the police on anyone."

"Well, then," she said, rising from her chair. She went to a nearby cupboard, pushed things aside and pulled out a box, which she set upon the table. "That's the box I found with the letters in it."

It was a metal box, "Japanned," in black lacquer with scenes of happy oriental peasants tending a garden. Jasper lifted the lid and saw a bunch of letters tied together with string.

"They're all there," Lizzie said. "Leastways, all I found."

Jasper took another sip of coffee, rose from his chair and tucked the box of letters under his arm. "Then I believe our business is concluded."

Lizzie appeared reluctant to see him go. "I don't know what to say. I'm truly sorry for what I did, but…" She pushed a string of hair off her damp forehead, "…life's hard, you know."

Jasper nodded, understanding. He thought to suggest to Lizzie that her luck might change, but they both would know it to be a false promise. Fortunately, he was saved having to respond, by the buzzer.

"Oh, drat her!" Lizzie exclaimed. As she rushed off once more to do her mistress' bidding, Jasper made his exit.

Clear skies and a westerly breeze had greeted Jasper that morning when he left the Palace Hotel, and he had returned to his room to leave the coat he would not need. But now it was quite chilly in the garden alongside the house on California Street, and he was glad of the warm sunshine when he emerged out onto the street. As on the day before, the old woman sat on the park bench, her face to the sun. Jasper decided to stop and say hello.

"Good morning," he said. "Do you remember me?"

The woman studied his face. Clearly she did not.

"I had a coat on, yesterday. You mentioned–"

"Oh, yes, I now remember. You are the soldier."

Jasper smiled. "I *was* a soldier. Now I am a prospector, looking for gold."

The woman's eyes lit up. "Really? I once had a friend who was a prospector. Please, do sit and tell about your work."

Jasper sat and placed the lacquered box on the bench between them.

The woman gasped. "That box! Where did you get it?"

Feeling protective, Jasper picked the box back up.

"Please," she said, "I must know where you found that box. I thought I'd lost it."

"Lost it?"

Stiff with age, the old woman yet managed to turn about and point back across the park to the house at 1817 California Street. "I used to live in that house there, up until it just got too much for me, what with maintenance and staff and all. So, I moved to the Fairmont Hotel, only in the move I lost a box, which I am certain is the one you have there."

The light of revelation entered Jasper's brain. "You are Esmeralda!"

The woman placed a hand over her heart. "My goodness, how on earth did you know that?"

Jasper's head spun. "Then... then you are still alive."

She smiled. "My doctor assures me that I am, though I do sometimes wonder."

Jasper slid toward her the box containing the letters. "Then this belongs to you."

Esmeralda stared down at it. "But how ever did you come by it, and how did you know my name?"

As Jasper was about to reply, the hotel limousine pulled up to the curb.

"Oh, dear," Esmeralda said. "Well, Robertson will just have to wait." She looked at Jasper, waiting for him to answer her question.

"Let me start at the beginning. You asked me earlier to tell you of my experiences as a prospector. That I have succeeding in becoming one is due to my meeting a man named Eros Slaughter."

Upon hearing the name of her former lover, tears filled Esmeralda's eyes. She took a small handkerchief from her sleeve. "Pay no attention to the sentiments of an old lady," she said. "Please continue."

Jasper told of his being mentored by Eros, and about that night Margaret and Jasper shared a campfire with Eros and listened while Eros told the story of his perfidious mining partner, Herman Eberhardt, and how Eros eventually lost Esmeralda's hand in marriage to a rich man. As Jasper unraveled the long string that tied his meeting Eros to the matter of the letters, it seemed to him that Esmeralda appeared to grow younger, her waxy skin more opaque, her watery green eyes to clear and to sparkle like gems.

"Hearing your story brings back such memories," Esmeralda said, once Jasper concluded his tale. "It's been many, many years since I last heard from Eros, and I have often wondered what became of him. Time is like a river, my young friend; we drift along together in our little boats, hardly realizing when we start to drift apart. Too late we realize a wide sea now separates us from those we once loved."

"I am certain Eros has never forgotten you, and he will be delighted to know that I met you."

Esmeralda, with a faraway look, nodded. She then turned to Robertson, who had been standing, waiting patiently. "Robertson, if you would be so kind as to help an old lady to stand."

Jasper stood and waited while Robertson folded the lap robe then offered Esmeralda his hand. But when Jasper held out the box containing the letters, Esmeralda shook her head.

"The letters belong to Eros now. Let them be for him a keepsake, a remembrance of a time long ago when two young people found some happiness in each other's arms. But do send Eros my love, and tell him should he ever come again to San Francisco, I should be more than glad to see him."

Jasper promised he would, and as soon as the limousine pulled away, he rushed off to the nearest telegraph office to relate the wondrous news. Esmeralda lives!

Later that evening, a bellhop delivered a reply from Margaret:

"NEWS OF ESMERALDA SADLY COMES TOO LATE STOP EROS PASSED AWAY THIS MORNING STOP HE HAD A GOOD LIFE STOP WE WILL MISS HIM."

Job

To say it is hot in the California desert in the summertime is to state the obvious, yet there came a particular day when Jasper felt certain that Apollo had once again given over the reins of his fiery steeds to his son Phaethon who, unequal to the task of controlling them, was proceeding to scorch the earth.

On the hottest days, Jasper would vary his work schedule, rising before the last of the stars faded from the sky, working until it was too hot, then holing up in whatever shade was available until after sunset, when he would return to work again. But on this day, the temperature forbade even this accommodation to the heat. To expose himself to the sun's harsh rays was to risk burning a hole in the top of his hat, or so it seemed. Certainly, his pick handle was too hot to touch, never mind trying to swing it. All Jasper could manage was to shrink back into the shade of a large boulder and—there was no other word for it—suffer.

Esmeralda, usually quite the stoic, suffered also. While sharing the boulder's shade, she would frequently stamp her feet and shake as if tormented by flies, though not even a fly dared to be abroad on such a day. Then she would voice her complaint with a few mournful hee-haws before stamping her feet once more.

Jasper did not know what to do for her. It was this damnable heat! He was curious to know the temperature. Then again, he was not sure he wanted to know. He removed his bandana, which he wore around his neck to keep the sun off, immersed it in a pot half filled with warm water and ran it over his face. It was a Sisyphean effort, for within seconds his face was dry and the bandana not long afterward. But for a brief time, he felt a little relief. The spring, from whence came the water, was called Job's Well, and like many he had come upon, showed evidence of manmade improvements. This spring had a catch basin made of actual concrete, which trapped a few gallons of spring water in a wide but shallow trough. Jasper wished the catch basin deeper so that he might immerse his whole head, but the maker, who might well have been the Job for whom the spring was named, had chosen a wider surface area over a deeper.

Esmeralda let loose with another string of lamentations.

"I am in perfect accord," Jasper told her. "Perhaps this wicked heat is to warn us of the damnation that awaits the wayward, though why the Good Maker should serve us with this warning is a mystery, since I believe you and I have had little opportunity to stray from the paths of righteousness."

Esmeralda appeared to consider this then, in response, urinated.

"Oh, Lord!" Jasper exclaimed, waving his bandana across his face. The smell did not last long; what urine that did not soak into the sand quickly evaporated. Jasper noted it was the second time Esmeralda had urinated that day, though he did not recall seeing her drinking from the spring. What trick was her body playing to deprive her of needed fluid on this day of all days? He knew nothing of the physiology of a donkey and made a mental note to someday purchase a book on the subject.

Thinking of a book reminded him of the one he had been trying to read. He had made a point of purchasing a book or two whenever he visited a town to replenish his supplies. Second to Esmeralda, a book had become his companion. On the whole, he preferred poetry over other forms of literature. A book of poetry was usually a slim volume, easy to carry about. More importantly, a good poet, with just a few well-chosen words, could conjure up whole worlds, could set a mind to wondering, could pry into a man's soul.

What was it he had read a little while ago? He picked up the book and opened it to the page he had bookmarked with a letter from Shoshone Sam.

"I cast my own shadow upon my path, because I have a lamp that

has not been lighted."

What had the author meant by this? The shadow had to be trouble, but a disturbance of one's own making. A man makes trouble for himself because he has no light to guide him. But like the trouble he creates for himself, the light must also be of his own making. He cannot expect another to light the way for him, for how then could a man trust in his own light? No, a man must light his own way upon the paths of this world.

Or so Jasper had interpreted the author's intention.

He turned the book over and reread the author's name: Rabindranath Tagore, an Indian chap. He had met a few Indian soldiers while serving in the army. He had always found them polite, but stoic, and fiercely brave in battle, which was surprising given their limited reasons for being loyal to the British Crown. Their paths seemed darkened by fate, not from a lack of an inner light.

The Tagore book, entitled *Stray Birds,* had been a gift from Shoshone Sam, sent along with a wedding invitation in care of the Inyo post office. Sadly, the day of Samuel Agullo and Sarah Petruzelli's wedding had passed by the time Jasper retrieved his mail. He had sent his regrets along with a wedding present of a large cluster of indigo-blue tourmaline crystals.

Shoshone Sam had also passed on a note stating he was now a student at Los Angeles University. Jasper had to smile, thinking of Shoshone Sam, who had never completed high school, sitting in a classroom alongside students nearly half his age. Though likely far better read than most of his classmates, he had lacked the prerequisites for admission. Yet it had not been hard for Shoshone Sam to finagle admittance when added to his admission application was a check in an amount sufficient to build a whole new university library.

Esmeralda once again voiced her frustrations. Hee-haw! Hee-haw! Hee-haw!

Jasper covered his ears. "Be still you blasted animal! If it is the heat that is bothering you, there is nothing to be done about it, so you may as well quit your yammering and suffer along in silence."

Ignoring Jasper's advice, Esmeralda perked up her ears and looked intently at something in the distance. Jasper squinted to see what had caught her attention. He made out a distant cloud of dust.

"What do you make of it, Esmeralda? A dust devil?"

The dust cloud appeared to be moving slowly toward them. Perhaps it was a car or truck making its way toward the spring. If so, the driver was going well out of his way, for Jasper knew of no road within a radius of one hundred miles.

Esmeralda again sang out. Hee-haw! Hee-haw! Hee-haw!

From a distance came a response: a whinny.

"Why, they are wild horses!" Jasper declared.

Esmeralda, not waiting for Jasper's confirmation of what she already knew, went racing toward the herd, now visible through the dust.

"Esmeralda!" Jasper cried, jumping up. He should not have risen so quickly. The world whirled about him.

Oblivious to the heat, Esmeralda ran as if she had just beheld long lost friends. A solitary stallion came forward to guard his mares from this unexpected visitor. As Esmeralda drew closer, he reared up, hooves flashing. This did not slow Esmeralda one bit. To her, this hostile reception might have been the stallion actually bidding her welcome.

Jasper feared the stallion might harm, even kill, Esmeralda. He snatched up his twenty-two-caliber rifle, purchased to kill rattlesnakes, and heedless of the heat, ran forward. "You, there! Be gone! Shoo!"

The stallion along with his harem stood staring at Jasper as he raised his rifle and fired a shot in the air. In response, the entire herd turned tail and raced away.

Esmeralda stood with drooping ears as she watched her new friends gallop off. Then, as if convinced it must be all a misunderstanding, she went running on short legs after them.

"Esmeralda, come back!" Jasper shouted, running in pursuit. But Esmeralda was soon out of sight, swallowed up in a sea of creosote bushes.

Jasper stopped and rested with hands on knees as once again the world spun around him. What was he thinking, running in this heat?

"That wee beast is going to be the death of me," he muttered. Yet it was not anger he felt so much as fear, fear that Esmeralda had chosen to run off and join the herd. It was not just that he relied upon Esmeralda to carry his gear, for she was more than a beast of burden. She was his companion in the desert wilderness, a friend to talk to. She had only been gone a few minutes, and already he was feeling lonely. As he staggered back toward the spring, he wondered what had made Esmeralda run off like that? He knew that equines were herding animals. Perhaps Esmeralda had felt the pull of her true nature.

Jasper again stopped to rest. He was surprised at how far he had run.

"Damn this heat!" he muttered.

Heat. The word had more than one meaning. For a moment, he forgot about the sun's scorching rays as he contemplated the other kind of "heat." He had been around horses enough that he should have recognized the signs of estrus. For days, Esmeralda had been restless, and she had urinated excessively. These symptoms of estrus explained Esmeralda's eagerness to approach the stallion. He did not know whether this knowledge made matters better or worse. Should Esmeralda mate with the stallion, she might choose to stay with the herd. Then again, she might just enjoy a bit of a fling, then return to the one creature who favored her with candy. He would just have to wait and find out.

One factor which might sway Esmeralda to return was the spring. Likely it was the reason the herd had been heading this direction. On a day like this, the animals could not go long without water. Perhaps Jasper need only to wait until the horses returned then separate Esmeralda from the rest of the herd.

But how? He pictured himself, hat in hand, pleading with Esmeralda, trying to make a case for her former life of servitude. Put that way, he would not be surprised if Esmeralda responded by turning up her nose then galloping off into the sunset with her new beau.

Jasper shook his head. It had to be the heat, he thought, for here he was, imagining Esmeralda, the stallion and himself as characters in a moving picture. He returned to the shade of the boulder, sat down and tried to think straight. Judging by the herd's reaction to seeing him, they would not return to the spring while he was still there. Consequently, if he wished to see Esmeralda again, he needed to gather up his belongings and move far enough away so the horses would feel safe enough to approach.

That was all well and good, but it would be foolish to try moving until the sun had set. In the meantime, he scanned the area, looking for a place where he might spy upon the herd unobserved. A nearby ridge seemed a suitable spot. Then, if lucky, he might sneak down and reclaim Esmeralda.

Satisfied with his plan, such as it was, Jasper covered his face with his bandana and dozed until sunset. Then he gathered up his belongings and stashed them out of sight behind the sun-bleached remains of a wagon abandoned not far from the spring. Even lugging his goods that short distance left him reeling, and as he rested, he looked upon all the trappings of the lone prospector and realized how much he relied upon Esmeralda.

With just his canteen and an army cot, he started up ridge. He did not bother with a blanket, knowing that the nighttime temperature would not dip much below one hundred degrees. The army cot, however, he must have because of his fear of rattlesnakes. He had purchased it right after hearing a tale of a rattlesnake insinuating itself into a man's bedroll as the man lay upon the ground asleep.

The first of the stars had appeared in the sky by the time he unfolded his cot on the ridgetop. In the west, an afterglow edged a distant range of mountains, above which a wandering star glittered in the heated air. As it grew darker, the constellations Scorpio, Sagittarius and Lupus were visible above the southern horizon. Overhead, a triangle was formed by the bright stars Altair, Vega, and a glittering Deneb, the bright star in the constellation Cygnus, the swan, whose long neck stretched out as she winged her way southwest.

Jasper sighed. A scorpion, a wolf, a swan–they offered little company. He missed Esmeralda.

He slept in fits and starts. Every time he awoke, he looked down upon the spring. There was no moon, but the stars were bright enough to cast shadows. Jasper studied the ground below, but nothing moved, nor were there any sounds other than the occasional thrum of a soaring nighthawk. A little before dawn, a breeze, refreshingly cool, almost chilly, swept along the ridge, a sign that the coming day would not be nearly so hot. This would have cheered Jasper had he not been so concerned about Esmeralda. He closed his eyes and concentrated upon visualizing Esmeralda, mentally willing her to return. All he succeeded in doing was to make himself fall asleep, and the sun was well up when he again awoke.

He immediately looked down. There was no sign of the horses. Feeling achy from a restless night spent in worry, he stood, folded his cot and made his way down off the ridge. The area around the spring revealed the tracks of jack rabbits, quail, and the small footprints of a kangaroo rat. But there were no hoof prints to show that the horses had visited during the night.

Jasper debated what to do. He was tempted to follow the horses' tracks across the desert. But at this point, they could be miles away, and he could not hope to overtake them on foot. There was nothing to do but to patiently go about his business. He mixed up bread dough in his Dutch oven. Every few minutes he looked up, but nothing moved save the occasional bit of brush pushed along by the wind. It was while he was on his second cup of coffee that he noticed something on the horizon which had not been there before. He jumped to his feet, heart pounding. He tried not to get his hopes up. It could be anything: a coyote, an antelope, even a tumbleweed. A whiptail lizard went racing across his boots, but he took little notice.

Then the wind carried to his ears the unmistakable sound of a donkey's bray.

Hee-haw! Hee-haw! Hee-haw!

Seconds later he saw Esmeralda, long ears erect, her familiar swaying gait. Jasper tried not to show how concerned he had been. But that did not prevent him from voicing his pleasure when Esmeralda was within earshot.

"You are a shameless, old trollop! But I am quite happy to see you, regardless."

Esmeralda answered: "Hee-haw! Hee-haw! Hee-haw!" Then she nudged the pocket he kept his hard candy in.

"I might have known it was the candy, and not me, that brought you back," Jasper said, as he unwrapped one of his hard candies.

From camp came the smell of bread baking, and Jasper realized just how hungry he was.

"Come," he said, leading Esmeralda by her halter. "This once I'll share some of my bread with you."

Eleven months later, Esmeralda foaled a healthy hinny, whom Jasper named Job after the spring. Or maybe the name was a reminder of how a donkey can try a man's patience.

Ode to Cholla

Following four years in which so little rain fell as to be almost immeasurable, the heavy winter rains of 1926 brought an end to the drought. The result was a desert wildflower display not seen in years. Every arroyo was a river of color, every jumble of boulders, a rock garden. Across the broad alluvial plains, desert gold, that singularly inconspicuous, daisy-like flower, carpeted the ground in numbers uncountable and turned hard, rocky soil into fields of gold.

Jasper hardly knew where to step for fear he might tread upon some delicate blossom, and at times he was forced to stop and to close his eyes lest his senses be overwhelmed. As he stood, looking across the broad valley that separated Mt. San Jacinto from Mt. San Gorgonio, he asked himself whether there was such a thing as too much beauty. He was convinced the gods must have been intoxicated when they brushed the valley with such striking hues. Pollen-heavy bumble bees swarmed over evening primrose, tobacco weed, poppies and lupine, all of which grew thickly in beds of gravel. Where the soil was softer, sand verbena competed with desert lilies and spreading purple mat. The arroyos were choked with mallow, indigo bush, chuparosa and paintbrush. And towering above this vast painter's canvas were the snowcapped Saints and a sky as blue as cathedral glass.

And if all this were not enough, lingering blossoms of night-blooming sacred datura permeated the air with a fragrance as heady as any to be sampled in a French perfumery.

He wondered how a man could live knowing that, in all likelihood, he would never experience such a sight again? How could he go on, knowing that, as each day grew warmer, the flowers would diminish, the glory fade? He longed for a way he might capture the beauty, wishing he were a master painter able to color the canvas as nature colored the plain. Instead he did his best to place this ephemeral gift in his memory, so that when the heat of summer came and all that remained of the fields of wildflowers were desiccated twigs, he would be able recall the wonder of this spring and comfort himself, knowing that the beauty was not truly lost, but stored away in the sands, in tiny seeds that would need only the right conditions to burst forth in splendor once more.

Jasper turned east and led Esmeralda and Job, her colt, toward Palm Springs, for he wanted to see the fabled Palm Canyon. Where he had wintered, south near Borrego Springs, he had visited small palm oases, but nothing prepared him for the extensive groves of palms he found in the canyons above Palm Springs. It was strange for a desert dweller to walk along a stream in the cool shade of sixty-foot palm trees. Jasper imagined himself in Egypt along the banks of the Nile, or perhaps on a tropical island where palm trees swayed in response to a gentle sea breeze.

Jasper relieved Esmeralda of her packs and let her and Job fend for themselves while he went exploring. In the slow-moving stream, fed by the snows of Mt. San Jacinto, there grew horsetail, ragweed, red willow and tangles of floating watercress. He ambled upstream, following a well-worn path that eventually branched off into separate side canyons, each lined with palms. Eventually, Jasper emerged into full sunlight and stood looking down on the tree-lined stream and, in the distance, the mud-colored buildings of the village of Palm Springs. Sweat beaded on his forehead, for here the elevation was only a couple of hundred feet above sea level, and even in early April, heat rose off the rocky ground. Continuing along the stream, Jasper came upon granite basins carved by the force of sand and water, creating perfect swimming holes.

Jasper took off his boots, rolled up the cuffs of his jeans and waded in, then waded right back out, for the crystalline water was icy cold. He wetted his bandana, cooled his face and arms then lay back upon a stone ledge with his feet dangling inches above the stream. Mt. San

Jacinto towered above him, its thickly wooded slopes a marked contrast to the openness of the desert lying at the mountain's feet. It had been seven years since he had first come to California, and in all that time, he had not lost his wonder of the land's diversity. One had only to gain elevation, and the vegetation changed from cactus to pinyon-juniper woodlands, or to ramble across miles of gravel devoid of vegetation, save for leafless twigs, and suddenly come upon an oasis, filled with greenery and stately palms. Jasper thought that if there ever came a time when he could no longer wander the desert, he might do well to settle in Palm Springs and join the few hundred souls sequestered in beauty and quietude.

A hummingbird, no bigger than a half dollar, appeared and hovered inches from his face. Jasper lay perfectly still as the purple-throated hummingbird attempted to pluck hairs from his beard. Finding them too firmly attached, it flew away, leaving a sound streak of trilling wing beats.

Jasper called after the hummingbird. "Had I known you were after soft nesting material, I'd have trimmed my beard for you."

The next day Jasper and his companions headed east, for Jasper hankered to see the mighty Colorado River. The way was easy, for the flat plateau gradually tilted downward toward the river. About midday, he came to another palm oasis, small, just a few trees, but offering water to fill his canteen and in which to soak his feet as he sat, admiring a nesting pair of northern orioles.

Refreshed, he continued on, crossed a shallow ravine and found himself at the edge of a garden of cholla cacti. Esmeralda, having learned to follow along without need of a lead rope, quickly turned aside and Job followed her. But Jasper, charmed by the abundant cacti, entered into the garden without a second thought. The height of a single cactus varied from three to six feet. Each cactus exhibited a multitude of distorted limbs so thoroughly covered with needle-sharp spines, it appeared to be wearing a coat of fur, hence the name teddy bear cholla. Another name was jumping cholla, for these cacti were rumored to shoot their spines at anyone who ventured near. This was not true, of course, though the cacti were quite willing to transfer their needle-sharp spines onto the sleeve of anyone foolish enough to brush up against them. Such a fool was Jasper. So accomplished are these hitchhikers, that Jasper did not realize he had been offering a free ride until he looked down and saw his sleeve had become a pin cushion. Attempting to brush off the spines resulted in impaled hands and fingers.

"Hell and damnation!" he yelled.

The inch-long spines required a surprisingly strong pull to extricate, for the spines had nearly invisible barbs. Mindful of their needle-sharp points, he pulled the remaining spines from his sleeve. Unfortunately, he failed to notice that other spines had attached themselves to the underside of his other sleeve until he lowered his arm and pushed the sharp spines into the fleshy part of his underarm.

"Hell and damnation!" he reiterated.

Esmeralda, who had been watching from a safe distance, voiced her amusement. "Hee-haw! Hee-haw! Hee-haw!"

A note is required here concerning the cholla's unique method of propagation. Though the cholla does produce fruit, these green and yellow, egg-shaped pods contain few viable seeds. The principal means of regeneration is by means of "joints," segments of the cactus, four to six inches in length, which frequently break off and root themselves in the ground. So productive is the cholla of these spiny joints that the ground around each plant is often littered with them, sometimes in piles from years of accumulation. Should a person happen to step on a joint, he will find it very difficult to remove it from his boot, for the barbed spines adhere to the shoe with a ferocity that is almost demonic, and one cannot simply pluck it out with one's fingers, for the joint, having parasitized its host, is not about to surrender its place without a fight. To pry this nuisance from the sole of a boot requires at least a sharp stick, preferably a crow bar. Thus, a person would have to be very careless or a fool to step on one of these cholla joints. Such a careless fool was Jasper. A joint, six inches in length, lodged itself in the arch of his boot, forcing him to walk on his heel. Fortunately, the soles of his boot were of good thick leather, impenetrable by even the cholla's rigid spines. Balancing himself on one foot, Jasper reached down to yank out the offending stem and, of course, immediately jabbed his finger on a spine. This time he managed to hold his tongue, for he did not wish to add to Esmeralda's amusement. But the pain caused him to lose his balance, and he went hopping about on one foot, picking up stems the way a cotton picker plucks up tufts of cotton.

Esmeralda found this much more amusing than any cry of anguish. "Hee-haw! Hee-Haw! Hee-Haw!"

"Curse you, infernal animal!" Jasper yelled, but only half-heartedly, for he was intent upon getting stopped, which he managed to do by dropping his other foot down into a whole bed of cholla joints. Jasper now found himself considerably taller, as if he were walking on short stilts, something that under normal circumstances requires practice. But this was not a normal circumstance and neither was there time to practice. It is not surprising then that Jasper should stumble and fall, landing on hands and knees. By good fortune, he did not land in a bed of cholla joints, but upon just two, each taking up residence in the palm of each hand.

By now he had almost gotten accustomed to the pain of being pierced. His concern was how to remove the stems, for this required, at the very least, a free hand, which he did not have. He tried to shake the stems loose, but they clung to his hands the way bulldogs grip tasty bones. He attempted to use fingers to get in under the stems, but found no way to maneuver the fingers through the tangle of spines. A fool might have tried prying them off with his teeth. Jasper was not that much a fool.

Finally, he could think of but one way to liberate his hands. Steeling himself for the pain to come, he smashed both hands together. The joints, being now affixed to themselves, fell to the ground when he jerked his hands apart, leaving behind but a few spines, which he was able to pluck out.

From a kneeling position, Jasper took a moment to access his situation. With cholla joints stuck to the soles of his boots, he dared not attempt to stand lest he take another tumble. He decided the best way to proceed was to exit the cholla garden crawling on hands and knees. This proved laborious, for he had to take infinite care to avoid picking up a host of cholla joints. Esmeralda, who had never seen her master ambulate in such a manner, moved closer to get a better view.

"Come to watch me in my humiliation, have you?" Jasper said.

"Hee-haw! Hee-haw! Hee-haw!"

"Cursed beast!" Jasper muttered.

After what seemed an eternity of crawling, Jasper made his escape. So glad was he, he thought nothing of the dozen or so cholla joints which, despite his best efforts, had attached themselves to his pants and shirt. Having now become somewhat adept in their removal, he managed these without too much loss of blood. He next removed his boots and, with a great sense of relief, stood up.

"Well, that has certainly taught me a lesson," he told Esmeralda, who had moved away after Jasper had thrown a few cholla joints at her. "From now on I shall stay well clear of all cactus gardens." Then to justify having imperiled himself in the first place, he added. "Understand, it was my innate curiosity, my need to get to know the way of things, which caused me to enter the garden in the first place."

Jasper arched his back to get out the kinks. "At any rate, I shall rest before trying to remove those blasted bits of cactus from my boots."

A nearby flat rock offered a perfect place to sit. Had Esmeralda been able to speak, she might have warned Jasper of an unseen hitchhiker he had failed to remove. Then again, perhaps not, for it was amusing to see Jasper's reaction when he sat down upon another cholla joint.

Utterly Brilliant

Over the years, Jasper had found a ready market for his most unique mineral specimens, mostly with rock collectors in the Los Angeles area. Sometimes a collector made a specific request, which is why Jasper found himself east of Barstow, looking for "bombs." It is an area interspersed with once active volcanoes, which, eons ago, shot globs of lava twirling through the air like cannon balls out of a cannon. Hence the name "bombs." Depending on how viscous the magma, these bombs took on different shapes as they spun and cooled. Some looked like thin ribbons, some like giant almonds, and some were nearly spherical. Many bombs have at their core harder minerals, and when broken open give the appearance of chocolate-coated candy. It was these specific bombs which Jasper sought.

There is quite an element of fun in breaking open a bomb. Like a grab bag, one never knew what one is going to find. The core of many bombs consists of the mineral olivine, which looks like tapioca colored black and dark green. Jasper's best discovery was a bomb that contained not only the granular form of olivine, but several large crystals, perfectly translucent and pale chartreuse in color.

When Jasper was satisfied that he had a sufficient quantity of bombs, he loaded them upon Job, who had learned the duties of a pack animal, and having grown larger than Esmeralda, his mother, could manage heavier loads. That done, Jasper and his two companions headed for the nearby desert town of Kelso, which owed its existence to two things: water and the railroad. Trains stopped there to fill their boilers before attempting the steep grade to the east.

But before getting to Kelso, there were the Kelso Dunes to be explored. Previously, Jasper had only seen these high dunes from a distance, but now his path led right past them. The Kelso Dunes are like a small range of mountains, rising to a central point. Jasper left Esmeralda and Job to browse on galleta, a shrubby grass growing out of the sand, while he took up the challenge of climbing to the top. Though it was late October, the hot sand could be felt through the soles of his boots. He sank ankle deep in the sand, and this, combined with the steepness of the slope, made progress slow. More than once, he lost his footing and slid several feet down the slope, causing the grains of sand, grating over each, to utter a deep growl. The sound was so strange, Jasper slid on purpose just for the fun of hearing the dune voice its complaint.

At last, he made it to the knife-edge ridge, which he straddled as he made his final ascent to the very top. From there the view repaid all his efforts. To the northeast, beyond a sandy playa, lay the Kelso Depot, looking from this distance like the layout of a boy's toy train yard; farther to the northeast was the Cima Dome bordered by the chocolate-colored Mid Hills; to the south, and closer in, lay the Granite Mountains, grayer in color; and to the west and north, smaller mountains rose up out of dry basins nearly devoid of vegetation.

As Jasper took in the view, a golden eagle, wings unmoving, glided directly toward him. As Jasper leaned back to follow the eagle's path, he lost his balance and fell backwards down the near vertical face of the dune. Had this been a mountain of solid rock, who knows what injuries he might have sustained, but as it was, he only slid a few feet in the soft sand. Dusting himself off, Jasper recalled a travelogue he had once seen wherein a skier, with a camera strapped to his chest, had raced down a mountain. Had Jasper possessed skis, he could have skied down the Kelso Dunes. Lacking skis, he did the next best thing and went running down the slope. It felt more like flying than running, for each stride carried him fifteen feet or more. With arms outstretched, he was his own eagle. From down below, Esmeralda and Job looked up as Jasper howled with delight, and when he reached the bottom, he turned right around and climbed back up to do it again.

The Kelso train depot was a long, two-story Spanish-style building with a colonnade supporting a lengthy covered walkway. The depot featured a lunch counter, and Jasper, who had visited the depot several times before, was eager for a taste of something other than his usual fare of bread and beans. He arrived just as a westward bound freight was starting to pull out. Atop a long line of flat cars, Jasper counted over thirty men. Some were lying down, sleeping; some reading; others just sat and watched as the scenery began to roll by. One man, barely out of his teens, said something to his companions, which Jasper could not hear, and the men turned to stare at Jasper and his donkeys.

"Hey there, sourdough," hollered the young man, standing up, "got any gold for me?" The other men laughed.

But as a matter of fact, Jasper did have gold, for he always carried a few nuggets around with him. He pitched one to the young man who caught it with one hand. When the young man realized he was holding actual gold, he swayed a little, and one of his companions had to reach out and steady him lest he fall off the train.

Having recovered his balance, the young man waved. "Hey, thanks mister!"

Jasper saluted the young man then waited for the caboose to pass and crossed the tracks. He left Esmeralda and Job to graze on the watered lawn while he made his way to the lunch room where the attendant, whose name Jasper recalled was Bill, was absently wiping off the empty lunch counter when Jasper entered.

"Hey there, stranger," Bill said, "long time, no see."

"And a good afternoon to you, Bill," Jasper said, plopping himself down upon a stool. "Is there a chance of getting one of those beef steaks like the last time I was here?"

"Sure thing. With all the trimmings, right?"

"That would be heaven," Jasper said.

"How you like your steak?"

"Just enough to stop it from bleeding."

"You got it." The waiter turned. "Hey, Roy! One steak, rare, with all the fixings."

Roy, a cigarette dangling from his lips, peered through the opening in the wall between the kitchen and the lunchroom and gave Jasper a wave.

"Coffee?" Bill said.

"Absolutely," Jasper said.

"You take it with cream and sugar, if I remember right."

"You have an excellent memory."

"Well, it ain't often we get an old-time prospector coming in here."

Jasper spooned two teaspoons of sugar into his coffee followed by cream. "I saw a small army of men atop the railcars of that train that just left. What was that about?"

"A bunch of bums!" said Roy, who had been listening from the kitchen.

"They ain't bums," Bill said, as he went about placing knife, fork and spoon before Jasper. "Just a bunch of guys who can't find work."

"Bums!" Roy reiterated.

"And why can they not find work?" Jasper said.

Bill stopped and stared at Jasper. "When was the last time you looked at a newspaper?"

Jasper had to stop and think. "I cannot remember. Several years, I think."

Bill shook his head then reached under the counter, pulled out a newspaper. "Here, read this. They're calling it 'The Great Depression.'"

"The Great Fiasco, if you ask me," Roy said.

The paper was open to the editorial page, which demanded government action to create jobs. He turned to the front page and read of bank foreclosures, factory layoffs, a protest in Minneapolis that had turned into a riot. It seemed that while Jasper had been living the life of a hermit, the world had gone topsy-turvy. Then he remembered the last time he went through Inyo and a cryptic note he had received from Sarah Agullo, née Petruzelli: "Not to worry. Your money is in blue chip stocks. They will rise again."

Jasper set his newspaper aside and cut into the steak Bill had placed before him. "So what is to be done about this 'Depression'?"

Bill shrugged. "I don't know. Maybe get in some new leadership, somebody with some new ideas for a change."

"He'll just be another rich, eastern political hack," Roy said, wiping his hands on a towel as he ambled into the lunchroom.

"Well, whoever he is couldn't be worse than Hoover," Bill said, "who just sits around on his hands all day, scratching his head."

Jasper restrained from commenting upon the difficulty with this scenario. "This steak is cooked to perfection, and I have not tasted potatoes so good since I was a boy in Wales. Might I have a bit more butter on them?"

Bill scooped out butter from a tub and set it in a saucer. "Ah, this 'Depression' thing will blow over, you mark my word. We've gone through rough patches before. Next time you're here, it'll be something else we'll be worrying about."

Roy shook his head. "Not this time. This ain't gonna blow over anytime soon." He took off his apron. "I'm going outside for a smoke."

"When do you ever stop smoking?" Bill said.

"When do you stop yapping?"

When Jasper finished his meal, he went to the office of the freight manager and arranged for his rock specimens to be shipped to the rock collector in Los Angeles. That done, he rested on one of the chairs set out on the walkway and gazed out upon the Kelso Dunes. Such a pleasure to sit upon a comfortable chair rather than a hard rock!

An eastbound train pulled into the station and two railway workers began to fill the boiler with water. When the train left the station, Jasper saw a lone figure standing on the far side of the tracks. Dressed in suit and tie, he clearly was not a railway worker. He looked to be about Jasper's own age, maybe a little younger, and similar in height, but lacking Jasper's rugged physique, and judging by his pallid complexion, spent most of his days indoors.

The young man, oblivious of Jasper's attention, appeared to be having a conversation with himself as he paced back and forth. Abruptly, he turned and marched away from the depot and out into the empty desert.

"Now, that is an odd thing," Jasper muttered. He watched, expecting at any moment the young man to turn back, but the young man kept on walking until he was but a speck in the distance. Jasper wondered about the man's destination, for there was nothing in that direction for thirty waterless miles.

Jasper walked over to Esmeralda. "It might be best if we follow that young man and see what he is up to."

Jasper and his companions caught up with the young man about four miles south of the depot. He was sitting on a rock, crying. The man looked up and, seeing Jasper, announced "I'm going to kill myself!"

"Are you, now?" Jasper replied, seating himself upon another rock.

"Yes, I'm going to keep walking out into the desert until I perish from thirst, just like Harry Carey in *Marked Men.*" The young man blew his nose on his handkerchief. "Or maybe it was Charles Le Moyne, I forget."

Jasper shook his head. "From what I have been told, dying of thirst is not a pleasant way to go about leaving this world."

"I don't care," the young man said, waving a damp handkerchief. "I'm ruined. Finished. Washed up. Done for. Bested. Wrecked. *Comprende?*"

Jasper nodded. "Yet to end your life seems a pity, young as you are. When I was in the army, I served with many a man who–"

"You were in the army?" the young man said, perking up considerably.

"Aye, that I was."

"Then maybe you saw the motion picture I made for the War Department: *Maintaining Sanitary Conditions in a Field Hospital*?"

"I am afraid I missed that one."

The young man sighed. "Yes, it did have a rather limited distribution. How sad that an utterly brilliant piece of directing went largely ignored. I believe that had I been allowed to add a few creative touches, *Maintaining Sanitary Conditions in a Field Hospital* would have appealed to a wider audience, but tragically I was overruled by the usual cabal of soulless Babbitts." He knotted his handkerchief in his fist. "Bureaucratic Philistines!"

"So you make motion pictures, is that it?"

"I do more than just make motion pictures, I bring magic to the silver screen. I was all set to make my first full-length picture, the one that was going to launch me into ranks of the world's great directors." He stood straight and tall and gestured with one arm. "Ladies and gentlemen, I give you the greatest directors of our generation: John Ford, Maurice Tourneur, Cecil B. DeMille, and Mortimer Peabody III." He tapped his chest. "That's me, by the way, Mortimer Peabody III, though you can call me Mortie."

"And you can call me Jasper. So, what happened to your motion picture, Mortie?"

Mortie sat back down. "The bastards pulled the plug on it. Said it was this economic depression; they couldn't afford to invest in an 'unknown quantity.' Imagine calling the utterly brilliant director of *Maintaining Sanitary Conditions in a Field Hospital* an 'unknown quantity!'" He fell to weeping again. "Oh, what am I going to do?"

"But surely an able young man such as yourself can find other ways to use his talents."

Mortie shook his head. "All I know is pictures. And now if I don't kill myself, I shall be forced to go crawling back to Mother, a fate worse than death!" He stood again, and this time he began to walk slowly forward, placing one foot directly before the other. "Picture if you will a scene from Maurice Tourneur's *Treasure Island*, and I'm Jim Hawkins being forced to walk the plank by Long John Silver, played by Charles Ogle, who's an utterly brilliant actor, though I thought him too short for the part."

"I read *Treasure Island*," Jasper said "though I do not recall Jim Hawkins having to walk the plank."

Mortie waved his handkerchief. "An insignificant detail. The point is, walking the plank would be infinitely preferable to going home to Mother." He stopped and pointed downward. "There she is! Can you see her, there in the water? She's that big shark, the one with all those nasty teeth." He waved his fist. "You'll not get me, Mother, not this time, you old toothy devourer of men's souls! I shall count to three and all this water will disappear, and you shall be left to writhe in the burning sand! One... two..." And on three he leaped aside, landed on one foot, fell, rolled and came up sitting.

"Is she gone?" he said, looking around.

Jasper nodded. "She is indeed. But would not a quick death by shark bite be preferable to a slow death by thirst?"

Mortie stood up and began to dust off his clothes. "If you knew Mother, you wouldn't ask." He took off his jacket, loosened his tie. "I say, it's rather hot in the desert, wouldn't you agree?"

"You should be here in July."

"I don't suppose you have any water?"

Refraining from stating the obvious, that a drink of water now would only delay Mortie's efforts to do himself in, Jasper stood and went to Esmeralda to fetch his canteen.

When he returned, he found Mortie staring through a frame made with his hands. "You know, this would be a great place to film a remake of *Marked Men,* only I'd call it *The Three Godfathers,* same as the book, which is what John Ford should've called it the first place." A stricken look came into his face. "What am I saying? No one is going to let me do a remake. I'm finished! Ruined! Kaput!" Mortie grabbed the canteen and raised it over his head. "Would this were whiskey to drown my sorrows!"

"Have you ever thought about a career on the stage?" Jasper said. "You have quite a flair for the dramatic."

Mortie wiped his wet chin with his handkerchief. "Done that. Lousy pay, endless travel, dressing rooms smelling of moldy cheese, and fat directors with sweaty palms. No, the theater is as good as dead. Motion pictures is where it's at, where an utterly brilliant director like myself can make his mark." Mortie stepped back and looked Jasper over. "You know, in that outfit, you would be perfect as one of the Three Godfathers. You'd have to color your hair though; red doesn't show up well on the screen. Makes you look like you have mange."

"I shall try to remember that."

"Yes, see that you do." Mortie took another swig. "By the way, what is it you do, Jasper?"

"I am a prospector. I go about looking for valuable minerals."

"Utterly brilliant! You know, my uncle Lucius is a prospector or something of that sort. He made a bundle with a company called…" He tapped his chin. "Minnesota Mining… Minerals… Milk Teeth… I can't remember. Anyway, perhaps you've met uncle Lucius?"

"I cannot say I have had the pleasure."

"Then count your lucky stars. Talk about Philistines! To Uncle Lucius, something is not art unless Jesus is at least hovering around somewhere in the background."

"Perhaps your uncle would be willing to underwrite the cost of your motion picture?"

"Uncle Lucius? Not likely! Not unless I were to direct some weepy morality story plucked out of the Bible, and the market is already awash with religious pictures." He sighed. "No, my utterly brilliant career as a director is over, so I may as well get on with the task of killing myself."

"But surely you must have a friend, someone you can turn to until you can get back on your feet?"

Mortie shook his head. "I am but a poor lost lamb left to wander alone in the wilderness, which is to say that when my picture deal got axed, all my so-called friends deserted me faster than you can say, 'Greta Garbo wears galoshes,' which she does, by the way. Even my Mary abandoned me."

"I am sorry indeed. To be deserted by the woman you love just when you need her the most—surely that must have felt like the last straw."

"Woman I love? What are you talking about? Mary is as old as dirt and not nearly as attractive. No, Mary is my casting director. Utterly brilliant! It was her idea to use real doctors and nurses in *Maintaining Sanitary Conditions in a Field Hospital.*" Mortie blew his nose. "Say, you wouldn't happen to have a spare handkerchief? This one is getting rather soggy."

Jasper dug his out of his back pocket. Mortie looked over the offering then shrugged. "Beggars and choosers and all that." He blew his nose then pocketed the handkerchief. "I must say, you've been ever so kind, lending an ear to my tale of woe."

"I only trust you are not still planning to kill yourself."

Mortie looked around. "I guess not. If I were to die out here, who would witness it? No, when I make my exit it will be with six white horses, a marching band and a gaggle of weepy maidens."

"So what do you plan to do now?"

"I guess I shall have to 'bite the bullet,' as they say, and crawl on home to Mummy. But never you worry. I shall be strong." He began to walk slowly forward, shoulders back, head held high. "Picture, if you would, me as Sidney Carton on his way to the guillotine. ' 'Tis a far, far better thing–' " He stopped. "By the way, which way is it back to the train station?"

Jasper pointed out the buildings, just visible in the distance.

"Egad! 'Tis a damn long way to the guillotine. Oh, well." He continued his march. "Will you join me, friend? No man wants to go to his death alone."

"Do not forget your jacket," Jasper said, picking it up where Mortie left it.

"Right you are," Mortie said. "I must look my best for the beheading."

They reached the station just as another westbound freight train was pulling in. Mortie studied the score or more of men perched upon the flat cars. "I suppose I shall have to join the ranks of the great unwashed, for I spent my last *centavo* on a ticket to get here."

Jasper pulled out his wallet and drew out five, twenty-dollar bills. "Here, take this."

"No, I couldn't possibly take your money," Mortie said, eagerly reaching out a hand to take the bills.

"If you like, you may consider it a loan, or, better yet, an investment. I am investing one hundred dollars in the career of an utterly brilliant director. And someday, when the world is singing your praises, drop me a note in care of general delivery, Inyo post office."

Mortie brushed a tear away. "I don't know what to say."

"Say nothing, but go purchase your ticket before the train leaves."

Mortie grasped Jasper's hand. "May all the saints in heaven dump buckets of blessings upon your head. Don't forget what I told you about red hair. And should you ever get to Hollywood–"

"I believe the train is getting ready to leave."

"Yes, so it appears. And so, with a heavy heart, the utterly brilliant Mortimer Peabody III must now make his exit. Good-by, dear friend. *Adios. Au revoir. Arrivaderci. Sayon–*"

"Skedaddle!"

"That, too!"

The following year, Jasper was in the town of Inyo, picking up supplies and checking for correspondence. The postmaster handed him a large envelope which contained one hundred dollars and two tickets to the premiere of *Jungle Passion*. A note read:

> Dear Jasper,
>
> Never let it be said that Mortimer Peabody III does not pay his debts!
>
> I had this utterly brilliant idea of getting Uncle Lucius to finance my new motion picture. He thinks it's about missionaries bringing the good word to the heathen. By the time he learns otherwise, I shall be able to placate the old Bible-thumper with a whopping return on his investment. Then again, if *Jungle Passion* should flop–which it won't, for it's utterly brilliant–I promise not to kill myself, though I may be forced to join the Foreign Legion.
>
> By the way, I'm sorry but I won't be able to use you in *The Three Godfathers*, as John Ford appears intent

upon holding on to the rights. Alas and alack!

Hope to see you at the premiere. Best leave your donkey friends at home.

Your fellow desert rat,
Mortimer Peabody III

A Few Consequential Errors

To a passenger, traveling through on a train, the desert may appear a monotonous moonscape, and time better spent in glancing at the advertisements in a magazine than gazing out the window. It is a fact that the desert is rarely depicted in such advertisements. If the ad-man wishes to sell cigarettes by suggesting there is something sublime about inhaling smoke, he would be better off showing a rugged hiker astride a majestic peak, celebrating his triumph (while you languish in the office) with a well-deserved puff on his Pall Mall. An ad showing someone smoking a cigarette in the desert would be redundant, for it is usually hot enough in the desert without the addition of a burning plant dangling two inches from one's nose. The desert, with its heat and the suggestion of needed refreshment, would be better suited for selling soft drinks, especially in winter when sales are down. But it seems the ad-man prefers to show a sweaty skier, fresh off the slopes, being greeted by a beaming blonde with her offering of an ice-cold Pepsi-Cola.

Outside of a few weeks in spring, and sometimes not then, the desert, generally, does not dazzle the senses. To truly appreciate the desert requires time and a receptiveness to subtle forms of beauty: the pastel hues in a sandstone cliff, the sparkle of salts on a dry lake bed, the motes of dust shimmering in a summer sunset, the unexpected flower sheltered in a crevice.

Yet to say the desert is lacking in evident splendor is only to consider it during the daylight hours. The opposite is true at night, for nowhere else on earth are the stars more radiant as when seen through clear, dark, dry, desert air. No one knew this better than Jasper, yet there came a night when the glory of the night sky was lost upon him, when all he could think of was whether he would make it to tomorrow.

The trouble began at Fort Piute, a long-deserted army outpost at the edge of the Lanfair Valley near the California-Nevada border. Here he had made the first of a few small, but consequential, errors. Admittedly, it had been a trying morning. Job, for some reason, had been refusing to perform his duties as a pack animal, and unlike his mother, could not be induced with the offer of a hard candy. Quitting before he succumbed to the temptation to "wallop the hell" out of the brute, Jasper instead loaded his goods upon Esmeralda, failing to check the level in his two water bags. This was his first mistake.

His second mistake was one of complacency. The Lanfair Valley is located in what is referred to as "high desert," being nearly four thousand feet in elevation. Temperatures, even in the height of summer, usually do not get above the high nineties. The relative coolness made Jasper less concerned about the need for water, that and knowing the route he would be traveling and the locations of the springs along the way.

"Enjoy your freedom while you may," Jasper told Job, who larked about as Jasper led Esmeralda down a broad wash. "I assure you tomorrow you will resume your duties." Yet Jasper could not hold a grudge, for it was a fine August morning, and the firm sand beneath his feet made walking a pleasure.

Because the rewards of prospecting had been meager of late, Jasper thought he might try his hand at looking for fossils. With that in mind, his destination was the fossil-rich Marble Mountains, approximately fifty miles to the southwest in a straight line. But the direct route crossed a wide plain as dry as a Welshman's wit. The need for water forced Jasper to choose another, longer route. First he would bear west and a little south to Desert Spring, where he planned to spend the night. Tomorrow he would cross the Providence Mountains by way of Foshay Pass, stopping at Dam Good Spring. The following day he would head south, skirting the Granite Mountains, to Willow Springs where he would be but ten miles from his destination.

In the desert, there are a surprising number of springs, though not always do they accommodate the thirsty traveler. There are several reasons for this. Some springs are only seasonal. Some flow some years, other years not. Even the most reliable springs can suddenly go dry. Earthquakes have been known to cause this, shifting the earth, closing off underground fissures, the result being that one spring dries up and another appears in a new location. Because of this, the experienced desert traveler has an inviolate rule: to carry enough water so that if one spring proves dry, he will still have enough water to reach the next one. Jasper, in his complacency, was not carrying enough water, but it did not even cross his mind to worry, for he had visited Desert Spring before and found it a reliable water source with patches of greenery providing forage for his donkeys.

As the sun reached its zenith, he passed Billie Mountain, a solitary butte to the east. Opposite were the Vontrigger Hills where an abandoned mine was revealed by tailings fanning out like a woman's red skirt. A little farther on he crossed the old road leading to the mine in whose ruts grew rivulets of cheesebush, some with a few clusters of pearly-white blossoms. In the scant shade of a Joshua tree, Jasper stopped to rest and to quench his thirst. It was then that he realized his error in not filling his water bags when he should have. Still, he was not overly concerned. He poured a little water into his palm and offered this to Job, who stood leaning over his shoulder.

"Well, if that is not gratitude for you!" Jasper exclaimed, as Job turned away from this offering. "Just for that, you will have no more water until we reach Desert Spring, and let that be a lesson to you not to turn your nose up when someone offers you precious, life-giving water."

The irony of this punishment was that when Jasper reached Desert Spring, just before sunset, he found there was no water for Job to turn his nose up at even if he wanted to. Absent too was the green grass, which had withered and died. Esmeralda nosed a few dry blades then snorted, sending up a little cloud of dust. The only sign of life was a few sickly green leaves on an all-but-dead willow.

Jasper set to work to open up the spring. He worked for an hour, but the only water he drew was the sweat that flowed down his back. Tired, he sat down upon the dry ground. If he was not worried before, he was now. Throughout the day he had drunk water whenever he felt the need with the result that he had hardly any left.

He licked his dry lips and tried to ignore his thirst. The sensible course would be to return to Piute Spring, but it irked him to think of having to retrace his steps. He also had to consider the fact that the distance back to Piute Spring was less than the distance forward to Dam Good Spring, making an argument for his continuing on. But what if Dam Good Spring should also prove dry? Yet what were the chances of two springs being dry?

Jasper was too tired to make a decision. He stood up and dusted himself off then ate a cold dinner before unfolding his army cot. The glare of a nearly full moon kept him awake, that and a headache. He slept fitfully and was awoken shortly after moonset by a wind that whistled about his head. Above him, the Milky Way, luminous like electrically charged gas, spanned the sky. Staring up into this fiery firmament, Jasper recalled something Emerson had written about beauty, calling it "God's handwriting." Jasper had not much of an opinion about God. He had seen too much killing to believe in an active, benevolent God. It was obvious that if God existed, He did not wish to trouble Himself with mankind's malevolence. Perhaps God was but a creative force, forever brushing the canvas of the universe, signing, "I was here!"

It was a nice thought, a liberating one, freeing him to act without fear that God was always looking over his shoulder, judging him. At the same time, it left him on his own, with no divine intervention should there be a need. And knowing this, he knew what he must do about his water situation. He cast aside his blanket, stood and began to fold his army cot in the predawn light.

"I have decided that our best course of action is to go back the way we came," he announced to Esmeralda and Job, who were moving about in search of food. Jasper leaned his cot up against a rock and began to roll his blanket. "As soon as it's light enough—"

A violent gust of wind blew over his cot. As Jasper made a grab for it, the wind took his blanket, and it sailed away like a kite off its string. He chased after it as it undulated across the ground like a sidewinder rattlesnake until being snagged in a bush. Jasper disentangled his blanket and began to pick out the burrs.

"This wind could change matters," he thought. As if to confirm this, a blast of wind nearly tore the blanket out of his hand. Finding the shelter of a boulder, he sat and waited for dawn to come. It was not the usual sun that greeted him. Shrouded by a great wall of wind-driven sand, it was a dull glow, varying in color from orange to nearly brown. He now had to rethink his plans. To return to Piute Spring meant he would be headed straight into the wind. He pictured himself having to breathe through the fabric of his bandana as he struggled to keep the sand out of his eyes. On the other hand, should he decide to go west toward Dam Good Spring, he would have the wind at his back.

Horace Greeley's famous command, "Go west, young man," came to mind.

"I doubt this is what old Horace meant," Jasper muttered, but nevertheless, he believed going west was now the better option.

Remembering his frustration with Job the day before, he took the easy way out and once again loaded his gear on Esmeralda. Then he started west, following the rise of the ground toward the Providence Mountains and Foshay Pass, faint in the distance. For a man accustomed to long treks, the pass was not far, straight as the crow might fly, not that a crow could fly straight on a windy day like today. But the possibility of heading in a straight line was negated by the presence of Mojave yucca, catclaw acacia, burro bush, silver cholla and a myriad of lower-growing shrubs, all of which were obstacles he must go around. Then there were the innumerable ravines and washes which added half as much vertically to the distance as horizontally.

As if these were not sufficient impediments, there was the wind, which preferred to make its assaults in fits and starts. The sound was like that of an approaching freight train, getting louder and louder until with blast of driven sand, it slammed against him, plastering his pants and shirt to his tall frame and forcing him to grip his hat to keep it from being carried away to the heavens. Then this wind-train would pass on, yet never out of earshot before another came on, louder and louder until once again Jasper found himself struggling to maintain possession of his hat as he dug in his heels to keep from being blown over.

When the sun was well overhead, he stopped in the shelter of a boulder to rest. The boulder gave him some respite from the shrieking wind, but could do nothing for his thirst. He had squeezed the last few drops from his water bags when not half a mile from camp. He had thought to put this off for as long as possible, but decided to go ahead and partake of this last swallow and thereby eliminate the added frustration of having to wait. He had once read that a person could live three days without water. He doubted such a figure was derived under conditions such as he was experiencing, and it disturbed him to think he might become the guinea pig for some experiment on the effects of severe dehydration, the results of which no one would ever know.

"Just put one foot in front of the other," he told himself, "and try not to think about water." Instead he thought once more about what Emerson wrote about God and beauty, but that only brought to mind something else Emerson had written, words to the effect that the man who is against himself finds the world against him. This seemed only too true. Oh, how he wished he had filled his water bags! Now he was paying a price made all the worse by this devil-sent wind!

He redirected his thoughts toward Foshay Pass and Dam Good Spring, imagining himself slaking his thirst then bathing his aching head. The headache, which had begun the night before, was now a throbbing torment, a sure sign of severe dehydration. There was, however, nothing to do but try to ignore the pain. In this, and this only, the wind was his ally, for it was a constant distraction. Uprooted plants hit against him or rolled across his path, creating a shifting obstacle course.

After climbing out of a particularly steep gully, Jasper found himself at the base of an alluvial fan, composed of rock fragments pressed flat into the ground, an arbitrarily patterned mosaic, reflecting back the sun's heat as if it were asphalt. He found himself increasingly blinking to clear his vision, and he did not know whether this was due to the sun's reflection, or was another symptom of his body's craving water. The air, which he had thought might cool a little as he climbed, seemed only to grow hotter. He would have liked to stop and rest, but there was not a dot of shade and little point in sitting on the ground, which had to be at least twenty degrees hotter than the air.

He came upon a well-worn trail leading straight toward Foshay Pass, the notch in the Providence Mountains which divided Fountain Peak to the north from the Winston Basin to the south. This was the same trail over which Father Garces and his Indian guides traveled in 1776, searching for a route from the Colorado River to Mission Monterey. In Jasper's current condition, such knowledge would have been of little interest. He thought only of the spring which awaited him at the top of the pass, and sought to shorten his suffering by trying to increase his pace. He managed only about fifty hurried steps before becoming overcome by dizziness. He stood, bent over, hands upon knees, waiting for his head to stop spinning. His body cast a long shadow, stretching out toward the Fenner Hills, surprisingly clear in the east. Only now did he become aware that the wind had ceased to blow.

It was nearly dark by the time Jasper entered Foshay Pass. Dam Good Spring, unless one knew its exact location, could easily be missed, hidden as it was up a narrow gully. Jasper, who had stopped at the spring once before, recalled it was not an abundant source of water, yet sufficient for the needs of man and animal, and refreshingly cool, having its source deep within the Providence Mountains. As Jasper entered the gully that contained the spring, he could dimly make out the tracks of animals, evidence that the spring was being used.

But whether the tracks were old, or whether Dam Good Spring had only recently dried up, it all amounted to the same thing, for all Jasper found was a water-stained basin where water had once pooled. Jasper's immediate thought was that he had made a mistake, that he had gone up the wrong gully. His head hurt so badly, it was difficult to think. Yet even in his confused state, he knew he had not erred. Dam Good Spring was now Done Gone Spring, and as he looked more closely, he found proof written on a rock where someone had scrawled, "Gone Dry," and had dated it a month earlier.

Jasper dropped down upon the ground and cradled his head. What a fool he had been not to fill his water bags when he could have. Now he had to consider that death was likely to be the result of his folly. This thought might have overmastered him had he not already encountered death countless times on the battlefield. Yet this was different; death on the battlefield came in an instant; death by thirst came creeping in slow agonizing steps.

With the tips of his fingers, he tried to rub away the white pain within his cranium, which made thinking a struggle. To return to Piute Spring was out of the question; he would never make it. The same was true of Willow Springs. The closest certain source of water was the depot at Kelso, but that was more than ten miles away.

Ten miles. On an ordinary day, he could walk ten miles between breakfast and noon. But this was not an ordinary day. Tired as he was, suffering as he was, he realized that if he were to stand any chance of surviving he would have to leave now and walk through the night, for he knew he would not last long come daybreak and the sun's return.

Jasper found his traveling companions waiting for him back where left them at the trail. Job was bedded on the ground while Esmeralda, encumbered by the packs, looked as if she would like to join him. Jasper wanted to tell them both how he sympathized with their fatigue, but a swollen tongue and a mouth painfully dry prevented speech. His dry swallows were like sandpaper scraping the interior of his throat. How long had it been since he had used up his last drops of water? Was it only this morning? It seemed much longer. And before that, when had he taken water? Was it thirty-six hours ago? Forty? Who said a man could go seventy-two hours without water? Not someone who had spent the day beneath a blistering sun while being pushed along by a wind sent from the devil's kitchen.

Jasper moved to get Job up. Though Job did not resist Jasper's urging, just the effort of leaning over and pulling on Job's halter set Jasper's heart racing. He rested, leaning upon Job, and watched as the moon rose clear in the sky. Jasper wanted to believe this was a hopeful sign. All day the world had been against him: the heat, the wind, the sun; and he against himself: his stupidity in not filling his water bags when he could have. But here was a bit of luck, for the moon would allow him to see his way forward.

"Come," Jasper whispered, leading Job by his halter.

The shadows of the three travelers stretched out before them. For a distance of a quarter of a mile, the trail passed through a section of twisting canyons then opened upon an alluvial fan which spread out and dissolved into the area known as the Devil's Playground. "Devil's Sand Box" might have been more apt, for it consisted of miles of sand dunes. The undulating mounds cast dark shadows. Darker was the sky in which stars glittered with spectral colors. Another time Jasper would have been enlivened by their beauty, but now he thought only of water's restorative power and the ten miles he must go before finding relief.

He tried to think of something to take his mind off his suffering. He thought of his old friends, starting with Jacob Harmon and their first meeting in his small Inyo store. He recalled the last words Jacob had spoken to him that day when he was about to set out across the desert: "Make sure you always carry plenty of water."

He thought of Shoshone Sam whose attitude on that same day was rather scornful. Yet it was Shoshone Sam who had come to his aid when a few days later Jasper, brash young fool that he was, thought himself like to die of thirst. How delicious had been that warm, metal-tainted water from Shoshone Sam's canteen!

He thought of Eros Slaughter, his mentor, who had spent a half century exploring the desert and never found himself in the situation Jasper now faced. Jasper wondered if somewhere Eros was looking down upon him, shaking his head and saying, "Didn't I teach you better?"

He thought of the town of Desert Rose and the wealth he and his partners had taken from the earth. It was that wealth which had given Jasper the freedom to wander where he would, never concerned about having to make a living as a prospector. But what was that wealth to him now? He would gladly have traded it all for just one long drink of water.

Water. No matter how much Jasper tried to think of something else, he always came back to that five-letter word.

The plain was deceiving in that, from a distance, it appeared smooth and even. Not only was the ground rocky, but gully after gully had to be crossed, some so deep that Jasper could not climb out of them without stopping repeatedly to rest. It was during one of these rests that he began to experience flashes of light, which seemed to emanate from behind his eyes. What did this mean, he wondered? Was he going blind? What chance had he of reaching Kelso Depot if he were to lose his sight? He closed his eyes, rested his chin upon his chest, but the flashes continued. His need for sleep was second only to his need for water, yet he must not sleep, for summer nights were short, and he dare not be caught out by the sun. Yet knowing this, he still slept, chin upon chest.

It was Esmeralda's nudging him that brought him awake. A panic seized him as he struggled to stand. How long had he been asleep? He held on to Esmeralda's halter for support, trying to remember where he was. His legs were trembling. He could scarcely breathe, so constricted was his throat. He could feel Esmeralda's warm skin against his hand, and a thought entered his mind that brought him wide awake. He might be able to save himself by sacrificing one of his donkeys, by cutting an artery and pacifying his thirst with blood. Then a feeling of revulsion swept over him, and he knew he could not sacrifice either of his friends, not even to save his own life. So, what was he to do? He would have cried had he been able to produce tears. What a fool he was to have put them all in such peril!

Yet there was one thing he could do for Esmeralda. He undid the straps that secured the packs and watched as they slid to the ground.

He could not voice the words he wanted to tell her: *Go, Esmeralda! Save yourself!* Instead, he struck her across her flank. Startled, Esmeralda bolted, but only a little way before turning to look back at her master. She would not desert him, Jasper knew, and for that reason he forced himself to go on.

He did not know how long he had slept, and could not tell by the position of the moon, for it had disappeared. The disappearance of the moon, which was not due to set until after sunrise, only added to Jasper's confusion and to his worry that he was going blind.

He told himself to just put one foot in front of the other and ignore everything else. But the flashes of light were coming more often, and each time they acted like an electrical charge, shattering his concentration. He decided to try walking with his eyes closed, one hand on Esmeralda, and this seemed to help with the flashes and to lessen the agony of his headache. On and on he staggered, half asleep. His brain was slow to register a change felt through the soles of his boots, the feeling of walking on sand rather than scattered rock. He opened his eyes and saw he was in a wide, sandy wash, and in the distance, there was the glow of lights from the train depot. How much farther was it? Seven miles? Maybe just six? Such questions were pointless, for Jasper knew he could go no further.

There was a large rock, sitting upright in the sand, looking like a tombstone. The symbolism was not lost upon Jasper. He knelt before the rock and leaned his head against it. It was surprisingly cool to the touch. In this position, he fell into a troubled sleep with flashes of light mingling with visions of watery oases.

It was Esmeralda who again brought him around, her hot breath blowing into his face. At first he tried to push her away, but she was insistent. He sat up. The moon, well in the west, had reappeared. In a little while, it would be daybreak.

The moonlight revealed what he had failed to notice before. Painted on the rock were pictographs, ancient paintings made by a long forgotten artist. Of the many figures, only a few could he recognize: a bighorn sheep with curved horns, a stick-figure man, squiggles like the ripples on a lake surface, and jagged lines suggesting lightning bolts. He closed his eyes, and when he reopened them he saw other things he had failed to notice. Near to the rock were clay pots decorated in geometric designs; a large woven basket, big enough for a child to hide in; smaller baskets, also with geometric designs. But most astonishingly, an old woman sat cross-legged upon a woven mat, winnowing seed with the aid of a flat basket.

Jasper knew he was hallucinating, yet the old woman looked real. He could see the spider web lines in her brown face, her gray hair cut short over her forehead. She took no notice of him, less than ten feet away.

"Water," he croaked. "Water."

The old woman stopped her winnowing, cocked her head, listening.

"Water."

Whether or not she saw Jasper, the old woman nevertheless appeared conscious of another's presence. She reached out a hand and spoke a few words he could not understand.

"Water," he pleaded once more.

She nodded, understanding. Then, smiling, she slowly tilted her winnowing basket. Out spilled grain, and as it fell earthward, it changed into water, far more water than the basket could have possibly held. Suddenly Jasper was surrounded by water, flowing over his hands, soaking into the legs of his jeans. He flung himself forward, face first into the inches-deep stream. First there was the agony of not being able to swallow, then his throat relaxed and he drank until he felt his stomach heave, and he retched. Crying, laughing, he drank some more. As the water flowed into him, he felt his body responding right down to the cellular level, as if he, a withered bush, were being miraculously restored, every capillary, fiber, stem and leaf, greening and returning to life. When his thirst was sated at last, he lay down at the water's edge and slept.

The sun was well up when he awoke. His head hurt, and he craved water. The stream had come and gone, yet here and there, in the depressions of rocks, small pools of water remained. Jasper crawled to the nearest and slaked his thirst. Then he sat looking about him. The pictographs still adorned the rock, but as for the rest: the pots, the baskets, the old woman–there were no signs of them having existed. They had been just hallucinations, delusions from the mind of a man at the end of his rope.

But the flashes of lightning, which he believed to have emanated from within his brain, had not been hallucinations, for while Jasper had been stumbling about, monsoon winds had brought a summer storm to the Providence Mountains, and to the accompaniment of lightning, rain had lashed the mountain tops in amounts too great for the soil to hold, and the surplus had raced down the canyons to spread out in the washes below.

Thus, it was nature, and not an old woman's magic, that had saved him.

Yet this logical explanation did not satisfy Jasper. Questions remained. Why had the water come just as the old woman appeared to have released it from her basket? What would have happened to Jasper had he not been exactly where he had been, kneeling before the painted rock, standing upright in the sandy wash? Why had his hallucination taken the strange form that it did? Though he had met many native Americans as he wandered about the desert, all had adopted the white man's apparel and none looked as had the old woman, a figure from a bygone era. Even now, Jasper could clearly see her face, could visualize her arthritic fingers as she tilted her winnowing basket and let the saving water flow forth. If she had not been real, from where in his brain had he drawn her likeness?

Jasper stood up. He was weak, but felt confident his strength would return. Plants, which made their home in the wash, were already starting to green. Like him, they had been brought back to life by the restorative water, and whether Jasper owed his life to forces natural or mystical, or to just plain luck, nevertheless, he was most grateful to be alive.

An Unlikely Parade

Time, the ordering of the year into months and days and hours, grew to have less and less relevance for Jasper. If there were any temporal order to his life, it was largely structured around temperature, for during the hottest part of a year he would invariably find himself migrating toward northern Nevada or eastern Oregon—those sections of high desert that were cooler in summer—and conversely going south when the weather turned chill.

This freedom from the tyrannies of calendar and clock was one of the joys of Jasper's life, and he guarded this freedom to the extent that he scrupulously avoided newspapers and calendars upon those infrequent occasions when he needed to visit a town for supplies.

One date, however, he wished he had known, for the sake of its commemoration. That was the day when his long-serving companion, Esmeralda, died. Jasper comforted himself with knowing that, for a beast of burden, Esmeralda had had a pretty good life. Jasper had never once laid a hand on her in anger, had rarely even raised his voice. For the last years of her life, Esmeralda did not even have to carry Jasper's gear, that job falling to the much younger and stronger Job. And every day, whether or not she had to carry supplies, Jasper always gave her a piece of hard candy, right up to the day when she refused her treat, a sure sign she was ailing.

Jasper spent a whole day digging Esmeralda's grave, all the while thinking how much he would miss his companion. And this led to thoughts about whether he should make changes in his solitary lifestyle. A fondness for animals was good, but might his affections be better placed on those of his own kind?

The answer to this question came not too long after Esmeralda had been laid to rest with a small bag of hard candies at her side. Ever since Eros Slaughter had shown Jasper a large pyrite crystal he had once found, a perfect metallic cube measuring three inches a side, Jasper had itched to find one himself. With that in mind, he set off toward an abandoned iron mine in the eastern Mojave where previously he had luck finding pyrite crystals. Much to his surprise he found the mine being worked.

He approached a young man, hardly old enough to shave, who sat in the shade of a bulldozer, eating his lunch.

"What all is going on here?" Jasper said, pointing to the work being done.

The young man shaded his eyes from the sun as he looked up. "We're mining iron."

Jasper thought there were better iron deposits elsewhere. "Whatever for?"

"For steel. For the war."

"War?"

The young man gave Jasper a funny look. "Geez, pops, where you been? The war against the Japs and the Gerrys." The young man gave him a big smile. "Come my birthday, I'm joining up."

So, it was happening again, Jasper thought, another war: more bloodshed, more slaughter, a whole new generation scarred by madness let loose. Jasper had a mind to plead with the young man to go as far away from the war as possible, but he recognized the look on the young man's face, that eagerness for adventure. He once possessed that look himself. Instead Jasper turned away, sick at heart, vowing to sever himself from all human contact, as much as possible.

About five years later, he found himself once more in the town of Inyo. Somehow, it seemed much smaller than it appeared on his first visit. Long ago, Jacob Harmon, successful with his supermarket chain, had sold the old general store. The current owner looked at Jasper's dirty and threadbare clothes then demanded that Jasper produce some silver before he would wait on him. Jasper was more amused than offended. He pulled from his wallet a one-hundred-dollar bill and listened with amusement as the bug-eyed storekeeper stammered an apology.

Jasper next went to the post office, and was given two bundles of letters, the larger from Sarah Agullo, and, much to his surprise and delight, a smaller bundle from his stepbrother Delwyn. Thanks to the education fund Jasper had set up for him, Delwyn had gone on to receive a degree in physics and recently been attending graduate school in Massachusetts, studying aeronautical engineering. Sitting outside, Jasper opened Delwyn's latest correspondence, dated two months earlier.

> Dear Aurfryn,
>
> I hope this letter finds you because, guess what, Aurfryn? We're neighbors! Or nearly so. I am living about one hundred miles north of Los Angeles. Or maybe I should say I'm trying to live. How do you stand the heat, Aurfryn? What makes it all bearable is that I love what I'm doing now. If you had gotten my last letter, then you would know that I completed my degree last May and am now working for McDougal Aviation here at Muroc Army Airfield. It's an exciting time to be in aeronautics. You probably read that just this year we broke the sound barrier for the first time. I'm sure it won't be long before our planes will be flying twice that fast, if you can believe it.
>
> I would very much like to see you, Aurfryn. It's been decades since you left, and I doubt you'd recognize the little boy you used to bounce on your knee back home in Wales. I pray that you'll get this letter and come visit me. Most days you can find me at Muroc. Just tell the guard at the station I'm your brother, and someone will come fetch me.
>
> Please, come soon. We're doing wonderful things

(most of which I'm not allowed to talk about), and I want to show you that all that money you spent on my education was not wasted.

   With great affection,
    Delwyn

  Smiling, Jasper folded the letter and put it his shirt pocket. *My baby stepbrother, an aeronautical engineer!* He went back inside the post office where he found the postmaster helping a customer. "Excuse me, but do either of you know the location of …" he consulted his letter, "… of Muroc Army Airfield?"

  The postmaster leaned forward over the counter. "I sure as hell do. Spent three years of my life in that hellhole during the war. Why do you want to know?"

  Jasper waved his letter. "My brother Delwyn works there, and has invited me to visit him."

  "Well, let me finish with this lady, and I'll show you on a map."

  "I'd curious to know, too, Clem," said the woman.

  The postmaster produced a road map and spread it out on the counter. "Muroc is pretty easy to get to from here," he said, pointing. "Just follow highway 395 south to highway 58, near where the borax works are, and you're about there." With a finger, he outlined a shaded area roughly in the shape of a rectangle, the longer sides going east-west. "This whole thing is the air base, but the airfield is way over here on the west side."

  "How far do you think it is?" Jasper said.

  "I'd say somewhere between one hundred and fifty miles and two hundred miles."

  Jasper thanked the postmaster then purchased a postcard and wrote a note to Delwyn saying he would arrive for a visit in about a week or so.

  Six days after leaving Inyo, Jasper found himself staring at a sign.

RESTRICTED MILITARY AREA

No Admittance Beyond This Point

————

Trespassers Will Be Prosecuted
To the Full Extent of The Law
Muroc Army Airfield

Jasper had trespassed upon restricted areas before. Not to do so often necessitated a lengthy detour, as a restricted area might cover hundreds of square miles. Usually Jasper did not even know he was in a restricted area, for most were too vast to fence, and he rarely encountered keep-out signs like this one, which looked serious.

"It seems as if someone is really wanting to keep us out," Jasper said to Job. He tugged on his beard, thinking. By his estimate, it would take him another day to reach the main headquarters of the air base, that is if he continued straight ahead through the restricted area. If forced to go around, he could expect to add at least another day to his travels.

Yet it was not the added distance that bothered him, but a feeling he had not experienced in a long time, an eagerness to be somewhere. He was anxious to see his stepbrother and was unwilling to tolerate any delays.

He turned to Job. "Now, Job, if they toss you in jail, just tell them it was all my fault." He gave a little tug on Job's halter. "You see, I am forcing you to trespass. I, myself, shall claim military exemption and trust they will not put an old soldier in jail. I am certain that such reasonable defenses will get us off with just a few words of warning should we get caught." He released Job's halter. "Then again, they may just decide to shoot us."

Before them was a dry lake bed stretching to the horizon, which meant there was nothing to block the wind that picked up just before sunset, bringing with it fingers of icy air from the snowcapped San Gabriel Mountains to the south. It was late November, a month which, in Jasper's experience, was often the coldest in the desert. Jasper pulled up the collar on his denim jacket, but it failed to protect his ears as the wind blew unchecked across the playa. As the shadows of the hills stretched out before him, Jasper feared he would be forced to make camp in the open. Thus, it was a relief when he came upon the rusting hulk of an abandoned army truck, half buried in the sand. Though there was no wood for a fire, the truck provided shelter from the wind, and after dining on cold beans and day-old sourdough bread, Jasper lay upon his cot, warm under his blankets, and watched as the first stars appeared.

Fifteen miles to the southwest, just outside a Quonset hut, which served as headquarters for the Muroc Flight Test Center, Delwyn Owen also was looking up at the stars, though his mind was elsewhere. Tomorrow would be a big day, the culmination of countless hours spent by McDougal's design team, of which he was the most junior member. To old hands, Delwyn was the "Kid," an appellation not without affection, but given to let him know there was a world of difference between a fresh-out-of-school "rookie" (something he had also been called) and a veteran design engineer with years of hands-on experience. Not that book learning was unimportant; in fact, it was essential. But matters in the air often defied the most studied predictions, which was the reason for tomorrow's test flight. The engineers of McDougal had been working on a new fighter for the U.S. Air Force, one that would achieve and maintain supersonic speeds using a jet engine, not a rocket engine such as the one that powered the Bell X-1, the plane Chuck Yeager had flown when he broke the sound barrier.

Their fighter, christened the D-1 Thunderbolt, featured wings with a thirty-five-degree sweep to lessen the dangerous tendency of a plane's nose to suddenly pitch downward as it approached the speed of sound. The plane's stability was also enhanced by the wedge design of the tail. It was this design that created some friction between the veteran members of the design team and their junior partner. Delwyn believed a thicker wedge was needed for stability at supersonic speeds. Delwyn's superiors countered, rightly so, that a thicker wedge would produce unnecessary drag at lower speeds. Delwyn agreed, but he thought stability more important than drag if the D-1 was not to fall out of the sky.

The cold desert wind seemed to pass right through Delwyn's jacket. During the heat of summer, he thought he would never be cold again. It amazed him how temperatures could fluctuate here in the desert, not just month-to-month, but day-to-night. He reasoned it had to be the lack of moisture's moderating influence.

Delwyn thought he should get some sleep, but knew sleep would not be easy, as wound up as he was. If lucky, tomorrow's test flight would answer the question about the design of the D-1's tail, along with countless other questions. In the meantime, he decided he would stay outside and look at the stars until the cold drove him in.

The wind stopped blowing sometime in the night, and the day broke cold and clear, so clear Jasper could see the folds in the hills of the San Gabriel mountains far to the south. Jasper longed for a cup of hot coffee to take away the chill, but it had to wait until midmorning when he and Job succeeded in crossing the lifeless lake bed. Then he was able to gather dead brush for a fire and sat drinking coffee while waiting for his sourdough bread to rise. It was while he was enjoying his second cup that the stillness of the morning was shattered by a sonic boom, causing Jasper to spill hot coffee on himself. Job, who had been browsing on blades of dried grass, bolted. He came to a stop after running one hundred feet or so, then voiced his indignation with a chorus of obstreperous hee-haws.

Jasper stood and looked to the heavens from whence came the boom, but saw nothing in the cloudless sky. Then he heard a high-pitched whine, like wind whistling across the sharp edge of metal, and saw high above him, a fighter jet plane banking sharply. The plane was so high up, Jasper would not have been able to see it had not sunlight illuminated its silver body as the pilot made his turn. As Jasper watched, the plane went into a steep dive, leveling off just a few hundred feet above the ground then immediately shooting up into the heavens like a rocket off its launch pad. So high did the pilot push his craft, he passed out of sight, and only the distant rumble of the engines was evidence of his still being there. Then even that faded away.

Jasper thought this the end of the air show, but a few minutes later there was another sonic boom. The reverberation slowly died out, leaving the rumble of the jet's engines. Then the rumble ceased, and there was an odd quiet, lasting perhaps half a minute, before the sound of the engines briefly punctuated the stillness before cutting out again.

Even before he saw the jet tumbling out of the sky, Jasper knew the pilot was in trouble by a sound familiar from his days spent on the battlefield: the whine of a large object freefalling to earth. When the jet plane came into view, Jasper saw its nose pointed straight downward while the fuselage revolved in lazy circles. When it appeared that the plane was just about to crash, the engines fired once more and with a scream like metal being tortured, the jet plane swooped back up into the sky seemingly inches above Jasper's head. Then the engines cut out again, and there was another explosion as the jet plane separated into two pieces. The larger piece, the jet plane without its cockpit, continued to corkscrew as it began a slow dying descent. Jasper did not see the plane crash, for it disappeared behind a mountain ridge miles to the west. But the sound of it striking the ground was like another sonic boom, only this time lasting for well over a minute as the grumble echoed and reechoed through the canyons. When Jasper turned to look where the other part of the jet plane had gone, he saw a parachute floating to earth, a limp human figure dangling underneath.

At the Muroc Air Force Base, members of the flight test team, perhaps twenty in all, sat in stunned silence. Their precious jet plane fighter, costing hundreds of thousands of dollars, had disappeared off the radar. Up until seconds ago, everything had been going swimmingly. The test pilot, Bob "Ding" Rogers had been putting the craft through a series of turns, dives and ascents, and reporting back, with obvious glee, the jet plane's superb handling.

"This baby's gonna fly me to the moon!" was the last complete sentence the flight test team heard before communications got disrupted. Then there was just radio static interspersed with a few words spoken in alarm: "fuel tanks...control...engine..." then nothing, not even static. There followed two minutes of silence before the radar operator announced, "She's gone off the radar!"

"What do you mean she's gone?" yelled Colonel Miles Kniesel, Army chief liaison officer working with the McDougal team.

The radar operator pointed to his empty radar screen. "We lost her, sir. She's gone."

Everyone in the room started yelling at once.

"Silence!" the colonel roared. The colonel pointed a finger at Harris, the communications specialist. "Get China Lake on the line. See if they got anything." China Lake was the location of the Naval Air Weapons Station located just south of Death Valley.

After a minute Harris reported back. "They got nothing, sir. Radar reports our fighter disappeared off their screen, too."

Throughout the room there was a buzz of anxious chatter.

"All right, gentlemen, listen up," the colonel commanded. "We've got a missing plane. I want a chopper in the air in two minutes, and I want to know exactly where that plane was when communication was lost. Now, get to it!"

There was a mad scramble for paper and pencils. Maps were brought out and laid across tables. Communications reviewed. While all this was going on, Delwyn, junior member of the design team, stood in the back of the room and tried to look inconspicuous. What had gone wrong? he wondered. Up until they lost contact, the D-1 Thunderbolt had been performing flawlessly. He recalled the pilot Ding Roger's last words: "fuel tanks...control...engine..." Delwyn mentally reviewed the Thunderbolt's fuel systems. The Thunderbolt's sleek fuselage limited its capacity for carrying fuel, a mixture of aviation fuel, alcohol, and liquid oxygen. To increase its long-range capabilities, additional fuel tanks had been mounted beneath the wings. Ding Rogers had been pushing the Thunderbolt to its limits. Perhaps stress had caused a break in the fuel lines or damage to the external tanks.

Delwyn knew and liked Ding Rogers. In fact, he did not know anyone who did not like the test pilot. Like other members of the small fraternity of test pilots, Ding had a "devil may care" attitude towards the perils of his job, an outlook he combined with a great deal of gallows humor. It sickened him to think Ding might have been killed, or perhaps was lying injured somewhere in the desert with no one knowing where he was. Delwyn wondered what he might do to help, but could think of nothing but to keep out of the way as the senior members of the flight test team pored over maps, trying to determine the D-1 Thunderbolt's last position before contact was lost. That position would act as the center from which search efforts would extend outward. But at best that position could only be an estimate, and if the Thunderbolt had continued its supersonic flight after contact was lost, it could be almost anywhere, and it might be hours, or even days, before they discovered what happened to it.

As it turned out, it was just one hour before the pilot of the helicopter reported the wreckage of the D-1 Thunderbolt. Pieces of it were littered throughout a remote canyon.

"Any sign of the pilot?" the colonel said, speaking into the communication microphone.

"Negative," replied the chopper pilot. "It doesn't look good, colonel. There's debris scattered all over the place. I'll try to get a closer look, but there's no place for me to land."

After a while, the pilot reported back, but could add nothing new. The Thunderbolt had crashed in a canyon so remote, the only way to get into it would be on foot. The colonel ordered the pilot to return to base then set about organizing a crash investigation team. As the colonel and members of the flight test team were formulating a plan, the communications operator interrupted.

"Excuse me, Colonel, but the helicopter pilot reports an intruder to the west of him. It looks to be a man with a horse. They appear to be heading this way."

"Christ!" the colonel muttered. "Just what we need, some desert rat who can't read a no-trespassing sign!"

"The pilot wants to know if he should investigate further."

"Negative. Tell him I want him back here at the base. Somebody notify security. They can deal with the bastard." The colonel turned back to working with the flight test team, the intruder already forgotten.

Delwyn, listening in the back of the room, got a sick feeling in the pit of his stomach upon hearing the communications operator's announcement of a man with a horse. He knew from a postcard he received earlier in the week that this "desert rat" might well be his stepbrother Aurfryn. But would Aurfryn be so foolish as to trespass into a restricted area?

Delwyn sidled over to the radar operator and leaned in over his shoulder. "Where was the chopper when he saw the man and horse?"

The radar operator pointed to a blip on the screen. "Right about there."

"Do you suppose you could show me on a map?"

"You got a map?"

Delwyn went to the table and got one.

"Okay, there," the operator said, pointing.

Delwyn thanked him and took the map and spread it out on an unused table. Gone was the ache in his belly, replaced by a tingle of excitement. If Aurfryn was off to the west of where the chopper pilot had reported seeing him, then he would not be far from where the D-1 Thunderbolt was thought to have been when communications were broken off. Perhaps Aurfryn had seen something that might be of help.

This, of course, was pure speculation, certainly, not something to trouble his superiors with. Still, Delwyn had little to do and thought it would not hurt for him to do a little investigating on his own.

No one noticed Delwyn slip out, nor took notice when he began to peddle his bicycle north across the hard pan of the desert floor. If Delwyn had had any authority, he would have commandeered a jeep. But he did not, and thus had to make do with the bicycle he used to get around on the base. Perhaps this was just as well, as he did not want anyone to know what he was up to in case his course of action turned out to be a wild goose chase.

Having trespassed into restricted space, Jasper might have been alarmed to see a helicopter not too far off. But, in fact, Jasper had tried his best to get the pilot's attention, waving his broad-billed hat and shouting for all he was worth.

"Might as well save your breath," Ding Rogers had said, from his perch atop Job. "It doesn't look like he's seen us."

Ding was clad in a tattered flight suit minus the right pant leg, which Jasper had cut away and used to bind Ding's broken leg with a splint, which in this case happened to be the small rifle Jasper carried with him for rattlesnakes.

"I sure hope this thing ain't loaded," Ding had said, as Jasper was binding his leg. "I can take the embarrassment of crashing my plane, but I don't think I could survive the humiliation of shooting myself in the foot."

Jasper was both amazed and amused by this character he chanced to rescue. Ding had been unconscious when Jasper had found him. The first thing Ding said when he came to and saw Jasper's weather-beaten face was, "Well, my ex-wife told me I was going to end up in hell, and it looks like she had it right." Since that proclamation, Ding had hardly stopped talking, not even when Jasper applied stinging rubbing alcohol to Ding's cuts and abrasions then went about straightening and binding his broken leg. The worst complaint Ding had uttered concerned the indignity of a test pilot having to ride on the back of a mule. Then as Jasper led Job toward the airfield, Ding regaled Jasper with war stories, off-colored jokes, and discourses on the virtue of being a pilot as compared to mere mortal occupations. It was more talk than Jasper had heard in the last twenty years.

It was the abrupt halt in a story Ding had been telling about the time he flew through a typhoon over the South China Sea that caused Jasper to turn and look back at him. Ding was rubbing his eyes.

"What is the matter?" Jasper said.

"I'm seeing things."

"What sort of things?"

Ding pointed. "First there's you and a mule, and now I'm seeing a damn bicycle. Tell me are we living in the jet age, or did I slip back through time when I crashed the sound barrier?"

By late afternoon, the head of the crash investigation team, a senior official working for McDougal Aviation, reported in that they had arrived at the crash site. "It's a holy mess!" he reported. "There's bits and pieces scattered from hell to eternity."

"Any sign of the cockpit?" the colonel said, speaking into the microphone.

"Don't know yet, colonel. I'll inform you just as soon as we find something."

The colonel was a patient man. He had to be, working as he did with civilians, especially the aeronautical engineers who, in the colonel's mind, ranked somewhere with amoebas when it came to social skills. Engineers were like little boys more concerned with their widgets than with people. He could just imagine certain members of the investigation team picking over debris and trying to figure out what went wrong rather than looking for signs of the pilot. After half an hour, the colonel's patience ran out.

"Don't you have anything for me yet?" he barked into the transmitter.

"Colonel, it's hard going. The terrain is really steep. But so far we've not found any of the cockpit. I think the pilot must have bailed."

The D-1 Thunderbolt was designed so that in case of an emergency, the pilot could blow the cockpit free from the rest of the fighter then bail out. If Ding Rogers had bailed, where was he, and just as important, what shape was he in? It would soon be night and temperatures would fall to freezing. The colonel was just about to order out another helicopter to do a search when he was interrupted by Deke Foster, head of the design team.

"Colonel, what do you think that is?"

The colonel looked out through the window to where Deke was

pointing. Far out on the dry lake bed, walking in a line, were two people and another on a mule. The colonel picked up a pair of binoculars. "Jesus, Mary and Joseph!" he exclaimed. "It looks like a goddamn parade!"

"May I see?"

The colonel handed Deke the field glasses. Deke first saw Delwyn, pushing a bicycle, followed by Jasper leading a mule, and atop the mule none other than Ding Rogers, who was talking and waving his arms around.

"It's Ding and the Kid!" Deke exclaimed.

"The Kid?" the colonel said, taking back the field glasses.

"Yeah, the one pushing the bike. Delwyn… something or other. I forget his last name. But he's on our design team."

"Well, Deke, while everyone else has been running around like decapitated chickens, it looks like the 'Kid,' as you call him, just found our missing pilot."

Sonya

The century reached its midway point and began to wane. Likewise did Jasper's passion for finding gold, for Jasper had grown to love the desert for itself and not just its valuable minerals. To chance upon a desert tortoise or a bighorn sheep was just as thrilling as finding a gold nugget in an ancient riverbed; to bathe in the cool waters of a palm oasis as pleasurable as discovering gem-quality turquoise. Could one ask more of life than to witness the desert celebrating in riotous color following a particularly wet winter?

It was during such a wet winter that Jasper decided to satisfy a long-held wish: to start near California's border with Mexico, where the wildflowers were first to bloom, then travel north with the spring as the wildflowers rolled out before him like a welcome mat.

Jasper had spent many of the rainiest winter days with his stepbrother Delwyn and Delwyn's American wife, Carol, who was expecting their second child. In the years since Jasper had gone to visit his stepbrother at Muroc Army Airfield, renamed Edwards Air Force Base, Delwyn had moved up through the corporate ranks of McDougal aviation to head his own design team, and now he and his family lived in a spacious ranch-style house not far from the base.

Delwyn had hinted at an addition to his already commodious house which Jasper could live in. But as nice as it was to sleep with a solid roof over his head, Jasper preferred to keep company with the stars. To soften his refusal of Delwyn's offer, Jasper agreed to extend his Thanksgiving stay through the Christmas holidays. Yet as Christmas approached, he found himself wishing more and more that he could get away. What ameliorated his restlessness was time spent with his five-year-old niece Ceinwen, who was a child after his own heart, being quiet and thoughtful. When the weather was clear, they wandered the desert together, always in the company of Job, whom Ceinwen loved to ride. Joshua trees dotted the landscape, and Jasper explained to Ceinwen how the native Americans used to prepare the tree's blossoms by roasting them in a pit. This triggered a whole flurry of questions from Ceinwen about other desert plants, and Jasper found himself struggling to dredge up what knowledge he had garnered over the years.

But the primary shared interest of uncle and niece was in prospecting for minerals. Once Jasper revealed to Ceinwen how small treasures, such as translucent chips of gypsum or shiny flakes of mica, could be found, Ceinwen could hardly be coaxed away from what she called her "digs." For Christmas, Jasper bought Ceinwen a child's-size pick and shovel. Jasper's hosts were at a loss as to what to give Jasper, whose needs were so few. They decided upon a new hat to replace the one Jasper had purchased from Jacob Harmon all those years ago.

New Year's Day broke cold and clear, a perfect day to travel. Jasper bid his relatives farewell, promising not to let so many years slip by before his next visit. Once Jasper had gone about a mile or so from Delwyn's house, he flung his new hat out into the desert and replaced it with his old one. Not only was the old hat more comfortable, but Jasper felt the need of making a symbolic gesture: tossing away the trappings of civilization in favor of his rustic ways.

He traveled east, across the plain that separated Edwards Air Force Base from the San Gabriel mountains to the south. Occasionally he happened upon a stray cow. More and more sections were being fenced with barbed wire, the bane of the traveler, but thankfully it was still open range here. Toward evening, Jasper veered south to make camp along one of the snow-fed streams. He was surprised at how tired he was, and attributed this to the rich food and lack of exercise of the last six weeks.

The sun was just about to set when he found a good place to camp. He also discovered he was not alone. An oriental man, dressed in a monk's robe, was sitting beside the stream, smoking a cigarette and studying the purple shadows stretching out across the desert.

"Good evening," Jasper said.

The monk stood, bowed to Jasper in recognition, but said nothing.

"Is this your land?" Jasper said. "Would I be trespassing if I were to make camp here?"

With a smile and a gesture the Chinaman indicated Jasper was welcome.

Jasper did not quite know what to make of this silent reception. He relieved Job of his packs then set about gathering wood for a fire. When he had gathered an armful, he returned to camp and found the monk gone. He gave this little thought as he set about making coffee. The water had just come to a boil when the monk returned and with an armload of wood.

"I hope you did not think me rude when I did not say anything to you before," the monk said. "Prior Dominic says I talk too much, and as a consequence I decided to spend the day in silence. But now that the sun has set, I can indulge my love of conversation, that is if you do not mind my company."

"May I offer you some coffee?" Jasper said.

"I would enjoy that."

The monk found a place to sit by the fire, and Jasper poured the coffee. "You said, 'Prior Dominic.' Then you are not a…"

"A Buddhist monk? Though I come from a family which was marginally Buddhist, I am a Catholic by faith. My given name is Yang Gao, but since 1926, when I was ordained a priest, I have been called Brother Peter."

"I am Welsh myself, born Aurfryn Owen, but prefer to be called Jasper."

"Ah, then you are a man of wisdom."

Jasper smiled. "I have spent much of my life wandering the desert, looking for valuable minerals. I am not sure if you would call someone who adopts such an occupation a man of wisdom."

"Have you had much success in your search?"

"I was fortunate to have success early on, but that was…" Jasper made a mental calculation. "My goodness! Has it been over thirty-five years?"

"The time has gone quickly for you?"

Jasper blew on his coffee, took a sip. "I suppose it has. It is not something I think much about." Jasper threw a couple of sticks upon the fire. "You speak English very well. You were born in this country?"

Brother Peter shook his head. "I have been living here for only about a year. But I studied English at the university in Louvain, and before the war I visited the United States to solicit funds for our mission in China." Brother Peter set down his cup and stood. "I am sorry to have to end our conversation so soon, but it is time for evening prayers."

Jasper stood also. "It was very nice to talk to you, Brother Peter, if only briefly. Perhaps we shall have the chance to talk again some time."

"Would you care to join our small community for breakfast?" He pointed toward a thinly wooded hill. "The priory is just over that ridge."

"Thank you, I would enjoy that."

"I must warn you, we observe a silent breakfast." He smiled. "But thankfully there will be time for conversation afterward."

"Silence has been my friend for many years." He gestured toward Job. "Silence and a faithful mule."

Jasper did not know what he had expected to find when he arrived at St. Anthony's Priory next morning, but it certainly was not a sun-bleached ranch house and a couple of old barns still smelling strongly of manure. Brother Peter was waiting for him and silently ushered him into the ranch house where a dozen or so monks, robed as Brother Peter, were just now seating themselves at a long table covered in a yellow oil cloth. With a smile, one of the monks gestured for Jasper to sit at a space reserved for him on a crude bench. Breakfast was as much a surprise to Jasper as the appearance of the priory. He had been expecting a bowl of porridge or some such humble fare he thought befitted the habits of ascetics. Instead he found a wide variety of boxed cereals, platters stacked high with pancakes, a covered dish filled with sausages, a pitcher of milk, jars of jams and jellies, and lots of coffee to go around. And no one, when they began to tuck in, appeared to exercise much self-restraint.

Another surprise was to discover that what the monks called a "silent" breakfast did not involve the absence of speech, for while the brothers ate, one of the monks read to them, and not from holy scripture, but in this instance from Hildegard's *Physica* on health and healing.

At the conclusion of the reading, the monk who sat at the head of the table, whom Jasper assumed was Prior Dominic, asked Brother Peter to introduce their guest. Brother Peter first introduced Jasper by his Welsh name. "But our guest prefers to be called Jasper. Jasper is a ..." he searched for the word to describe Jasper's occupation.

"A prospector," Jasper said. "Someone who wanders around the desert looking for something that is usually not there."

The monks laughed then went around the table introducing themselves. There were lots of saints' names–Andrew, Anthony, Thomas and the like, but also a Schuyler, a Mies, and a Roberto, these last three names spoken with foreign accents.

After introductions were concluded, Prior Dominic assigned the monks their morning tasks, which primarily involved building projects.

"Jasper, you are welcome to join us in our labors," the Prior said, "or, if you prefer, you can wander around and enjoy the beauty that surrounds us. Whatever you decide, feel free to come and go as you please."

"Thank you," Jasper said. "It would give me pleasure to be of help, though I am afraid I am not much of a carpenter. But I can certainly hold a board while someone puts a nail in it."

Prior Dominic smiled. "Then I will assign you to work alongside Brother Andrew."

Brother Andrew appeared to be about the same age as Jasper, somewhere in his fifties, but any similarity between the two ended there. Brother Andrew was short and stout, with a round, smooth face that looked as if it never needed a razor.

"We're working on converting one of the barns into a chapel," Brother Andrew explained, as he and Jasper made their way from the ranch house. He pointed. "The bigger of those two barns eventually will be our living quarters."

Jasper studied both barns. At one time, they had been painted, but little of the paint had survived years of sun and wind. There were missing boards in the weathered siding of each barn, and both roofs sagged. To Jasper's way of thinking, it would be better to tear down both barns and start from scratch.

Brother Andrew read Jasper's thoughts. "The barns are sturdier than they look. The basic structures are sound. Isn't that right, Brother Mies?"

They had been joined by Brother Mies and Brother Roberto. Brother Mies appeared to be the oldest of the monks while Brother Roberto the youngest.

"Oh, ya," Brother Mies said, "plenty of good wood in that old barn." With his hands, he outlined the pitch of the roof of the smaller barn. "It will make beautiful chapel."

"Before Brother Mies was ordained, he was a carpenter," Brother Andrew explained.

"Ya. I learn from a man in my village. He was a master builder."

The men's task that morning was to remove the exterior boards of the barn. The three monks attacked the old siding using crowbars while Jasper was assigned the task of driving out the rusty nails once the boards were liberated. Then he sorted the boards according to Brother Andrew's simple criterion: "If you think any of the boards salvageable, Jasper, then stack them here. Otherwise you can throw them over there, and we'll eventually use them for firewood."

The three monks kept Jasper busy, yet it was pleasant work. The temperature was neither too cold nor too hot; the sun-bleached wood gave off a pleasing smell; and during pauses in his work, Jasper could admire the snowcapped San Gabriel Mountains in whose shadow the priory was situated.

The brothers worked until a bell called them to noontime Mass. Jasper was invited to participate, but he chose to wander about the priory grounds. A large flat area, which looked as if it had once been a corral, was starting to green. Beyond was a stream, nearly hidden by thickets of willows and overhung with leafless sycamores whose round spiky seed heads dangled in a light breeze. Jasper found a comfortable place to sit with his back against a sycamore and listened to the shallow stream as it flowed over its bed of granite cobbles. The murmur of the stream provided an accompaniment to the voices of the monks chanting the Mass. Both spoke of peace. He fell asleep and did not awake until roused by Brother Peter shaking him by the shoulder.

"You were sound asleep," Brother Peter said. "I fear we are working you too hard."

Jasper stretched then slowly stood up. "No, I came under the spell of your singing. That and the music of the stream acted as a lullaby."

Brother Peter laughed. "I shall have to tell that to the others, for I doubt most listeners would find our voices so soothing."

Brother Peter led Jasper back to the ranch house where lunch was already prepared. In contrast to breakfast, lunch was a time to socialize. Two other guests were present, both women, one older, one younger. Jasper sat quietly, listening to the conversations going on around him.

After a while, the older woman, seated across from Jasper, spoke. "You don't say much, do you?"

Brother Peter, seated to Jasper's right, answered. "Jasper is a prospector. It is a quiet life."

"Can't Jasper speak for himself?"

Jasper smiled. "Brother Peter is kind to defend my lack of social graces Mrs...."

"Just call me Liz. What brings you here to this ramshackle excuse for a priory, Mr. Prospector?"

"Sheer chance. I happened to be passing this way when I met Brother Peter who invited me to visit."

"Well, I'm here to check up on my brother, making sure he's staying out of trouble." She jabbed an elbow into the side of Brother

Mies, seated beside her. "Isn't that right, big brother?"

Brother Mies did not look happy. "It's you who should worry about trouble, Lijsbeth. You and that rich husband of yours."

Liz laughed. "Mies forgets that that "rich husband" of mine has been dead ten years."

"It's all your money that troubles me, Lijsbeth," Mies said. "The Bible says, 'It is easier for a camel to go through–' "

"I know, I know, 'for a camel to go through the eye of a needle than for a rich man to enter the kingdom of God.' "

"The same is true for a woman, Lijsbeth," Mies said.

"Well, don't worry, big brother. I don't plan on buying any camels."

The brothers, listening to this exchange, all laughed. Jasper later learned that Liz and her husband Axel had once been prosperous Belgian tulip farmers, though they and their daughter had lived mostly in England. Before the outbreak of World War II, they had followed Brother Mies to California, Mies having emigrated years earlier. There Axel increased his wealth, buying and selling real estate. Much of the cost of converting the old ranch into a priory was being financed by Liz.

"Jasper, this here's my daughter," Liz said, indicating the woman sitting beside her.

The woman, whose short black hair was just beginning to show signs of gray, smiled, but said nothing.

"Good grief, Sonya," Liz said, "Can't you even tell Jasper your name?"

"Sorry, Mother. I guess I'm just used to you doing all the talking for me."

"Oh, fiddlesticks! You've always been too shy for your own good. I swear, you and Jasper are a pair." She rose and picked up Jasper's plate. "You're done, aren't you?"

Jasper was, but only just.

"Sonya, help me clean up these dishes so these men can get back to work."

If Prior Dominic was offended by Lijsbeth usurping his authority, he made no sign. The monks returned to work, Jasper along with them. By the time the bell rang, announcing the end of the work day, the barn, which would one day be the chapel, had been stripped of its exterior siding, save for up high at the gable ends. Without its siding the barn's post and beam framing was revealed, making it possible for Jasper to imagine the old barn a chapel. The last rays of the setting sun streamed through an opening high in the west gable end, and Jasper thought it a perfect spot for a stained-glass window.

Until called to evening prayer, the monks had this time as their own. Most chose to rest after their labors, but a few of the younger monks got together an impromptu game of soccer on the open field. Brother Peter, who was young at heart, joined in, laughing whether he outmaneuvered his opponent or was outmaneuvered by him. He called for Jasper to join the game, but Jasper declined the invitation, as he needed to exercise Job, who had spent the day cooped up in a small corral. Jasper led Job down the dusty road that led to the open desert, still bright in sunshine. He came upon Sonya sitting on a rock, lost in thought.

"Do not let us disturb you," Jasper said, as he ambled past. "I am just out to give Job some exercise."

Sonya stood and dusted off her slacks. "May I tag along? I have been sitting too long and wouldn't mind stretching my legs."

"I would enjoy your company."

Walking alongside Jasper, Sonya said, "There must be a story behind your mule's name. Some tale of long suffering, perhaps?"

Jasper smiled. "It comes from the name of a place, Job's Well." Jasper told her of his first donkey, Esmeralda, and of her being seduced by wild horses with Job being the consequence. As he talked he struggled to lead Job over the rocky, uneven ground. Finally, he gave up and let Job run free.

"So, how long have you been a prospector, Jasper?"

"Well, I came to California just after the Great War."

"My, that's a long time!"

Jasper laughed.

"What?" Sonya said.

"You make me feel old."

"I did not mean to. I only meant that you have found something you liked and stuck to it. I admire that. I wish I could say the same."

This last statement created an opportunity for Jasper to learn something of Sonya, about whom he had yet to form an impression. But before he could pose his question, Sonya changed the subject.

"Have you ever been in this area around April or May? The display of wildflowers, particularly the poppies, is spectacular."

Jasper shook his head. "In terms of prospecting, there is little of value here. I only came to visit my stepbrother who works at the air base. The fact is I find this area too crowded."

Sonya laughed. "Too crowded! There's not another building in sight."

Jasper smiled. "Maybe 'crowded' is not the right word, but look." He pointed northwest where there was a glow of lights. "All that light is coming from the town of Palmdale, which seems to have doubled in size since I last time I visited my stepbrother." He pointed east. "And those lights over there are from Victorville, and it too seems to be growing by leaps and bounds. And every year there are more paved highways bringing more people and more cars to places that never used have any roads at all."

"But, Jasper," Sonya said, pointing to the line of asphalt to the north. "There is not a single car out on that highway." She gripped his arm, stopping him. "Stand still a moment and listen." The only sound was Job pulling up a clump of grass. "You can hardly get quieter than that."

Jasper smiled. "True." He pointed to a large flat rock. "Would you like to sit down while Job makes the most of that patch of grass?" Once they were seated, Jasper continued. "It is not just the quiet, it is the sense of…" What was the right word to describe how he felt when completely alone in the desert? 'Freedom' came to mind, but the word was overused. "Many is the time when I have climbed a desert mountain and felt as if I were the only person on earth. I've looked out over desert plains so vast and…" He tugged at his beard in frustration. "I am sorry. I have been so long in my own company I have lost my way with words."

"You are doing fine. Plains so vast and… empty?"

Jasper shook his head. "Plains vast and filled. Filled with beauty. I admit it may not seem like beauty to some. Perhaps it is only the peculiar shape in the trunk of an old sagebrush, or the swirl of colors in a small rock, which is not to say there are not places of grand beauty, painted deserts and vast canyons and the like, but I have come to favor places of more humble beauty, beauty that–"

"Fills the heart."

Jasper nodded. "Places that fill the heart with an immeasurable sense of peace." He was surprised he was telling her all this, yet felt compelled to say more. "I was a soldier in the Great War. I came here ostensibly to look for gold, but the truth is I came to find some peace after that living nightmare."

"And did you find it?"

Jasper turned to look directly into Sonya's eyes. "Yes, I did. I found peace in the vast healing power of nature, and so it troubles me when I look out there and see the lights of those growing towns, or see paved roads where there used to be no roads, for it means I must retreat deeper and deeper into the desert to find that peace, and I fear there will come a day when there will no longer be places where a man can find himself alone in nature."

"But that will not be in anytime soon. Surely not in our lifetime."

"Perhaps. But just this afternoon Brother Andrew was telling me about a four-lane highway they are building that will connect Los Angeles to Phoenix. Why, I remember when the only road east of Palm Springs was just a dirt wagon track!"

Sonya sighed. "Well, that's progress, I guess. But no matter what happens, Jasper, there will always be a way for a person to find peace. Have you talked much with Brother Peter?"

Jasper smiled. "He seems to me to be one of the happiest men I have ever met."

"Do you know anything of his history?"

"A little. I know he only came to this country only recently from China."

"Yes, where he spent seven years in prison for practicing his faith. The Communists, as you know, are fiercely opposed to religion, and they tortured Brother Peter, trying to force him to renounce his belief in God. When ultimately they failed, they expelled him from the country."

"I did not know that," Jasper said.

"Yet despite all his suffering, Brother Peter is a man at peace with the world, which is what I meant when I said there will always be a way to find peace. Brother Peter finds peace through his faith."

The light on the desert was nearly gone, leaving just a rosy glow that seemed to emanate from the land itself.

"I suppose I should be getting back," Sonya said.

Jasper stood and took Job by the lead rope.

"I feel that in terms of finding peace, I share something in common with both you and Brother Peter," Sonya said, as they walked toward the priory.

"How so?"

"Well, I have certainly never experienced such horrors as you and Brother Peter have. I've had it easy, perhaps too easy. When you grow up rich, it's hard to be motivated to take a great interest in anything. At least, it's been that way with me. That said, like you, I find peace in nature, which is why I suppose I join Mother on her little outings to the priory. But like Brother Peter, I also find peace in what I believe, which is not just what I was taught in Catholic school. If anything, my faith is an adverse reaction to that teaching. I don't believe there is but one church, or one particular religion. But I do believe there is someone, far greater than any human or any institution, in whose loving hands is the governance of the world, even though it often does not seem that way. But when I come across true goodness, whether it be in the beauty of nature, or the beauty of a human spirit, then I feel the presence of God's hand and draw comfort from it." She turned to look directly at Jasper. "Does that make sense?"

They had come to the edge of the priory grounds and could hear the voices of the brothers chanting evening prayers. Jasper stopped and stood where he could see Sonya's face illuminated by the light coming from the ranch house. "Yes, it does make sense."

"Tell me, Jasper, do you believe in God?" Sonya said.

"You mean, God as a being who governs the world?"

"I mean God as you perceive Him."

Jasper took time before answering. "I did not come from a religious family, yet I do recall being told that God is love, a statement that always struck me as curious."

"How so?"

"To say that God is love is different than to say that God loves. 'God loves' suggests there is a being who acts. Whereas 'God is love' is like an equation: one is the same as the other."

"So you mean that God is not a being, but a force."

Jasper smiled. "I am not sure what I mean. But I do know this: The Great War left me in a great need of healing. Perhaps a doctor might have helped me, or I might have found solace in religion. But something told me to seek healing here, here in the desert. Tell me, do you believe God created the desert?"

"Not as it says in the Bible, not in seven days, but, yes, God created the world and all its wonders."

"I believe the opposite; the creation created God, or more to the point, God is the creation. God is the force that creates and continues to create, and often, when I am alone in the desert, I can feel that force. I do not know if you would call it love, but I do know I have often drawn great comfort and healing from that force. I am certain that if I were a creature far more comprehending than a human being, I could perhaps peel back the fabric of nature and behold the hand of the Creator creating. As it is, I am grateful to be able to partake of the 'wonders,' as you say, of this world."

Sonya smiled. "I understand, now, why you care so much about the wheels of progress making their way into the desert."

"Yes, it is as if I were a truly devout person having to watch the object of my worship being torn down."

A bell sounded, inviting all to dinner. Jasper offered Sonya his arm, and they returned to the ranch house and entered. Like breakfast, the meal was taken in silence. Following dinner, Sonya's attention was demanded by her mother, and Jasper did not see Sonya until the next morning when she came to say goodbye.

"We're going back to L.A.," she said.

Jasper set down the hammer he was using to remove the nails from the boards he had not gotten to the day before. "It grieves me to hear that."

She gave him a wistful smile. "It's all your fault, you know."

Jasper was taken aback.

Sonya explained. "Mother saw us out walking together last night, and now she suspects you of prospecting for my inheritance."

"You surely do not believe that!"

"Of course not. But I shall be the obedient child and return with her to the city."

Jasper saw Sonya's mother, standing next to her large automobile, watching them both. "I cannot tell you how much it meant for me to talk to you last night, how much I enjoyed the pleasure of your company. I shall miss you, Sonya."

"And I you, Jasper." She stood a moment, undecided, then quickly planted a kiss on his rough cheek. She walked away, leaving Jasper with a feeling he could not remember having last felt: loneliness.

Brother Andrew appeared, crow bar in hand. "How goes the work?"

Jasper did not immediately reply, but watched as Sonya and her mother got into their car. "Sonya's mother appears to be a rather dominating woman."

Brother Andrew laughed. "That is like saying a shark is a rather carnivorous animal. Knowing Liz's penchant for bossing people around, I'm surprised she didn't stick around longer. I consider that a small miracle."

Jasper touched the cheek where Sonya had planted her kiss. "A miracle to some." He retrieved his hammer. "I understand our task today is to take the roof off the barn."

Brother Andrew nodded. "It's a big job. I doubt we'll finish it today."

Jasper looked at the sagging barn roof and the layer upon layer of cracked and peeling shingles. "Finish today? Now, *that* would be a miracle."

Right-O, Daddy-O!

J asper enjoyed his time with the brothers of St. Anthony's Priory and might have stayed with them longer had he not been on a mission to make the most of what was likely to be a spectacular year for desert wildflowers.

The end of February found him and Job in Anza-Borrego State Park, near California's border with Mexico. There he found the desert floor already carpeted in wildflowers. The usual goldfields, in countless numbers, provided a yellow background to bright blue phacelia and white cryptantha, the latter growing on wire-thin stems and looking like bits of cotton floating in the air. Gravelly dunes, sunbaked and devoid of vegetation most of the year, were now blanketed with brown-eyed primrose, white oenothera, lavender sand verbena and desert lily on whose tall stalks snow-white flowers were just starting to unfold.

The Anza-Borrego is noted for its wealth of barrel cacti and tall spiky ocotillo, but these would not bloom until April when most of the annual flowers would have already withered. Yet even without blossoms, the ocotillos' spiny stalks, which earned its nickname "Jacob's Staff," and the ribbed columnar barrel cacti, some nearly as tall as Jasper, were living sculptures amidst a flower-filled rock garden. Not for the first time, Jasper pondered nature's ability to surpass even the most gifted of landscape architects. It was, in fact, the absence of human intrusion that made this protected portion of the desert so special, for nowhere was there the usual detritus that signified man's consideration of the desert as a dumping ground: the rusty tin cans, dumped auto parts, half-buried box springs and abandoned refrigerators. The Anza-Borrego was one of those rare places where

Jasper felt himself to be the first person to partake of untrammeled wilderness.

Thus, it was much to his chagrin that he stumbled upon a boy, aged thirteen or there about, idly ambling up a wash. The boy, a pudgy creature with thick eye glasses and exhibiting a good case of adolescent acne, was intently fiddling with his camera as he walked along, and he failed to notice Jasper and Job until they were almost on top of him.

The boy, startled at first, hurriedly adjusted his glasses then exclaimed, "Hey, like crazy man!" He held up a hand, getting Jasper and Job to stop while he took their picture. Releasing his camera, held by a strap around his neck, he lumbered forward. "Ain't this a blast! So, what's your tale, nightingale? You two look like you just walked off the set of *Gunsmoke*."

Before Jasper could manage a response, the boy answered his own question. "I know, Daddy-O, you're like one of those…" He snapped his fingers a couple of times. "…one of those… prospectors! Yeah, that's the handle. Like that cat at Knott's Berry Farm, only he's just a show-off and you gotta slip him a thin one to take his picture. But you look like the real deal, Big Daddy!"

Big Daddy? *Knott's Berry Farm*? *Slip him a thin one*? To Jasper, the boy may as well have been talking Mandarin.

"So what's buzzin' cousin?" the boy continued. "Don't tell me you live out here in Nowheresville."

Jasper was growing irritated with the boy's obvious infatuation with what must be the current slang. "Excuse me, son, but are not you supposed to be in school?"

The boy grinned. "Hey! You make like the King's jive. How cool is that?"

Shaking his head, Jasper attempted to put some distance between himself and the boy.

"Hey, Daddy-O!" the boy yelled, running after Jasper. "I didn't mean to rattle your cage."

Jasper stopped and faced the boy. "Perhaps we should reach an understanding, young man," Jasper said. "I am not your daddy."

"Hey, no need to get frosty! That's just the handle we use for cool cats. Dig?"

"Dig?"

"Yeah, dig."

"Is that a question?"

"What is?"

"You just asked if I dig. 'Dig?' you said."

"Yeah, like 'dig,' dig?"

Exasperated, Jasper began to move away again.

The boy ran after him. "Hey! I'm just trying to show I'm hep, you know." The boy kicked at a piece of wood. "Like James Dean, or maybe –Ow!"

Jasper stopped and turned around.

"Ow! Ow! Ow!" the boy yelled, hopping about on one foot while rubbing the ankle of the other. "Something stung me!"

Jasper looked to where the boy had been standing. A scorpion, exposed by the boy having kicked away the piece of wood, was posed ready to strike again.

The boy saw what Jasper was looking at. "What on earth is that?"

"It is a scorpion," Jasper replied.

"A scorpion! Oh, my god! I've been stung by a scorpion! Where's the nearest hospital?"

"Shhh!" Jasper said. "Try to remain calm. Take a seat on that rock there and take off your shoe and sock."

The boy hopped on one foot over to the rock. "Scorpions are poisonous, aren't they? Am I going to die?"

"Yes," Jasper said, as he plucked a handful of leaves from a nearby brittlebush.

"What?"

"You are going to die in your bed at the age of one hundred and nine. Now calm yourself while I make up a poultice to draw out the poison." Jasper crushed the brittlebush leaves and made a paste of them with a little water.

"I think my ankle is starting to swell," the boy said.

"That's a natural reaction. Now, hold still." Jasper placed the paste over the affected area. "You should not be wearing this kind of shoe if you're going to be walking about out here in the wild."

"They're loafers, just like Elvis wears."

"Then you should let Elvis take care of you when you get stung. Now put your hand over these leaves and hold them there."

"What are they supposed to do?" the boy said.

"As I said, the leaves will draw out the poison."

The boy nodded, understanding. "I get it. I read somewhere that in nature the antidote for any kind of bite is always nearby in some kind of plant."

"Hmm," Jasper replied.

"Ow! The bite feels like it's on fire."

"Good! That means the leaves are doing their job."

The boy pointed to the scorpion, which had not relinquished its defensive position. "Aren't you going to kill that thing?"

In response, Jasper picked up the piece of wood the boy had kicked and gently returned to the scorpion the roof of his home.

"You mean, you aren't going to kill it?"

"It is not the poor scorpion's fault that you disturbed his home and threatened to step on him."

"But it's poisonous!"

Jasper sat down on a rock opposite the boy. "You would be surprised how many things are poisonous out here. I once had a great fear of rattlesnakes and wanted to shoot every one I came across. But over time, I came to realize that all creatures, even poisonous ones, have a right to live. Moreover, every creature has a role to play for the good. If it were not for rattlesnakes, and snakes in general, the world would be overrun by rodents."

"Have you ever been bit by a rattlesnake?"

"Thankfully, not. A rattlesnake is a real gentleman, always warning you when you are intruding upon his territory."

"Well, you'd probably feel different about rattlesnakes if you'd ever been bitten by one." The boy peeked under the paste of leaves. "How long do I have to keep this on?"

"A little while longer, until the stinging stops."

"It's mostly stopped already." The boy raised his camera to take a picture of his injured foot and discovered dust on his lens. He took out a handkerchief and carefully removed the dust. "I gotta be real careful with this camera. It took me a year to save up for it. It's a single lens reflex. What you see through the lens is what you get in the photo. Someday I'm gonna be a sports photographer. I'm already covering high school sports for the local newspaper."

The boy took a picture of his foot then one of Jasper. "I want to document all this," he said. "First, my bite, then my rescuer. I wish I'd snapped a photo of the scorpion. Say, I don't suppose you'd care to lift up that piece of wood again?"

"I believe we have tormented the scorpion enough for one day," Jasper said.

The boy lifted up a few of the wet leaves. "Can I take these off now? The bite has stopped hurting."

"You may as well. I would be quite surprised if those leaves did any good."

The boy looked alarmed. "But you said they'd draw out the poison."

"Hmm. Did I?"

"Yeah, you did. And they worked, didn't they?"

"I confess I grabbed a handful of leaves from the nearest bush not knowing if they had any medicinal properties or not. Scorpion bites are rarely more harmful than a bee sting, but you were quite upset, and I thought my appearing to administer an antidote for the sting would serve to calm you, which it did."

Indignant, the boy started to rise, realized he was not wearing sock and shoe, and sat back down again. "Well, thanks a lot!"

"You are most welcome," Jasper said, and started to laugh.

The boy studied Jasper not knowing if he should continue to be angry or join Jasper in his merriment. The humorous side of his nature prevailed, and he joined in, laughing.

"But I was in no danger, right?" the boy said, once he stopped laughing.

"If that had been a bark scorpion, you would have been in trouble," Jasper said. "But you were stung by a little striped-tail scorpion. Just as a warning, when out here in the desert you should always check for scorpions before putting on your shoes."

The boy, who was just about to put on his shoe, flung the shoe aside.

Jasper laughed again.

"Ha! Ha! very funny!" the boy said, retrieving his shoe. Nevertheless, he inspected his shoe before putting it on.

"Well, then," Jasper said, "now that we have shared our little adventure, I best be getting along."

"But what are you going to do," the boy said, quickly getting to his feet, "look for gold?"

Jasper shook his head. "Not today. I came here strictly for the purpose of enjoying all these beautiful wildflowers." Jasper gestured to the field of flowers with a sweep of his arm.

"Would you mind if I sort of tagged along?"

Jasper did not want really want the boy's company, yet he sensed the boy was something of an outcast and perhaps lonely. "What is your name, son?"

"Robert." Robert spoke his name as if it were a question.

"Well, Robert, do you not think your parents would mind your keeping company with a total stranger?"

In response, the boy shrugged then once more pushed his ill-fitting glasses higher up on his nose.

Jasper sighed. "I'll tell you what, Robert. You can keep Job and me company so long as you attempt to limit your speech to commonly accepted vocabulary."

Robert grinned. "That's easy. I just use slang to show that I'm cool, I mean 'with it' you know."

Jasper started to move off.

"What a sec," Robert said, hurrying after. "You know my name.

What's yours?"

Over his should Jasper replied, "You can call me Jasper."

"And your horse is called Job?"

"Job is not a horse, but a mule—a hinny, actually."

"And you're really a prospector?"

"Yes, I am."

"Have you ever found any gold?"

"Yes."

"Very much?"

"Yes, but that was some time ago. Long before you were born."

"Cool! I mean… that's great!"

Jasper stopped and faced Robert. "Any other questions?"

The boy paused before speaking. "Is Jasper your real name?" Before Jasper could answer, the boy hurried on. "I'm only asking because I've never really liked Robert."

"And what would you rather be called?"

"Ace. Ace Moskowitz."

Jasper tried to stifle a laugh, could not.

"I know, I know," Robert conceded. "The two don't quite jive, but I'm working on a new last name."

"And is 'Ace' what your father calls you?"

The boy snorted. "Are you kidding? My old man's so square he's a cube."

"Meaning?"

"Sorry. It's just that Dad is out of it, you know. He doesn't know what's going on, what it's like to be a kid nowadays. It's like he was born last century or something."

Jasper smiled. "I was born last century."

"Oh, sorry. I just mean he doesn't know what it means to be cool. To be with it. To be accepted as one of the guys."

"To be popular, you mean."

"Right. I'd give my right arm to be like my sister's steady. Roy is practically radioactive. And on top of that, he's got this screaming ragtop."

"Translation?"

"Sorry. I mean Roy is really popular. All the girls practically drool over him. And he drives this cherry Chevy convertible."

"I see. Well, Ace, as you wished to be called, you should know that out here there is little value in being 'cool' in the sense that you mean. The flowers are indifferent as to whether you are cool or not. As for Job and myself, 'cool' suggests a shady spot out of the sun." Jasper turned and started to walk on. "Speaking of the sun, let us make the most of the morning while it is still 'cool' in the real sense."

They soon topped a rise and stood looking out over the desert. The wondrous display of color silenced even the loquacious Ace Moskowitz. Lupine, poppies, oenothera, chuparosa, purple mat, globe mallow, mimulus–flowers too many to name vied for their attention. And the smells! Those rare earthy aromas unique to the desert–in particular, the sun-warmed oils of woody sagebrush and brittle bush. Added to all this was a constant hum of bumblebees in a frenzy of nectar gathering, punctuated by the song of a cactus wren perched atop an ocotillo and giving voice to spring.

The only other sound was the click of Ace's camera. After each picture, he made a few notes in a small notebook. Jasper looked over Ace's shoulder to see what he was writing.

"Mom bought me this book on California wildflowers," Ace explained, "only I don't carry it around because it weighs a ton. So, I'm making a note of each photo I take so when I get home I can look up the flower's name. I'm doing a report on wildflowers for my earth science class. That's one of the reasons Mom and I were able to convince my dad to drive us out here."

"Perhaps I can help with the flowers' names," Jasper said. "Their common names, at any rate. I am afraid you will have to look up their Latin names later."

"Hey! That would be great!"

Jasper assumed the role of Robert's teacher, a role he was surprised to discover he enjoyed. Ace had an active mind and, when not trying to be someone he was not, turned out to be good company. Numerous lizards crossed their path, prompting Jasper to lecture on reptiles, which somehow led to a discussion of geology, a topic upon which Ace responded with as much interest as he did his lessons on wildflowers.

When they grew hungry, Jasper shared chunks of sourdough bread along with the cheese he had purchased the day before in the nearby village of Borrego Springs.

Sitting atop a gravel bed, Ace spoke with his mouth half full. "So, as a prospector, you just go wandering around, looking for gold and minerals and things?"

Jasper admitted that this was a fairly accurate description of his occupation.

"Not to sound too much like my old man," Ace said, "but what if you don't find anything? What do you do for bread—I mean, money?"

Jasper tossed a bit of bread to a scrub jay who was showing an interest in their lunch. "A prospector's needs are few, basically the food we are eating now. I doubt I have spent as much as fifty dollars on necessities within the past year."

"Jeez!" Ace exclaimed. "My camera cost more than that!"

Jasper grinned. "On the negative side, I am sadly lacking in cherry Chevy convertibles."

Ace bit off another piece of bread and sat thinking. "Fifty bucks in a whole year! Don't tell my dad that. He'll cut my allowance."

"Speaking of your dad, don't you think he might be getting worried about you?"

Ace shrugged. "I don't know. What time is it?"

Jasper looked at the position of the sun. "I would say about three, maybe four, o'clock."

"What?" Ace yelled, jumping up. "Where'd the time go? I thought it was only about noon!" He turned in a circle, studying the horizon. "I've no idea where we are."

"We are in the desert."

"I know that. But where's the parking lot? I think it's that way." He pointed east, the opposite direction of the parking lot.

With a sigh, Jasper stood. "I can see I am going to have to accompany you to keep you from getting lost." He gathered up the remains of lunch and slowly walked over to where Job stood dozing in the shade of a palo verde tree.

Ace waited, anxiously shifting back and forth from one foot to another. "I don't suppose you could step on it a bit. I'm gonna catch it as it is."

"Do you hear that, Job?" Jasper said. "Our friend, Ace, who cannot keep track of the time, now wishes for us to make it up for him." That said, Jasper took up Job's reins and set out on a pace that Ace had to run to keep up with.

A half-hour later they were within sight of the parking lot where Ace's father, looking angry, and Ace's mother, looking worried, scanned the desert in search of their son. Ace's father saw Jasper and Job, grunted, then continued to survey the area. It was Ace's mother who spotted Ace trailing along behind Jasper, and upon seeing the company he was with, her eyes grew wide.

"Robert," she cried, starting to run forward.

Ace's father swiftly caught his wife by the arm. "Stay here, Miriam. I'll take care of this." Ignoring Jasper and Job, he advanced upon Ace.

Jasper, who had anticipated an angry response to Ace's tardiness, stepped before Ace's father and held up a muscled arm. "Whoa there, partner!" Drawing from dime novel Westerns he read as a child, he went on. "Jasper is my name and prospecting is my game. Now the Park Service has hired me to give all you tenderfoots an introduction to desert ways." He jabbed a thumb toward Ace. "Me and my new sidekick here have been learning all about plants and animals and rocks and things."

Ace's father, who had been too angry to pay much attention to Jasper and Job, now looked up at the tall stranger. "Park Service, you say?"

"Yeah, Dad," Ace said, creeping forward. "Jasper is like that guy at Knott's Berry Farm, only he's for real. You can't believe how much I've learned about desert plants from him."

Ace's dad looked somewhat mollified. "Well, if he works for the Park Service, then…" His anger flared back up. "But you shouldn't have been gone so long, Robert! Your mother's been worried sick!"

Jasper turned towards Ace's mother. "You got a mighty smart young'n here ma'm. He's been peppering me with questions, and I'm afraid we just plumb forgot about the time. I do apologize if we got you to worryin'."

Ace's mother gave Jasper a small smile. "Sometimes I think Robert is too smart for his own good, but we love him anyway."

"As well you should," Jasper replied. He turned to Ace. "Well, partner, I've sure enjoyed our time together, but I reckon me and Job best be moseyin' on."

"Wait a minute!" Ace's dad cried. He fished a small camera out of his pocket. "Let me get a picture of you and Robert together. I must say, Jasper, you do look like the real deal."

Jasper posed with a paternal hand resting upon Ace's shoulder.

"Take one with my camera," Ace said. He adjusted the camera's lens before handing it to his father.

"I don't know why you need this fancy thing," Ace's dad said. "I get just as good pictures with my little Kodak." Picture taken, he returned the camera to Ace then got out his wallet. "Let me give you a little something for your time, Jasper."

"Now, sir, that's not necessary."

"Five dollars!" Ace's mom cried. "That's too much, Harold."

"Nonsense," Ace's dad said, stepping forward and slipping the bill into Jasper's shirt pocket. "We all know what government work pays, right, Jasper?"

Jasper hitched up his jeans. "Well, thank'ee kindly. That'll sure buy a heap of beans."

Ace's father laughed. " 'Heap of beans,' that's a good one!" He turned toward his son. "All right, Robert, get in the car. You being late, we'll likely get stuck in traffic going home."

Ace dutifully followed after his parents before suddenly stopping. "My lens cover! I dropped it!"

"You and that stupid camera," Ace's father said, not bothering to stop. "Well, hurry up and get it."

Ace ran back to Jasper. "I didn't drop the lens cover. I just wanted to say good-bye and thank you for a great day and especially for saving my bacon with Dad." He grinned. "That was a great act you put on."

Jasper looked over Ace's head toward Ace's parents. As they walked along, Ace's mother leaned her head against her husband's shoulder. "Your parents seem like nice people."

"They're okay, I guess. Well, anyway, thanks again." He turned and ran after his parents.

"Ace!" Jasper called.

Ace skidded to a stop and turned.

"Be cool," Jasper said.

Smiling, Ace snapped his fingers and pointed back at Jasper. "Right-O, Daddy-O!"

Laying Ghosts to Rest

It had been many years since Jasper had last visited Kelso. Once the old steam-driven locomotives were superseded by ones powered by diesel, the depot ceased being the busy water stop it had once been. He entered the lunchroom and discovered that Bill and Roy, who had once served him steak dinners, seemed also to have gone the way of the steam locomotives. Their replacement was a young waitress who told Jasper he could not get a steak, and would have to settle for a sandwich.

So many other things had changed in the intervening years. That morning he had planned to climb the nearby Kelso Dunes, as he had done years ago, only to find them crawling with "dune buggies," as they were calling the stripped-down autos that raced over the sands, destroying the scant vegetation. Jasper had stood a while, sadly watching, before hurrying away from all the dust and noise.

It was that way with so many of his former haunts: a lot of dust and noise. Palm Springs, that once shy village of a few hundred souls was now a major resort town, the playground of Hollywood movie stars, with nearly as many golf courses as there had once been residents. Jasper tried to be philosophical about all the changes being wrought upon the desert, but it was hard to see the good when folks seemed intent upon bringing the confusion of the cities to the once peaceful desert.

The young waitress placed a sandwich before Jasper along with a small bag of potato chips. Jasper missed the mashed potatoes and gravy that Bill had served.

The waitress lingered. "Are you a hippy?" she said. "You look like a hippy, though you're a kinda old for one."

Jasper, who was having difficulty opening the bag of chips, looked up. "Hippy?"

The waitress snatched the bag out of his hands and with a quick jerk, tore it open. "You know hippy: Woodstock, Haight-Ashbury, sex, drugs and rock 'n' roll."

Jasper shook his head. Whatever a 'hippy' was, he was certainly not one. "I am a prospector."

"Oh…really," she said. "That's cool, I guess." And with that pronouncement, she left him to enjoy his sandwich.

Cool. The last time he had heard the word used in that manner had been by a lad he had met in the Anza-Borrego desert. How long ago was that? Ten years? Fifteen?

"Is everything all right?" the waitress said.

"What?" Jasper said, looking up.

"You were shaking your head."

"I was only trying to remember something and not succeeding."

"I get that way sometimes."

Well, Jasper thought, maybe I am not getting so old after all.

"Here's a newspaper if you'd like something to read," she said, placing a folded newspaper before him.

Jasper was about to say he did not wish to read when a caption caught his eye:

Fiftieth Anniversary of the End of WWI

"Thank you," he said, picking up the paper. The article was brief, a mention of events to be held in France the following month to commemorate the Great War's end. Jasper searched through the rest of the newspaper but could find no other mention of the bloodiest war in history. Had the world forgotten already?

Jasper set the newspaper aside, finished his lunch and left. Outside he picked up his backpack, left leaning up against the side of the building. Ever since Job died, Jasper had become his own pack mule. He had considered getting a replacement for Job, but could not bear the thought of losing another friend. And once he managed to lighten his kit, the backpack served his purposes well enough. Gone was the heavy pick and shovel, replaced with a simple rock pick; a lightweight mattress pad substituted for the old army cot; a small aluminum pot for the cast iron Dutch oven. Nearly the only article he had held on to was the small caliber rifle he had bought from Jacob Harmon so many years ago. He justified keeping the rifle in case the need should arise to augment his limited food supply with a jack rabbit, though he would be loath to do so. The truth was he still harbored a fear of rattlesnakes, and the rifle somehow made him feel safer.

As he laced his arms through the shoulder straps of his backpack, he recalled the time when he had performed a similar motion years ago in Jacob Harmon's store in Inyo. He smiled at what an innocent he had been back then. His smile dissolved as he recalled a letter from Sarah Agullo, relating the tragic news about Jacob Harmon. After Captain Jacob Jr. had been killed while fighting at Guadalcanal, Jacob Sr. had lost interest in his supermarket enterprise. He eventually sold his stores to a larger food chain. Then he succumbed to depression and…

Jasper shook his head. Best not to dwell on that. Best not to live in the past. Reminiscing was the pastime of the aged, and though he was old, Jasper did not feel old. Outside of a few minor aches and pains, he did not feel any different than when, as a lad of seventeen, he had gone off to war.

He headed northwest, planning to restock in Baker before continuing on to Tecopa and from there to Death Valley. But as he walked, he could not stop thinking of the past. It was because of that newspaper article. Over the years, his memory of the Great War had become less of a mental burden. Still, the war had been the defining moment in his life, the impetus for his coming to California, for his becoming a prospector, for fifty years spent wandering in the desert.

In an attempt to forget the newspaper article, he increased his pace to put more distance between himself and the Kelso Depot. But he had not gotten far before he stopped. He felt torn between going on or turning back, and not just in the physical sense. Continuing on meant a determination not to live in the past. Yet such a determination felt as if he were not only turning his back on the Kelso Depot, but on something consequential, as if he were forsaking an old friendship, or abandoning a sacred obligation.

An idea began to form in his mind, and, as strange as it seemed, it succeeded in taking hold of him. Doing an about face, he returned to the Kelso Depot and purchased a train ticket to Los Angeles.

"I'm so glad you came to see me," Sarah Agullo said, as she motioned Jasper to a chair. "I had not heard from you in so long, I'd actually been thinking of hiring somebody to go out and see if you were still alive."

Jasper leaned back in the comfortable chair and looked across the large desk where Sarah, whose appearance had changed little over the years, sat with hands folded in her lap. "I suppose I have been a little remiss in my correspondence."

Sarah smiled. "Just a little." She picked up a faded envelope. "Your last letter was dated April 8th, 1965. That's almost four years ago."

"Has it been that long?"

Sarah picked up another envelope. "Yes, but I suppose I shouldn't be too critical since this, your previous letter, was dated August 12th, 1958. In the last four years, you've managed to almost double your rate of correspondence."

Jasper scratched at the skin beneath his beard. He had managed a bath before coming to visit Sarah, and the soap had made his face itch. "I confess time does not have much meaning to me. I notice when the weather turns cool, and I notice when it turns hot, and that is about the only clock I live by. I'm sorry, though, if my lack of communication has made your work harder for you."

"Don't be. The truth is I'm rather envious."

Jasper looked around Sarah's large office, located within her palatial home. Not surprisingly, the room was lined with books, these positioned in handsome walnut cabinets softly illuminated by hidden lights. Through the large window, he saw three gardeners busy trimming the hedges that lined the long stone walkway leading to an enormous swimming pool, which glowed like a blue sapphire.

"I know what you're thinking," Sarah said, as she watched Jasper staring out the window.

Jasper turned back to Sarah. "You do?"

"Yes, and all that you see here, and much, much more could have been yours. It was you who chose to give up a life of ease in favor of the wide-open spaces."

"So why the envy?"

"I envy your sense of time. I feel time rushing by me like a jet plane, and ever since Sam died, it only seems to be going faster. That is why I am so glad you're here, so I can tell you that I have found someone else to handle your finances, for I no longer have the energy to handle them myself."

Jasper could see the truth of this in Sarah's tired eyes. "I see I have been more than just remiss in my correspondence. I have failed to realize how much of a burden I saddled you with, asking you to look after my fortune all these years."

Sarah waved this away. "As it turned out, I was much better at finance than at law. And it gave me something to do while Sam was busy with his teaching. But now, in the time I have left, I want to spend it with my family, with my grandchildren and great grandchildren."

"So what is it you need for me to do?" Jasper said.

Sarah leaned forward and rested her arms on her desk. "Have you given much thought as to what is to become of your wealth once you're gone?"

"It suppose it will go to my stepbrother and his children."

"That is a vast amount of wealth for just a few people. Have you ever thought about setting up a foundation, perhaps doing something to help protect the desert that you love so much? There is a growing environmental movement in this country. People, especially young people, are becoming more and more concerned that we're slowly destroying this good earth."

Jasper and Sarah talked about this and other things, and eventually outlined a plan to parcel out Jasper's wealth among three different nature conservancies and five charities, with the remainder going to his relatives.

"There, I feel much better about all this," Sarah said, once they had concluded. It was late afternoon. The gardeners had all gone home. "Will you stay the night? I've lots of spare bedrooms."

"I would like that," Jasper said. "And maybe in the morning you could show me where I might purchase a new suit."

Sarah laughed. "You, in a suit?"

Jasper smiled.

"Well, I suspected your visit wasn't solely to see me. But why the suit? Are you planning to get married?"

Jasper again scratched his itchy skin. "Let us just say that I have decided it is time to lay a few ghosts to rest."

Had Jasper realized the task he had set for himself in trying to purchase a suit, he would not have made the attempt. First was his discomfort with the press of humanity as he, accompanied by Sarah, negotiated the busy shops. Second was trying to find a suit without either the hip-hugging waists and flared leg bottoms, which he thought made him look a clown, or the slick and shiny fabrics that cast him as a used car salesmen in a worn-out suit. Finally, they located a shop that prided itself on offering clothes for "the distinguished gentleman," providing, of course, the distinguished gentleman was rich.

"Six hundred dollars for a suit?" Jasper lamented, as they emerged from the store. "They must think I am as rich as Croesus."

"The suit you bought could not have looked nicer on you had it been hand-tailored," Sarah said. "Besides, you seem to forget you *are* as rich as Croesus."

They could not take the suit with them, as the pant cuffs had to be hemmed. But the salesman assured them that if they were to return a little later, the job would be done. In the meantime, they found a restaurant in which Jasper, still in his prospector's garb, would not look out of place, which, given the current careless fashions of young people, left them a lot of choices.

"So, are you going to tell me why the new suit?" Sarah said, once they were seated.

Jasper explained about the newspaper article he had read and the idea which had taken hold of him: to go to France and take part in the ceremonies commemorating the end of the Great War.

"You know, I never knew you were a soldier," she said.

"It is a fact I usually kept to myself."

"Was it bad for you, the war?"

It was not something Jasper could explain to someone who had not experienced it firsthand. "Yes," was all he said.

"And thus your need to 'lay a few ghosts to rest.'"

Jasper nodded.

Their food came, and Sarah, who sensed Jasper's reluctance to talk about his war experience, changed the subject. "I shall have to go shopping soon myself for a new dress. While you're in France, I shall be in New York where my youngest granddaughter will be receiving a prestigious literary award."

Jasper smiled. "A literary award? Well, I am not surprised, given the passion for literature that runs in her family."

"Oddly enough, her mother rarely cracked a book. It seems these literary obsessions tend to skip a generation. Or maybe it was because Dorothy, the one getting the award, was the grandchild closest to Sam."

"Who shared his love of books with her?"

Sarah nodded. "But I think it was more of a personality thing, really. Dorothy doted on Sam, and she, more than my other grandchildren, loved the fact that he was a native American. Dorothy's book, the one she's getting the award for, is about the history of our treatment of native Americans, which, basically, is a history of persecution."

"I remember back in the heyday of Desert Rose and what Sam

had to go through," Jasper said. He remembered how Shoshone Sam, if not exactly persecuted, was nevertheless shunned by the nearly all-white population. "Do you remember his library? He had hopes of it becoming the intellectual center of Desert Rose, only nobody visited it because he was an Indian."

"I do remember," Sarah said. "And do you remember the night of the big fire?"

"How could I ever forget?"

"Sam worked like a demon that night, risking his life as he leapt from rooftop to rooftop, beating out the flames with a wet blanket. If it had not been for Sam, the whole town would have been lost. And do you think any of the citizens of Desert Rose ever thanked him for his efforts?"

Jasper wiped his hands on his paper napkin. "It makes me ashamed to think how I took Sam's generous nature for granted."

"Well, Sam always acted the Stoic, but deep down inside I know it hurt him. I thank God you all made the fortunes you did, for the money freed Sam to study Literature, and eventually when he was made full professor, and was beloved by his students, a lot of that hurt went away."

After retrieving Jasper's new suit, they returned to Sarah's home where she made arrangements for Jasper to fly first class on a nonstop passenger jet leaving LAX the following afternoon. Jasper spent the next morning having his locks trimmed. The barber argued for shaving off his beard as well.

"You don't want to look like a damned hippy, do you?" the barber said.

Jasper, who had been relaxing in the barber's chair, sat forward. "I will have you know that these whiskers have sheltered this poor face of mine well-nigh fifty years, and should you shave them off now, I shall either die of sunstroke or catch pneumonia." He leaned back. "But if it will appease your sense of propriety, you may trim them, but only a bit."

Sarah chose not accompany Jasper to the airport, but she stood outside with him as they waited for her driver to bring the car around.

"When do you think we'll see each other again?" she said.

Jasper wished to be honest with her. "I do not rightly know, Sarah. I am old. I do not feel old, but yesterday when the barber held up his mirror, I saw the passing of time deeply etched into my face. Right now, I just want to see what awaits me on the far side of the globe. Then, most likely, I shall return and take up my old occupation."

"Well, whatever you decide, drop me a note from time to time so I know you're still alive." She reached forward and straightened the lapel on his new suit. "You look very handsome, Jasper. No one ever would suspect you of being a one-jack-mule prospector."

Jasper arrived on time at the airport only to find his flight had been delayed. He took a seat in the waiting room next to a soldier in uniform. Jasper could not help but notice the occasional hard looks directed at the young man seated next to him.

"As if I'm the one who started this damn war," Jasper heard the soldier mutter. "Can I help it if I got drafted?"

Jasper sensed not only anger, but hurt in the young soldier's utterance. "Where are you headed?" he said, wishing to strike up a conversation.

"Fort Polk, Louisiana, sir," the soldier said. "I'm to get special training before heading off to Viet Nam."

"I have heard of Viet Nam. Isn't there a war going on there?"

The soldier turned to stare at Jasper, trying to see if he were being funny. "Yeah, a war with about thirty thousand American dead."

Jasper was quick to apologize, explaining that, as a prospector, he dwelled in remote places. "Sometimes I go for years without seeing a newspaper."

"A prospector? Without the beard, I would've taken you for a banker."

Jasper tugged on his lapel. "I assure you these togs are not my usual attire. But I thought them more appropriate for where I am going. You see, I served in World War I, and now I am going back to France to attend the ceremonies commemorating the fiftieth anniversary marking the Great War's end."

The soldier's attention was drawn toward a young woman in a heated conversation with the attendant at the ticket counter. "The Great War, huh?"

"Let me stress there was nothing *great* about it."

The soldier nodded. "Well, as one soldier to another, what can you tell me that I should know?"

Jasper's first impulse was to tell the soldier to flee, to get up from his chair right this moment and fly to some place far, far from any battlefield. But he knew his advice would not be heeded. "The time immediately ahead of you may likely be the most vital period of your life. For me, and those who fought beside me, it was a time when everything we ever thought about ourselves was stripped away, leaving us strangely open and vulnerable. Yet only then were we able to perceive what truly mattered: the human bond we shared with each other."

The soldier turned to look Jasper in the eye. "You almost make it sound as if war is a good thing."

"I do not mean to suggest in any way—"

Jasper was interrupted by the young woman who had been at the ticket counter.

"Jesus!" she exclaimed, plopping herself down on a seat directly across the aisle. "You'd think everybody and his damned uncle is going to France."

The clothes the woman wore were a parody of the young soldier's smart uniform. Her jacket, an army surplus jacket much too large for her, was half buttoned, revealing a necklace strung with what looked like dog tags, but upon closer inspection, proved to be the pop tops of soda cans. Upon her head was a sailor's cap festooned with dry flowers. The bottom edges of her raggedy blue jeans were as dirty as her sandaled feet.

"Where the hell are my damn cigarettes?" she said, as she rummaged about in a canvas knapsack. She found her cigarette pack and extracted a cigarette. "Hey, soldier boy, you got a match?"

The soldier took out a lighter, leaned across the aisle and lit her cigarette.

The young woman inhaled deeply and blew out a stream of smoke. "Thanks. Where you headed?"

"Louisiana. You?"

"I'm trying to get to France on stand-by, only so far today every flight's been full."

"Tough luck," the soldier said.

"Yeah. So, what's in Louisiana besides alligators?"

"Advanced training. What's in France?"

"Paris. The Eiffel tower. Artists along the Seine. Relaxed drug laws. I'm going to bum around Paris then head south, maybe even cross the Mediterranean to Morocco. I hear you can get great hashish in Marrakesh." She shot the soldier an impish grin. "Say, why don't you come with me?"

The soldier grinned. "I'd like to, but I've got this date with Uncle Sam."

The young woman blew out another cloud of smoke. "Aw, screw him. There's nothing Uncle Sam can do if you're in Europe."

The soldier shrugged. "Maybe not, but I'd like to be able to come home someday. See my parents."

The young woman shook her head. "If I never see my parents again, it'll be too soon."

A voice came on the speaker, announcing the departure of a flight to New Orleans.

"That's me," the soldier said, standing up. He turned to Jasper. "It was nice talking to you, sir. I'll remember what you said."

Jasper stood and offered his hand. "I trust all will go well."

"Thanks," the soldier said.

The young woman suddenly leaped up out of her chair and threw her arms around the soldier's neck. "You be safe, now, soldier boy. Come back in one piece, okay?" She kissed him full on the lips, then stuck one of her dried flowers in the breast pocket of his jacket. Jasper and the young woman stood watching until the young soldier was lost among the boarding passengers.

The young woman sat back down. "I hate this damn war!"

Jasper, taking his seat, nodded in agreement.

The young woman eyed Jasper. "You know, you look awful nice, I mean for an old guy. Though you kinda look like a banker."

Jasper laughed, but said nothing. In a little while, the young woman went off to harass the attendant at the ticket counter again, leaving Jasper alone with his thoughts. He wished he could have talked more with the soldier, yet what more could he have said that would have been of benefit, that would not have alarmed him? Had he continued talking more of "the human bond," he might have been led to sharing details of his own experience, of the friendships he had formed with beautiful and vital young men only to see them fall beside him as they rushed the enemy line.

And what could he have told the young soldier of the men he would be fighting? There were times when Jasper's unit had been so close to enemy lines, they could hear the enemy talking. Jasper did not speak German, but likely the topics of conversation were familiar: how bad the food was; how good a pint of bitters would taste right now; what they were going to do if they ever got out of these trenches alive. Jasper sensed that those German boys were really no different than him or his mates. They, too, were young men with hopes and dreams, and with much goodness, even greatness in them. How did such a thing as the Great War come to pass? Where was the need to sacrifice so many to placate the ambitions of a few?

The young woman, still unsuccessful at getting on a flight, sat back down and lit another cigarette.

What am I doing here? Jasper asked himself. *Why do I feel compelled to return to the scene of that lasting nightmare? No matter where I am, the ghosts of all those young men will continue to haunt me.*

Yet by returning to the field of battle, by walking over the once bloody ground, now covered with row upon row of white headstones, he might speak to the bones of those men he fought beside and perhaps give voice to what he had been wanting to say for a very long time.

Jasper shook his head. He did not have to go to France speak to the dead; the ghosts of those men lived right inside his skull. Closing his eyes, he saw one fellow soldier after another, as clearly as if they were standing right before him.

I am sorry, sorry for all your lives cut short. Sorry that you never got to see, as I have seen, the desert in bloom, or to lie, looking up through the dry desert air at a sky ablaze with stars, or to climb atop a mountain and look out upon endless sunbaked plains and feel as if the whole world was created just for you. I'm sorry you never got that decent meal we talked so much about, or the pint of bitters we craved, and that the bond of friendship we shared was broken and shattered there in the muck and the blood and the filth. You were such beautiful young men, and you were gone far too soon.

Jasper felt a hand upon his shoulder.

"Hey, mister, you okay?"

Through eyes blurred with tears, Jasper saw the young woman standing before him. "Eh? What?"

"You've been really crying," she said.

"Have I?" Jasper reached up and felt his wet beard. He could not recall the last time he had cried, yet he wished it had happened sooner.

He grasped the young woman's hand. "Why did we do it? What was the point? What did we hope to achieve?"

The young woman looked confused and a little embarrassed, but she made no attempt to pull away.

Jasper continued. "Why are we given this life? What is its meaning? Are we given it to suffer?"

The young woman's Adam's apple rose as she swallowed hard. "Well… I hope not."

"I hope not too," Jasper said. "Because in my heart I believe life a wonderful gift, meant to be loved and lived."

An image came into his mind of the great aspen forests on Table Mountain in central Nevada. Right now, the trees would be displaying their autumn colors of green, yellow and orange-red. And thinking of those aspen trees, Jasper was gripped with the need to go home. Not to Wales, certainly not to France, but to his true home, where peace was to be found: the desert.

Releasing the young woman's hand, he stood up and reached into his coat pocket. "Here," he said, thrusting his plane ticket into her hand, before walking away.

The young woman called after him. "Hey! Wait a minute!"

Jasper stopped and turned.

The young woman looked at the ticket then at Jasper. "You serious? This is a first-class ticket!"

Jasper smiled. "Yes, first-class. Enjoy your flight. Enjoy Paris! Enjoy your life!" Then with the smell of sagebrush in his nostrils he strode toward the airport exit.

The Colberts

It was late September with a bit of chill in the air, and a touch of frost on the ground, signs that it was high time for Jasper to head south. Yet he could not bring himself to leave the Okanagan Desert. For years, it had been on his mind to explore this arid region of British Columbia, knowing his experience of the American desert would be incomplete until he had visited the northern-most portion on the continent. The Okanagan Desert had shown itself to be a true desert, with prickly pear cactus, sagebrush, even rattlesnakes. Portions had been irrigated and turned into farmland, and, as a consequence, Jasper had added fruits and vegetables to his Spartan diet, purchased from roadside farm stands. Lately he had been enjoying crisp apples and succulent pears. These delights coupled with a glorious Indian summer had made him put off thoughts of migrating south.

Then one morning he awoke to find the water in his coffee pot frozen solid. That same day he purchased a bus ticket. At one time, he would have made the journey south on foot, arriving near the Mexican border when the spring wildflowers would be just starting, but nowadays allowances had to be made for age.

He got off the bus at Alturas. With temperatures in the upper nineties, it still felt like summer in this high-desert town tucked away in the northeast corner of California. Long accustomed to the desert heat, Jasper found the temperature to his liking, and when he visited nearby Lava Beds National Monument, he discovered he could not stay long within the lava tubes, for these underground tunnels, created by rivers of molten lava, were always cool, no matter the temperature outside, and the largest and deepest tubes had floors covered in ice year round.

Temperatures had moderated considerably by mid-October when Jasper stood looking out over the Black Rock Desert in northwest Nevada. The vast chalky playa, rimmed by dark mountains, appeared untouched until the appearance of a passing freight train set the ground to shaking. The brakeman waved in passing and peace ensued until a string of four-wheel-drive vehicles appeared and went racing across the hard-packed playa to the accompaniment of radios blaring out a pounding beat. This invasion was emblematic of the changes that had come to the desert: more and more people and cars, less and less peace.

Fortunately, Jasper still knew of places where human feet, not to mention car tires, rarely, if ever, trod. He thought he was in one such place a couple of weeks later while on his way toward Death Valley. Jasper did little in the way of prospecting anymore, but he still had the prospector's eye, and when late in the day a promising stretch of ground caught his eye, he stopped to investigate. He picked up a handful of soil and sifted it through his fingers. Nearly microscopic particles of gold clung to his fingers and glittered in the sunlight.

It must be understood that not all gold is alike. Veteran prospectors can tell where certain types of gold come from just by looking at them. To Jasper, this trace of gold, combined with its setting, sparked a memory. Following this dim line of remembrance, he strode east and came upon an old conveyor, used for loading ore, lying on its side and nearly hidden by brush. It was the same conveyor which, decades ago, Shoshone Sam and he had hauled off the Shoshone Reservation.

With a feeling of delight tinged by sadness, Jasper stood and surveyed the area. His delight came from his having found his way back to the source of his wealth, to the town of Desert Rose. The sadness came from discovering only rabbit brush and sagebrush where once a vibrant town had stood.

He had visited Desert Rose only once after he and his partners had sold the Three-Legged Dog Mine. At that time, the mines were still going strong, and the town boasted a population of nearly two thousand souls. Now, as he picked his way over the ruts, which were all that remained of Main Street, he could find little evidence of Desert Rose ever having existed. If his memory served him right, the Palace Saloon, built by Ezra Harris, once stood upon the level ground to his right, now the resting place of a jumble of weeds. A closer inspection yielded nothing but shards of broken glass, as if someone had been using bottles for target practice. Not even bits of glass marked where Countess Isabella's house of pleasure once served as the center of Desert Rose's spirited nightlife. All Jasper found was a piece of silk, tattered and sun-bleached, which may, or may not, have been part of a lady's fancy dress.

Jasper stood and slowly turned in a circle. He was not surprised that the buildings of Desert Rose, once abandoned, had been carted away, for good building material was not easy to come by in the desert. What surprised him was just how little remained: a few rusty pipes, small pieces of machinery, a short section of wall. The backstop for the baseball field was still there, largely intact, though the boards were warped and split. He hurried forward, anxious to see what remained of Shoshone Sam's library. He might never have found where it once stood had not Shoshone Sam insisted upon thick concrete footings to support the stone walls. The cut stone, which had made Shoshone Sam's library the most imposing edifice in Desert Rose, had likewise been hauled away, and the concrete footing now was cracked and weed-choked.

Jasper wandered back to the rusty conveyor. Even the Three-Legged Dog Mine had disappeared. Someone must have been troubled by its offending scar and had it bulldozed over. More likely, some government agency had feared the mine would collapse upon an unfortunate visitor and had taken measures to prevent such an accident.

Jasper sat on the conveyor and stared back over what was once Desert Rose. Here was a lesson in the temporal nature of all human endeavors, and thinking along these lines, he wondered just how many of the town's original inhabitants were still alive. Where was Countess Isabella? Where Ezra Harris? Where were all the young men and

women who danced beneath the electric lights at the Miners' Ball? He recalled how, on the night of the ball, a young girl and her brother had entertained the miners with a sentimental song, though he could not remember the song itself. Surely, the sister and brother must still be alive today. He hoped so. He hoped there were still people who remembered Desert Rose and would keep it alive, at least in memory.

A few weeks later, sitting atop a sand dune not far from Stovepipe Wells in Death Valley, Jasper was grateful for the warmth of the sand, for a late November wind whistled about his ears, forcing him to pull up the collar on his denim jacket. He recalled the first time he had visited Death Valley, back before it became a national monument. Thankfully, little had changed, for the Park Service enforced restrictions designed to preserve Death Valley's natural features. This meant, in terms of the sand dunes, a prohibition on dune buggies. This not only preserved the graceful contour of the dunes, but safeguarded the desert solitude, interrupted only by the wind and the occasional passing of an automobile on the nearby highway.

Two days earlier, while crossing the Panamint Valley, he had been tempted to climb the Panamint Dunes, but that had been at the end of a long day, and he had decided to save his energy, for he would need it for the steep climb over mile-high Towne Pass the next morning. He was not exactly sure when this parceling out of energy had been begun. Yet he could not fail to notice that he was moving slower. His familiar morning routine—setting dough to rise, gathering wood, building a campfire—was taking him longer to perform.

But why think such sobering thoughts on such a beautiful afternoon? Perhaps because of the influence of the somber mountains to the east: dark, craggy and foreboding. Jasper smiled, thinking that someone, judging by appearances only, might have described him using these same adjectives. But appearances are deceiving, particularly in the desert, and having twice explored the Funeral Mountains, as these austere mountains were called, he had always found them unsurpassed in unique geological features, particularly the colossal uplifted and bent layers of rock, which exhibited enough variations in color to inspire the most jaded artist. In fact, Artists Palette was the name given to a place near the base of the Funeral Mountains where colors swirled over the tortured earth like threads woven crazily by a drunken rug weaver.

Leaving the dunes, Jasper headed southwest toward Mosaic Canyon, within whose narrow canyon walls he planned to camp, out of the wind. A graded dirt road provided access to the canyon for motorists, but Jasper eschewed the easy path in favor of the untrammeled way, not that he expected to come across any tourists this late in the year, and with such a cold wind blowing.

Thus, it was a surprise when he saw a truck parked in the lot not far from the mouth of Mosaic Canyon. It was a park service vehicle. Over the years, Jasper had met many park rangers and counted a few as friends, or as near to friends as a solitary prospector had. He had always found the rangers to be cordial, interested in him and his doings, and eager not only to share their knowledge of the desert, but to learn from him as well. He was curious to know what brought a park ranger out here so late in the day.

Almost immediately upon entering Mosaic Canyon, the canyon walls closed about him, shielding him from the main thrust of the wind, which continued to whistle high above. Sections of the canyon were so narrow, he could touch both sides in passing, his left hand gliding over the smooth dolomite-marble wall while his right hand bumped along over the rough breccia of rock fragments embedded in a sandy matrix. Other narrower canyons entered from the sides, and within this maze of twisting corridors, sound echoed, making it difficult to tell the direction of its source.

At first, he attributed a peculiar sound to the keening of the wind. It reminded him of his friends, the monks at Saint Anthony's Priory, chanting the offices of the day. Yet the more he listened, the more there seemed something unholy in this particular chant.

As he drew deeper into the canyon, the sound grew in volume then abruptly ceased. A chill came over him, not attributable to the dropping temperature as night approached. With the cessation of the chanting he heard someone crying, though the crying was strangely muffled. He waited until the chanting resumed before quietly slipping off his backpack and leaning it against the wall of the canyon. He slid his small caliber rifle from his pack, then choosing his steps carefully, he stole forward. He now could discern a few words of the chant: "Praise thee… from the darkness… to thee we give…"

A woman's loud voice broke in, "Keep the damn thing on!" Followed by the voice of a young man or older boy, "It itches!"

The voice of the chanter, decidedly male, did not let this interruption keep him from repeating the same phrases, spoken in a near monotone, like a disobedient student forced to recite the same lines over and over: "We praise thee Dark Lord. We call upon thee from the darkness. To thee we give all praise and seek to do thy bidding." All the while, the sound of crying continued.

Jasper inched forward until the woman's voice, close by, stopped him in his tracks.

"I'll not tell you again! Keep the damn thing on!"

This warning seemed to come from just beyond the next bend.

There was the sound of a slap followed by someone crying out in pain. Unperturbed, the man continued his intoning, "We praise thee… We call upon thee… To thee we give all…"

Jasper felt himself trembling. He did not know what the people were doing, but clearly they were up to no good. Moving very slowly, he peered around the corner and saw three cloaked and hooded figures standing over a kneeling woman, whose hands were bound and head covered with a white cloth sack. The woman's uniform identified her as a park ranger. It was she doing the crying.

As Jasper looked on, the tallest of the three standing figures attempted up to pull back his hood only to be thwarted by the smallest, reaching up to slap the back of his head. Still the chant continued. "We praise… We call… To thee we give…"

Then from beneath his robe the chanter drew a long pointed knife and raised it above the kneeling park ranger.

Raising his rifle, Jasper stepped forward. "Now, you stop right there!"

The three cloaked figures turned as one. The man dropped his arm to his side and whipped back his hood. For a moment, Jasper was taken aback, for the man was beautiful of face, an Adonis with ringlets of black hair caressing alabaster skin and lips as soft and red as any woman's. But this remarkable beauty was spoiled by the man's eyes. No spark of life dwelled within them. They might have been the eyes of a corpse or of a discarded doll.

The man, noting Jasper's hesitation, smiled, revealing perfect teeth. "Come to join us, have you friend?"

"I've come to put an end to your shenanigans," Jasper said, training his rifle on the man's exquisite face. His aim hit upon a sensitive nerve, and the man's smile turned into malevolent snarl. At that moment, the smallest of the trio, a woman, launched herself at Jasper. What she lacked in size, she made up for in the ferocity of her attack. She did not go for Jasper's rifle, but with long fingernails like talons of a hawk, she sprang for Jasper's eyes. On a shorter man, she might have succeeded in causing great damage, but her claws only met with the flesh of his cheeks, scratching the skin and drawing blood.

Time had little diminished Jasper's combat training, honed on the battlefield. He pivoted the gun, jamming the point of the barrel down hard upon the woman's pelvic bone. Her scream was cut short by Jasper turning the rifle about and slamming the butt end against her left temple, knocking her down and unconscious.

With hatred ripping from his voice, Adonis sprang at Jasper, carving knife raised. Jasper had anticipated this, and before the young man could strike, he whipped around and smashed the butt end of the rifle into the man's face, mashing his nose and sending blood squirting every which way.

Stunned, the man took a step back. He brought a hand up to his ruined face then stared at the blood dripping through his fingers. He appeared amazed that he, a seeming immortal, could actually be made to bleed. Jasper did not wait for the man to resume his attack, but using his advantage of height and all the power of his muscled arms, brought the butt end of the rifle down upon the crown of the man's head. The man went down like a pole-axed steer.

All through this, the last member of the threesome had stood with his hood nearly covering his face. Now he threw back his hood and rubbed his scalp vigorously. "It itches!" he declared.

"Mongoloid" was the word that came to Jasper to describe the appearance of this young man, who was more concerned with his own discomfort than with the plight of his fallen comrades. Trying to rid himself of his cloak, he became entangled in its folds and in frustration started to whimper. Jasper was forced to set his rifle aside in order to help free him. Delivered from his itchy cloak, the young man scratched at himself as if he were covered in fleas which, judging from his neglected appearance, he may well have been.

Jasper picked up the knife, which had fallen from Adonis's hand, and used it as a pointer. "I want you to sit down on that rock. Do you understand?"

Moving slowly, the young man obeyed, and when seated, began another bout of scratching. Jasper picked up the young man's discarded cloak, and using the knife, he cut the material into strips and used these to bind the hands and feet of the unconscious woman. During the scuffle, her hood had fallen back. She, too, was exceedingly fair, but in contrast to the handsome man's raven black hair, hers was a blond of near transparency.

Jasper went to see if the man should be likewise bound. A large circle of blood stained the ground around his head. It was obvious this man would not rise again. Jasper had not meant to kill him; it had been the heat of the moment and his battle instincts coming to the fore. It sickened him to think that, having come to the desert to escape violence, he had been forced to kill again, even though the man, with all his mumbo-jumbo about a "Dark Lord," obviously was a monster bent upon murdering an innocent.

And what of this innocent? She was quiet now. Jasper cut away the ropes that bound her wrists then removed the sack covering her head.

Her tear-streaked face showed no sign of life. She was a small woman, and ordinarily it would have been nothing for a man of Jasper's size and strength to carry her, but his trembling legs nearly buckled as he lifted her then struggled to set her down where she might rest her back against a flat rock. She was so young, too young to his mind, to be wearing the uniform of a park ranger.

With a glance back at the young man, who appeared content to sit on his rock, Jasper took his rifle and went to retrieve his backpack. From it he removed a cloth, soaked it with water from his canteen, then applied the damp cloth to the young park ranger's face. With a jerk, she came awake, her eyes wide open, yet unseeing.

"You are safe, now," he said. "My name is Jasper, and I am here to help you."

The young park ranger did not respond. She was in shock, the same sort of shock Jasper remembered seeing on the faces of wounded soldiers.

"Here," he said, placing the open canteen before her lips, "try to take a sip of water."

The simple act of drinking resulted in her becoming more fully aware. She began to cry, her distress leading her to choke on the water she had only half swallowed.

Jasper took her small hands and rubbed them between his great big ones. "You have gone through a horrible ordeal, but you are safe now, I promise you."

The park ranger made no reply and appeared to lapse back into a state of semi-consciousness. Jasper realized this would never do. "Let us try and stand up together," he suggested, and bearing most of her weight, he helped her up.

To the young man, still sitting on the rock, Jasper said, "I want you to follow us. Do you understand?"

The young man pointed to the woman on the ground. "Sister."

"Your sister is fine. She is sleeping. She wants you to come with me."

The young man looked doubtful, but as Jasper started down the canyon, rifle in one hand, one arm helping to support the park ranger, the young man followed. The wind had died, but the evening remained cold. Jasper worried they might not make it out of the canyon before darkness overtook them, but there was still a bit of glow in the west when they emerged out into the parking lot. The park ranger was walking fully on her own now, but she still had not spoken. When they reached the park service truck, Jasper helped her into the cab then directed the young man to find himself a nearby place to sit.

The young man hugged himself. "Cold," he said.

The young man would be warmer in the cab, but Jasper did not want the park ranger to be forced to sit next to one of her attackers. Jasper looked into the bed of the truck and saw an old canvas tarp held down by a few tools. Setting his rifle alongside the tools he removed the tarp and offered it to the young man. "Here, put this around you. It will help keep you warm."

Jasper took a moment to wipe off the dried blood on his cheeks before letting himself in on the driver's side. Leaving the door part way open, he studied instrument panel by the overhead light. He wanted to transport the park ranger to a place where she might receive medical attention, but the last time he had driven a truck had been right after the Great War. His thoughts were interrupted by a cackle of static followed by a loud voice.

"Ranger Williams, this is park headquarters. Gail, do you read me?"

The truck had a communication radio. Jasper lifted the receiver and spoke into it. "Hello, my name is Jasper. I am with Ranger—"

"Ranger Williams, this is park headquarters. Gail, do you read me?" the voice repeated.

The young park ranger came to life. She took the receiver from Jasper. "You have to push the button on the side," she said. She pressed the button, spoke into the receiver. "Park headquarters, this is Ranger Williams."

"Gail, where have you been? We've been trying to contact you for hours."

"I—" Ranger Williams lapsed back into silence. As she stared out over the dashboard, the receiver fell from her hand.

Jasper retrieved it and pressed the side button. "Ranger Williams was being held captive by three people. I managed to get her away from them."

"Who is this?" the voice demanded.

"My name is Jasper, and I–"

"Put Ranger Williams back on!"

Jasper looked at Ranger Williams, who was still staring out over the dashboard. "Ranger Williams is unable to speak right now. She is very upset by her ordeal."

There was a moment of silence. "How bad off is she?"

"She needs medical attention. I suggest you send–wait a minute."

Park Ranger Williams was trying to tell him something. "Colberts," she managed to say.

"Colberts?" Jasper said. "I am afraid I do not understand."

"Tell headquarters that the people who held me were the Colberts."

Jasper relayed this information.

"Jesus!" the voice on the radio exclaimed "Are you serious? Where the hell are you?"

"We are located at the entrance to Mosaic Canyon," Jasper said.

"Are you safe where you are?"

"Yes, we are, but it's cold and getting colder."

"Understood. Do not go anywhere! Help is on the way!"

Help seemed a long time coming, but when it came, it came in force: a whole string of patrol cars and park service vehicles. Jasper got out of the truck to meet the first of the arrivals, a highway patrol officer, nearly as tall as Jasper.

"I am Sergeant Hagen. Who are you, sir?"

"My name is Jasper. I am a prospector who happened upon Ranger Williams up in Mosaic Canyon. She was being held captive by people who Ranger Williams said are the Colberts. They were about to kill her in some fiendish ritual when I came upon them." Jasper went on to describe subsequent events and the condition of the captors when they left them.

"It sounds like you did our job for us. Who's that kid over there with the stupid look on his face?"

"He was one of the three holding captive Park Ranger Williams, only I do not believe he knew what was going on. He appears to be mentally deficient."

Sergeant Hagen nodded. "He must be Jamie Colbert, Cindy Colbert's dumb brother. Is that Ranger Williams I see in the truck?"

Jasper nodded.

"I need to speak with her." Sergeant Hagen moved to open the truck door.

Jasper reached out to stop him. "I am not sure that is a good idea. She seems to be going in and out of shock. She needs medical attention."

"I see. We'll get her help as soon as we can. In the meantime, I'll ask you to stay with her. You'll also need to give a formal statement later on." Sergeant Hagen took Jamie Colbert away to his squad car around which other officers were gathered.

Another man, this one dressed in park service greens, made his way to the truck. "I'm Park Supervisor Paul Leclerc." He looked in through the truck window, then rapped on the glass and before Jasper could stop him, he opened the truck door. "Gail, are you all right?"

Supervisor Leclerc might as well have been addressing a manikin for all the response he received from Ranger Williams.

Jasper pushed the supervisor away from door before closing it. "She is in shock. As I told Sergeant Hagen, she needs medical attention."

"We've a couple of ambulances on the way. Unfortunately, they have to come all the way from Ridgecrest. Was Ranger Williams really being held captive by the Colberts? You know, it was rumored that they hung out here in Death Valley about five years ago."

"Who are these Colberts?" Jasper said.

Supervisor Leclerc studied Jasper, his well-worn denim, his unkempt beard, his misshapen hat. "Where have you been? Living in a cave?"

"I am a prospector. I do not get to town much."

"Then you've not heard about the Hollywood Murders, a series of satanic killings, the victims all young women trying to get into the movie business."

"And the Colberts are responsible for these murders?"

"Yes. Cindy Colbert is the leader of these devil worshippers. It's said she doesn't do the actual killing herself, but manages to get others to do the dirty work for her. Her followers are all dope fiends, which explains how she can exert power over them."

"There was another man with her." Jasper said. "The two seemed alike in many ways. I thought he might be her brother."

Supervisor Leclerc shrugged. "As far as I know Cindy Colbert's only got that idiot brother of hers. They say the two are inseparable."

Another park ranger appeared and spoke quietly to the supervisor.

"Okay," the supervisor said, nodding. He turned to Jasper. "I've got things needing doing. If Ranger Williams comes around, tell her an ambulance should be here any minute now."

Jasper judged there were now about twenty people on the scene with more arriving. A large generator, attached to the back of a truck, was started up, adding to the noise. Soon banks of lights turned night into day. A second group of officers, these with walkie-talkies, were preparing to follow Sergeant Hagen's contingent that had already gone up the canyon.

Jasper rubbed his hands together. The night was getting colder by the minute. He decided to get back into the truck. Ranger Williams was still staring out over the dashboard, oblivious to all the activity going on outside.

In a voice devoid of emotion, she spoke. "I've been thinking, and I've decided I'm going to leave the Park Service and go back home to Missouri."

"I understand," Jasper said. He could not fault Park Ranger Williams for having reached this decision. "Would it trouble you too much to tell me how you came to be taken by these Colberts?"

Ranger Williams continued to stare ahead. "They were hiking along the road. I know we're not supposed to pick up passengers, but it was getting cold, and they looked like such nice people." Tears started down her cheeks. "Then that man, the handsome one, he pulled out a really big knife and ordered me to take them here. I thought maybe that would be the end of it, but the woman, she said that the Dark One was angry, that it was too long since he had had fresh blood." She shuddered.

Jasper quickly changed the subject. "Do you read much?"

Park Ranger Williams, in the process of wiping a tear away, half turned toward him. "What?"

"I know it is a silly question, but a book was a great help to me at a time when I felt as I imagine you feel right now. This was a long time ago, back when I was a soldier in the Great War. I am not saying what I experienced back then was the same as what you suffered tonight. Yet few were the times when I was not frightened, when I did not think I was going to die."

Jasper had Park Ranger Williams' full attention now.

"By some miracle, I managed to survive, and when the war ended, I went home to Wales where I got a job delivering kegs of beer to the taverns. Times were hard, and I should have been glad of the work, but all the while, I felt life was pointless, that it would have been better if I had died on the battlefield."

Jasper rested his hands on the steering wheel, thinking.

"So, what did you do?" Park Ranger Williams said.

"I remember a day right before Alban Eilir, which is the Welsh celebration of the first of day of spring. It was to be special celebration that year, in recognition of the war being over. For me, that meant a long day delivering extra kegs of beer for the festivities. But as I was driving along, something came over me, and I pulled over to the side of the road and got out and walked to the top of a tall hill, of which there are many in Wales. It was as fair a day as one could ask for, with the air as clear as glass, and white clouds drifting over hill and valley, a day to gladden the heart, yet it held no joy for me. As I stood there looking out at the scenery, yet not really seeing it, I was seized by a great anger, an anger that left me shaking, yet at a loss to explain it."

Jasper released the steering wheel and sat back.

"Then it came to me, it was Old Devil War whom I was angry at. War had robbed me of feeling. War had robbed me of joy. War had robbed me of seeing nature in all her beauty. Malevolent, evil, wicked War had done this to me.

"Well, that was an awakening, I can tell you. Right then I realized I had three choices: I could go on living the life of the dead, I could kill myself and finish the job that War had nearly accomplished–not a very attractive option–or I could try to take back what War had stolen from me."

Jasper smiled. "This is where the question I asked you about reading comes in. There was a book I had carried around with me during the war and read during lulls in the fighting. It was called *Roughing It* by Mark Twain. Have you read it?"

Park Ranger Williams shook her head.

"It is a wonderful book about the Old West, told with humor and youthful optimism. Standing on that hilltop in Wales I recalled how the book began with two young men, Mark Twain and his brother Orion, bumping along in a stagecoach, bound for Virginia City and high adventure. Well, I was young, and I was alive–at least in a physical sense–so, following those two brothers' example, I decided to set out on an adventure of my own, ostensibly to look for gold, though my underlying purpose was to take back what War had robbed me of."

"And did you take it back?" she said.

Jasper nodded. "It took a while, but I did. Here in the desert, I discovered the antidote to War's poison, which is peace and beauty and the great healing powers of nature."

Ranger Williams nodded. "I know what you mean. I've always loved nature. That's why I majored in botany. It's why I became a park ranger."

"And now you wish to give that up?"

Tears started down her cheeks once again. "I don't see how it could ever be the same after this."

Jasper rested his calloused hand upon hers. "True, it will not be the same, not for a while, at least. What those Colberts did–tried to do, anyway–was to kill you. On a physical level, they did not succeed. Now it is up to you to decide whether you are going to let them rob you of the life you truly love, which they will continue to do as long as you let them. If you will take the advice of an old soldier, do not let them. Do not let the Colberts of this world rob you of your soul!"

Jasper saw the flashing red light of an ambulance in the truck's rearview mirror. He opened the door of the truck. "Promise me you will think about what I said."

Park Ranger Williams nodded, then Supervisor Leclerc came and led her away. Jasper stood outside and watched the flow of human traffic going up and down the canyon. He saw Sergeant Hagen return and walk over to a group of fellow officers. A little later, paper cup in hand, the sergeant came to see Jasper.

"Thought you might like some coffee," he said. "It's not very good, but it's hot."

"Thank you," Jasper said, taking the cup from him.

Two men, carrying a body in a stretcher, passed by not far from them.

"You sure did a number on that one," Officer Hagen said, pointing to the man on the stretcher.

Jasper could see the man's scalp caked in dried blood. "I did not mean to kill him. It was the heat of the moment."

"Oh, you didn't kill him. More is the shame. But he'll live to stand trial."

Two officers appeared with Cindy Colbert walking stiffly between them, her wrists still bound by the strips of cloth Jasper had used. "Jamie!" she cried, looking frantically around. "Jamie! Where are you?"

Sergeant Hagen shook his head. "That psychopath is going to be facing trial for half a dozen murders, and all she can think about is that idiot brother of hers!"

"What do you think will become of him?"

"Jamie Colbert?" Sergeant Hagen shrugged. "Can't say. Maybe some institution somewhere." He spotted Jasper's rifle lying in the bed of the truck. "Is that the weapon you hit that bastard with?"

Jasper nodded.

"We will need it for evidence."

"You are welcome to it."

Sergeant Hagen gingerly picked up the rifle and examined it. "It looks old. There's a lot of rust on it. I'm surprised it still fires."

"It would be a miracle if it did."

Sergeant Hagen looked enquiringly at Jasper.

Jasper smiled. "It is not loaded."

Sergeant Hagen stared at the rifle then back at Jasper. "You mean to tell me you walked into that nest of vipers with an unloaded rifle?"

"There was no time to load it. Besides, the Colberts did not know it was not loaded."

Officer Hagen laughed. "Jasper, you got a lot of balls."

"And very little in the way of brains."

"Well, I'll see this rifle is thoroughly cleaned before it's returned to you."

A young officer appeared, bearing Jasper's backpack.

"Where do you want this, Sergeant?"

Jasper stepped forward. "That belongs to me." He took the backpack and leaned it up against the truck.

"Is that how you live?" Sergeant Hagen said, gesturing toward the backpack.

Jasper nodded. "I guess I am like the turtle, I carry my house upon my back."

The young officer interrupted. "Lieutenant Caruthers would like a word with you, Sergeant, when you got time."

Sergeant Hagen nodded. "Anything we can get for you, Jasper?"

Jasper shook his head.

"Well, one of us will be along in a while to take your statement."

Jasper waited until they had gone before picking up his backpack and slipping his arms through the straps. He chose his steps carefully as he walked slowly beyond the range of the portable lights then quickened his pace as he stole away from the scene of activity. He almost made it past the line of cars and trucks when he was stopped by a young police officer returning from one of them.

"Who are you, sir, and where are you going?" The officer quickly answered his own question. "Say, aren't you the fellow that saved that young ranger and captured those Colberts?"

Jasper acknowledged that he was. He pointed to a pickup truck, the last one in the line. "Supervisor Leclerc said I might stow my backpack in the back of one of the park service trucks."

The officer stepped forward. "Here, let me carry that pack for you, sir."

Jasper waved the young officer away. "I am sure you have more important things to do."

The officer hesitated.

"I wish to be alone with my thoughts, Officer," Jasper said, "to sort them out before I give Sergeant Hagen my statement."

"Oh, of course, sir."

As Jasper waited for the officer to join the others, he reflected that he had just told the young man a lie. Well, he was entitled to a lie every fifty years or so. When he was certain he would not be observed, he struck out northeast across the desert, away from all the hubbub, away from the Colberts, away from the world and what it had become. His eyes soon adjusted to the darkness, and the bright stars provided light sufficient to guide his steps across the open plain. A glow of lights, about two miles off to his right, marked the resort at Stovepipe Wells. Jasper knew he could find water there, but also people, and it was people he wished to avoid, particularly right now. Besides, he knew of another source of water, the Old Stovepipe Wells, rarely visited since the resort had been built.

Jasper, his eyes now fully adjusted to the darkness, increased his pace. In two hours or less he would reach the wells.

Sleep

The Cima Dome, an uplift in the earth's surface, was formed eons ago by the pressure of magma pushing up from below then later exposed by the forces of erosion. The dome has the distinction of being covered by the densest growth of Joshua trees anywhere in which this unique tree grows. From atop the dome the viewer has an uninterrupted view of the Mojave Desert. Looking east, there is Teutonia Peak, Then farther east, the New York Mountains, extending well into the state of Nevada. Southwest are the Kelso Dunes, just visible above the line of Joshua trees, and to the west are the Cinder Cone Lava Beds, black and red in the distance. Far to the north is Highway 15 with what appears to be determined ants following the scent of food, but are actually semis hauling double trailers. And to the southeast, are the Mid Hills, situated between the New York and the Providence Mountains.

The Mid Hills were Jasper's goal that day. In the shadow of these hills are many springs, bubbling forth with life-giving water. Most of the springs had names, but the one at which Jasper planned to camp was unnamed, as far as he knew.

But for now, Jasper was content to sit atop Cima Dome and enjoy the view. Lately, he had found himself in a nostalgic mood, returning to favored places with the thought that this might be his last chance to partake of their beauty. Age had bent his tall frame; his once red-orange beard had turned the color of alkali dust; and during the last decade the hair on his head had grown increasingly thin until now only his old hat, the same one purchased from Jacob Harmon all those years ago, protected his bald scalp from the sun's blistering rays. If necessary, he could still put in a good twenty-mile day, but experience had taught him to plan his routes to avoid his having to.

Along with the physical alterations had come alterations in his thinking. More and more he dwelt upon the past, to the time before he went off to war. Up until his mother died, when he was twelve years old, he had had a happy childhood. Twice he dreamt of himself and his school mates in an improvised game of football, using a ball made of rags. Together they played with such joyful abandon, Jasper was sad to awake and find them gone.

Perversely, he was also receiving nightly visits from his late stepmother, a woman he had always disliked and had little thought of since leaving Wales. In these visitations, she was still the wicked gossip, sharp-tongued and bossy, scolding him for acts he never committed and words he never spoke. It puzzled him why this harridan should have the privilege of invading his dreams rather than his natural mother, whom he remembered fondly, and whose photograph he had carried with him until it eventually fell apart.

Jasper watched as a raven, its wings glossy blue-black, glided unaware toward him then, startled by his presence, veered sharply away, cawing. He imagined what it would be like for a man to grow wings as he aged, so that when he reached the time of life at which Jasper found himself, he might fly about, relieving his legs of the burden of having to walk. And when the time came to join the celestial choir, he could just wing his way heavenward.

Acknowledging the similarity of this and the saying about pigs having wings, he sighed, then stood up, stiff from having sat so long. As he rubbed his aching muscles, he was grateful for it being mostly downhill from Cima Dome to the spring where he planned to camp, and for the fact that it was as pleasant a late autumn day as he might have wished for, warm, but with a cooling breeze and a sky laced with sweeping cirrus clouds. Near Wildcat Butte, he stopped to enjoy a lunch of crackers and sardines in the shade of a massive Joshua tree whose branches grew like the tortuous serpents upon Medusa's head. Gazing upward into the tree, he felt a lethargy, and though he doubted this strange Medusa tree had the power to turn him to stone, it certainly invited him to nap, which he did.

Though he did not sleep long, he slept heavily, and it took him several minutes to come fully awake. He would have liked to have slept longer, but it was still six or seven miles to the spring, and he wanted to get there before dark. He shouldered his backpack and staggered a few feet forward before getting his legs firmly underneath him. He knew it was his imagination, but his backpack felt heavier, as if, during his sleep, Age had crept up on him and added several pounds to his pack. He dismissed this notion and increased his pace, determined to show that Age would not get the better of him. As a consequence, he arrived at the unnamed spring before sunset and saw what he had come to think of as the scourge of the desert: a four-wheel-drive vehicle.

Jasper knew it was a selfish notion, but he felt a proprietary claim to the desert. It had taken him years and years to truly know the desert, to become acquainted with its springs and oases and to know the surest routes for getting from one place to another. And now any city dweller with a map and a tank of gas could just drive right up to a spring, or, in this case, near to one, for this spring was still several hundred feet up a boulder-strewn wash which, thankfully, not even four-wheel monstrosities could traverse.

He was not in a good mood as he followed two sets of fresh tracks leading up the canyon. He was tired and had been looking forward to an early dinner then lying out on his sleeping pad and listening for the approach of nocturnal creatures drawn to the spring. He noticed that one set of tracks was smaller than the other, which suggested the interlopers were a man and a woman. He found them picnicking on a blanket near the spring. The man, who looked to be in his early twenties, rose at Jasper's approach. Jasper received some satisfaction from the young man's obvious displeasure at having his intimate picnic interrupted. Or maybe Jasper was misreading the man's expression; perhaps it was fear he was showing.

Jasper stopped and held up a hand. "Do not be alarmed. I assure you I am quite harmless. I am just an old prospector needing to refill his canteens. I shall be but a moment, then leave you in peace."

He took his canteens, which were looped over the pack frame, and, leaning over, began to fill them from the spring. He could hear the young couple whispering as he worked. Out of the corner of his eye, Jasper saw that the young man's companion was at that stage of life where she appeared not a girl, yet not quite a woman. She also wore a long dress, which he thought novel, for the few women he had encountered in the desert invariably wore trousers. The dress, the blanket spread with plates of food, the intimate whispering of the young couple, these made Jasper feel that he, not they, was the intruder, and he felt ashamed of his earlier attitude.

Having finished filling his canteens, he straightened up and became so dizzy he would have fallen had he not been able to brace himself against a large boulder.

"Are you all right?" the young woman said.

Jasper took in a deep breath, let it out slowly. "I just stood up too quickly, and all the blood rushed from my head."

The young man cleared his throat. "We were just wondering whether you might like to join us for a bite to eat."

Jasper shook his head. "I can see you have come here to be alone, and I have intruded."

"Oh, that's all right," the young woman said. "We have lots of time to be together."

"And we've never met a real prospector before," the young man said.

Still Jasper held back.

"Do join us," the young woman said. "We've plenty of food." She held up a plate. "See, I've made lots of peanut butter and banana sandwiches."

Jasper grinned. "I can't say I've ever had the privilege of dining upon that delicacy. I must warn you though, it has been a while since I have had the luxury of a bath."

"You can't be any worse than us," the young man said. "We've been hiking all weekend."

Jasper took off his backpack, leaned it against a boulder then sat down on the edge of the blanket. The young woman handed him a sandwich wrapped in waxed paper.

"My name is Michael, by the way," the young man said, "and this is Elizabeth."

Jasper, his mouth stuck shut with peanut butter, nodded. He could taste the presence of honey in his dry sandwich, which, thankfully, provided sufficient lubrication to allow him to swallow. "My name is Jasper. I am pleased to meet you both."

Michael pointed to Jasper's backpack. "I've always imagined a prospector having a burro to carry his gear."

"I used to have a burro, two, in fact, but when they died I decided to simplify things."

"How long have you been a prospector?" Elizabeth said.

Jasper scratched his beard. "That is a good question. I came here to the desert in May of nineteen twenty."

"Good God!" Michael exclaimed. "That's fifty-two years!"

"You don't look that old," Elizabeth said.

"Well, I feel that old sometimes."

"And you've been prospecting all this time?"

"Yes, although for a number of years now I have not done any real prospecting. Mostly I walk from one place to another, taking pleasure in the desert's beauty and enjoying its great open expanse. Once the desert takes a hold of you, it becomes your true home, at least it has for me."

"Even in the summer when it is so hot?" Michael said.

"Especially in the summer, for that is when I have the desert to myself. But what of you two? Where do you call home?"

"We live in Santa Barbara," Elizabeth said. "I go to school there, and Michael works as a musician."

"I work *at* being a musician," Michael corrected. "Mostly I earn money landscaping."

"And are you married?" Jasper said.

Michael looked at Elizabeth and smiled. "We just got engaged last month."

Elizabeth placed her hand upon Michael's. "Michael proposed to me as we stood on Campus Point with a full moon making a path of light across the water."

Michael looked into Elizabeth's eyes. "I guess you could call me a romantic."

"We both are," Elizabeth said. She leaned over and gave Michael a kiss.

"My congratulations to you both," Jasper said. He found he was not fond of peanut butter and banana sandwiches, but he took another bite to be polite. He eyed his canteens hanging from his pack frame, wanting water to wash down the dry sandwich.

"Here," Elizabeth said, reading his thoughts. She handed him a can of cold soda taken from a small cooler. "I'm afraid all we have is diet."

Michael and Elizabeth looked on with amusement as Jasper fumbled with the tab.

"When was the last time you had a soda?" Michael said, once Jasper got the can open.

"It has been a while." He took too big a sip and some of carbonation went up his nose and set him to coughing. Michael and Elizabeth laughed.

"My goodness," Jasper said, when he got his breath, "that is certainly fizzy, is it not?"

Elizabeth handed him a paper napkin, then set before him a paper plate of cookies. "Take as many as you want," she said. "I made a huge batch, and we've been living off them all weekend. Right now, I'd be glad if I never saw another chocolate chip cookie as long as I live."

Jasper took a bite of the cookie. It was warm, the chocolate melting on his tongue. "Mm, this is a delight. I do not know about the soda, but this cookie definitely gets a high mark."

"Before we go, I'll wrap them up and you can take them with you," Elizabeth said.

"We should be going soon," Michael said. "We've got a long drive back to Santa Barbara."

Jasper was sad to hear this, for he had been enjoying their

company. "Why did you chose this particular spot to come to? It is very remote."

"That was the idea," Michael said. "We wanted get away from everyone and everything. And we have this map with symbols showing the location of springs. Here let me show you."

As Michael got out his map and shared it with Jasper, Elizabeth began to put the remains of their picnic back into their basket. She covered the paper plate of cookies with clear plastic wrap and handed them to Jasper.

"Are you sure you wish for me to have all these?" he said.

Michael belched. "Definitely." They all laughed.

Jasper stood and helped Elizabeth fold the blanket. "Thank you for sharing your meal with a stranger. Being of a solitary nature, I am generally wary of the people I meet out here. But I am very glad to have met you both, and if you will wait a minute, there is something I would like to give you in return for your generous hospitality." He rummaged around in his backpack and produced a gold nugget the size of a walnut.

"Here," he said, placing the nugget in Michael's hand.

Michael's eyes went wide. "Is this for real?"

Elizabeth looked over Michael's shoulder. "Jasper, we can't possibly accept that. It must be worth a lot of money."

"Please, consider it an early wedding present."

Michael and Elizabeth exchanged looks.

"You would also be doing me a favor," Jasper said. "You will be saving me from having to haul it around."

Michael smiled. "Well, thank you. It's awfully kind of you."

"Would you like a couple of peanut butter and banana sandwiches to take with you?" Elizabeth said.

Jasper grinned. "Thank you, but I think the connoisseur's appreciation of peanut butter and banana sandwiches is lost on me."

Elizabeth smiled. "They are kind of stale, aren't they?"

As they were saying their good-byes, the rim of a full moon rose in the east. They watched in silence until it cleared the horizon.

"The moon looks just like it did the night you proposed," Elizabeth said, leaning her head upon Michael's shoulder. Michael kissed the top of her head.

"I have traveled many a night by the light of the moon," Jasper said. "May it guide you safely on your journey home."

When Michael and Elizabeth were gone, Jasper rolled out his sleeping pad upon a section of sand between two granite boulders. The sand still held some of the sun's warmth, and the boulders provided shelter from the breeze that was blowing. As he lay, looking up at the patterns of moonlight and darkness upon the rocks, he thought about Michael and Elizabeth and wondered about the life he had chosen. Had he been right in trading a life of peace over a life of love? Would he have found the same power of healing in marriage that the desert had granted him? This begged the question of whether he was capable of loving another person. Conversely, could he have found someone capable of loving him? On a more general note, had he failed in his duty to the world by shutting himself off from his fellow man?

Such questions rarely troubled him, but tonight he felt a sadness and perhaps a sense of having missed out. His sadness might have had nothing to do with these questions, but with the time of year, for though he loved autumn, the season always made him a little sad, though he was never quite sure why. It was true that autumn was the time of the year when nature closed down in preparation for winter. But here in the desert, where the growing season was short, most of the plants had died back weeks ago, if not months. Still there seemed something mournful about autumn, especially now that he had arrived at the autumn of his years.

The sky was bright because of the full moon. He closed his eyes, hoping to sleep, but thoughts concerning love continued to engage his mind. He had once loved a girl in Wales. They had even talked of marriage. Then the war had come along, and he had returned from the battlefield broken in spirit with no room in his heart for love to take root. It had taken the desert to make him whole again, and, as a consequence, the desert became his one true love.

In all of this, Jasper could not disregard the hand of fate. There had been a war, and he had been fated to participate. And of all the books he might have come across, it was fate which had presented him with *Roughing It*, the book which inspired him to come to California. Why, if fate had truly wished for him to marry, did it lead him to the desert, where the chance of finding a bride was practically nil?

An interesting question popped into his head. Did he love himself? It was not a question he ever remembered asking, perhaps because he believed the love of self a given. If he had not loved himself, he might have ended his life during those dark days following the war. Instead he had come to the desert where he found not only peace, but joy in the desert's beauty. From that joy came a love of life, and was not a love of life the essence of loving oneself?

Jasper yawned. Content to have reached some resolution to his questions, he turned upon his side and fell asleep. Later he woke with a pain in his chest. It was all he could do to draw breath. For once, he wished he were not alone, that there was someone he could call upon. He looked up at the moon, now directly overhead, its light reflecting brightly off the granite. He had always received comfort from nature, and now was no exception. The moon bathed him in its great light, and his breathing eased. Then he felt another pressure, not within his chest, but coming from outside of himself, as if great arms were enfolding him.

Unbidden, an unfamiliar voice spoke. *You are loved!*

Three words, no more. But what words! They assured him that his life had been well lived. The words gave him peace. He felt a sudden joy. The moon bore witness to this, and as the great arms enfolded him like his old denim jacket, Jasper surrendered up the strength of his limbs and slept.

www.ingramcontent.com/pod-product-compliance
Lightning Source LLC
Chambersburg PA
CBHW070057260626
47160CB00004B/1240